Wanting
what's hers
derick's dilemma

KHARA CAMPBELL

Wanting What's Hers

THIS BOOK HAS BEEN REPUBLISHED WITH NEW COVER SINCE ORIGINAL PUBLISHED DATE IN 2016. CONTENT IS STILL THE SAME.

ISBN 9781092491341

Published by Writegal

Printed in the United States of America

One

The buzzing of the alarm clock drug him out of his deep slumber. His large hands swept the sleep from the corners of his eyes. He yawned loudly then blindly reached for the alarm on the night stand and pressed the button to shut the noise off.

"Hmmm, Derek, is it time to get up babe?" Breana yawned, then dug her head deeper under the covers.

The sound of his name on her tongue caused him to the cringe. The lustful haze from the past three days finally lifted. Derek slowly opened his eyes and allowed them to adjust to the sunlight creeping through the sheer hotel curtains. He sat up then placed his feet on the floor and continued to sit on the edge of the bed. He held his head in his hands, he could feel the onset of a headache coming on.

"Is it time to get ready to catch our flight?" Breana asked groggily.

Derek groaned. He pulled his head out of his hands and the sight of his wedding band caused his heart to constrict tightly in his rib cage. At that moment, he really wanted his heart to explode so he could just die. Because – he knew he was already dead. He committed the ultimate offense in his marriage. Guilt overwhelmed him causing him to sweat profusely with fear. He sprang from the bed and headed for the suite bathroom. He locked the door behind him, then looked at his reflection in the mirror.

Thirty-three years old, six feet tall, mahogany skin, bald head with a goatee trimmed to perfection, bare chest, and medium, muscular built with a little belly he was working on. But what stood out more than ever in his reflection – was the pain etched into his handsome face of what he'd done. He hung his head low, not able to look at himself anymore. *How the hell did I get here?*

Breana's knock on the bathroom door interrupted his thoughts.

"Babe, open up I've got to pee." He could hear the urgency in her voice.

How the hell did I get here? He questioned again. He slammed his hand on the granite countertop, but the pain of it didn't register, as his heart was already bleeding with grief, the blood was flooding his veins and suffocating the life out of him. *Nine years of marriage and two kids and I do this shit!?*

He unlocked then opened the bathroom door for her. Breana quickly brushed passed him and went for the toilet to relieve herself. Derek stepped out. He needed to get away from her – from this mess. His luggage was already packed from the night before, so he quickly pulled on the pair of jeans and polo shirt he had hung up in the closet.

"You're not going to take a shower with me? Our last before we head back to the states?" Breana asked. She stood in the doorway of the bathroom, completely nude, watching him quickly dress himself.

"You're right, this is our last. Matter of fact the last three days never happened." He stated matter-of-factly as he shoved on his shoes.

"Well in that case, let's have a sendoff in the shower and what happened in the Bahamas – stays right here in the sun, sand and sea," she enticed. She seductively rubbed herself the way he liked all weekend on their *business* trip.

They were in Nassau, Bahamas as Derek assisted her, as her business consultant, on a few business ventures Breana wanted to take on. She is a small time real estate developer in Maryland and with Derek's business as a consultant and his connections in the Bahamas, the business trip came about – which led to a little *personal business* on the side during their stay.

"This weekend was a mistake that should've never happened and honestly we're not going to be doing business together. I was able to get you connections here in the Bahamas, so you can move forward with your plans with them, if you so decide to do so." Derek looked around the room to ensure he didn't leave any personal items. Last thing he needed was being framed. "Look, I'm leaving to head to the airport—"

"Derek, we're both adults. I'm not going to ruin your marriage—"

"You sure as hell won't!" He barked which startled her a bit. He knew he already threatened his marriage so no way was he going to allow her to try to do anything vindictive to hurt his wife.

"All I'm saying is, the past few days was fun, but I don't want to break your happy home. I've been married before and trust me – I have no desires of being tied down ever again. So chill, this isn't my first fling, I know the rules."

He looked at her, stunned. He wasn't expecting that. Now he was making a mental note to get himself checked out to make sure he wasn't taking any diseases home. He used condoms – but he didn't want to take any chances. *Perfect time to wonder if she's clean Sherlock*, he scolded himself. *You're an idiot for being so foul!*

"Good! So we're on the same page. I'm out." He started for the door. He figured he'd get to the airport early and freshen up in the men's room. No way did he want to spend another second in the lion's den.

****

"Can we at least sit together and have breakfast?" Fully dressed in a sundress and designer sandals, Breana took a seat next to Derek in a café at Lynden Pindling International Airport as they waited for their flight back to Reagan National in Washington, DC.

He watched her as she moved to sit opposite him at the small table. He bit into the coconut tart he'd purchased.

"Plus we are sitting together on our flight..." Breana continued.

"I'm sorry for crossing the line with you, but it's best we cut ties—"

She held up her hand halting him. "You know Derek, that's one of the things I admire about you. I know you feel bad about what happened between us and honestly, I feel bad that we took things too far too. But like I said, no worries." She sipped from her paper cup of coffee.

He was still skeptical. "How are you so casual about this? I cheated on my wife with you." Saying it out loud only increased the guilt he felt. *Where was that guilt when you were screwing her?* He pushed that thought aside. He loved his wife, the only woman he'd ever loved and the fact that he cheated on her – disgusted him. He didn't know how he was going to face her. Just the thought made him sick to his stomach. *I'm such an idiot!*

"Trust me, having been a wife years ago – I'm not proud of what we've done. We got caught up, we are on a tropical island and we were staying at the Atlantis Resort – one thing led—"

"That's just it, how did one thing lead to another?" He muffled a curse under his breath. He always heard of people saying that crap whenever they got caught cheating and the fact that he was now part of that clique added to his turmoil. He never thought he would be someone to step out in his marriage. Yeah he admired a good looking woman like any hot-blooded man, but never did his thoughts take him to the place of undressing a woman. *I love my wife!* He proclaimed in his mind. Breana was definitely a catch. Brown skinned and curves in all the right places, plus she was well educated – but she didn't hold a candle to his bride. But still he cheated – three whole days he had repeated the offense. And now that he was finally back to reality – he couldn't figure out why. *Why and how did I fall into Breana's trap? Was it a trap?*

"I didn't seduce you Derek," she said, unknowingly answering his mental question. "We had amazing sex these past few days. But it's over. No need to beat yourself up about it."

He did curse out loud then, using every explicit he could think of. *Don't beat myself up about it?* "I cheated on my f–" He stopped his profanity when he noticed an elderly couple walking past their table. "I cheated on my wife! What the hell kind of BS is that to say? Don't beat myself up about it? The f–"

"Flight 242 to DCA is now boarding at gate seven." Was announced on the intercom.

Breana gathered her things. "All I'm saying is mistakes happen. Go home, buy your wife something nice and forget the last three days ever happened."

Is she for real?

Two

"Devon, get in the bathroom and brush your teeth, then get downstairs for breakfast." Angie called out to her six year old son from the doorway of her bedroom.

She pulled the hair scarf off of her head and started for the master bathroom to comb her bone-straight hair back into the bob-style from the wrap she combed her hair into the night before. At thirty-three she loved the cute classic style, it kept her looking young and fly but sophisticated at the same time.

"Okay Mommy!" Devon yelled back.

"I can't find my purple shoes Mommy," Dena, her eight year old daughter whined. She stood at the entrance for the master bathroom pouting.

"Check by the backdoor where you left them yesterday," Angie said over her shoulder. She picked up a brush to style her mane in place. Her bob-cut was stylish and easy for her to maintain, plus Derek loved it too – which was even better.

Angie smiled at the thought of her husband and of seeing him later that day. He had been gone a week on business. Two days in New York, two days in Georgia and three in the Bahamas. It was the longest they'd went without seeing each other. But she didn't complain much because she was so proud of her husband for growing and expanding his business consultant business to what it was today. Just a few years ago he was dreaming of doing what he was doing now – helping others live out their dreams of entrepreneurship.

"Mommy I need socks," Devon stated. He walked bare feet into the bathroom dressed in jeans and a t-shirt. Angie smiled, thinking of how much he looked like his daddy.

"Grab your shoes and backpack and go downstairs. There are some clean socks in the laundry room." Angie turned to look into the mirror to make sure she looked appropriate for the day. She was dressed in dark slacks and a yellow blouse with basic jewelry: gold studs in her ears, a gold necklace, a gold watch and of course her wedding band. She didn't overdo her attire as a fourth grade teacher. She liked wearing stylish but flexible clothing while teaching her students. She quickly applied some lip-gloss to her lips, once satisfied with her appearance, she exited the bathroom.

Angie flicked her wrist to look at the time on her watch. "Okay we don't have time for a big breakfast, so cereal it is." She pulled three bowls out of the cupboard.

"Mommy look, I made this welcome home card for Daddy," Devon said while he admired his artwork on the sheet of paper in front of him at the kitchen counter.

Angie walked over and looked at his picture. It was of two stick figures, one big and one small, and written underneath was: welcome home dad. Angie figured Dena must have spelled 'welcome' for him.

"I think Daddy is going to love it. He probably won't be home until dinner tonight."

"I can't wait!" Dena exclaimed. "He's been gone long."

"I know sweetie, but Daddy is away for business. But we'll have him all to ourselves later today." Angie poured cereal into the bowls. "Okay now eat up so we can get on the road for school."

****

"You're looking extra cheerful this morning," Pauline, Angie's co-worker and best friend since high school stated. She sat on the edge of Angie's desk with a huge mug of steaming coffee in her hand. "That must mean Derek's coming home today."

Angie couldn't help the smile that spread across her mocha complexioned face. "Yup, my boothang is coming back today." After just celebrating nine years of marriage a month ago – Angie was overjoyed with the fact that she was still madly in love with her husband. They weren't perfect – she'd be the first to admit that. And they'd had their struggles, but she was looking forward to many more years of marriage with her man. Not seeing him physically for a week was like torture.

Pauline laughed after brushing her brunette hair out of her pale, cream face. "Ah, do I need to babysit my god-kids tonight?" She winked.

Angie shook her head, then said, "No. They miss their dad, but I do have plans for him and me later when they're asleep. I just hope Aunt Flo holds off for a day or two."

Pauline took a sip of coffee from her mug. "Well for your sake I hope she doesn't pay you a visit just yet."

Angie pulled out her lesson plan binder out of her desk drawer. "This is one day I can't wait for three o'clock."

"Hmmm, fast tail!" Pauline mocked, then burst out laughing. She stopped when some of the coffee spilled onto her hand, burning her a little.

"Yeah, that's what you get," Angie laughed. "As if you don't be wearing poor Benjamin out every night."

Pauline licked the spilled coffee off of her hand. "Well that is a benefit of being married."

"Yes God!" Angie agreed. She imagined all the dirty things she wanted to do with her husband tonight.

"Good morning Mrs. Monroe," one of Angie's student greeted after he walked into the classroom, followed by his dad.

"Okay girl, we'll talk later. Let me get to my class." Pauline slid off of the desk and exited the classroom.

"Good morning Arnold. Good morning Mr. Taylor." Angie greeted both student and parent.

"A great morning to you Ms. Monroe," Aron Taylor greeted. He never acknowledged her as missus. His son, Arnold, busied himself with putting his things away into his cubby. "You look lovely this morning," Aron continued. He had a deep attraction for her ever since he met her at his son's fourth grade orientation. He knew she was married, but figured flirting was harmless.

"Thank you!" Angie replied politely. She was completely oblivious to his attraction for her. She took his charm as him being nice. Besides, Derek was the only man she was interested in. She got up and walked around her desk.

"How has he been behaving in class?" Aron asked, stalling his time to leave to head to work.

"Arnold has been great. I have no problems out of him. Trust me I would've called by now. He's three weeks in with no trouble." Arnold was actually one of her favorite students so far this school year.

"Good! He's my main man, I wasn't sure how the transition from him living with his mom to living with me would be, but so far things have been going well at home too," he confided.

"Oh, how long has he been living with you?"

"Five months. His mom wanted to focus on her acting career in LA and didn't have time to fit him into her schedule." He shrugged. "I can't say that I like him being away from his mom, but I'm happy with the opportunity to raise him fulltime."

Angie smiled. "Well he's blessed to have a father like you available to step in."

"That's what a parent is for."

"Good morning Mrs. Monroe!" Two more of Angie's students greeted. They went to their cubbies to put their things away.

"Well, I've got to get started with my day. Please if you have any concerns regarding Arnold contact me, and I'll do the same on my end," Angie told Aron.

"I will. Thank you."

Angie turned to retrieve a note from one of her students. Aron boldly checked her out, taking in every inch of her size eight frame. *Looking doesn't hurt either.* He bit down on his bottom lip when she bent over to pick up a pencil another student dropped on the floor. *And what a sight!*

Three

"Daddy's home! Daddy's home!" Both Dena and Devon exclaimed when they saw a car headlights reflected on the family room wall where they were sitting down watching TV.

Dena and Devon sprung up from the couch and sprinted for the front door. It was seven-fifteen in the evening. They had already completed homework, their extracurricular activities and dinner. Angie stood away off from the front door, allowing them the opportunity to greet their daddy.

Derek, unlocked the door and walked in and was immediately attacked with hugs and kisses from his children. "I've missed you both!" He told them, returning their kisses and hugs.

"Did you get us anything Daddy?" Dena asked.

"Yup, sure did." He handed them both a shopping bag filled with souvenirs from his travel.

"Thanks Daddy!" They both ran back into the family room to view all of their new goodies.

"Welcome home baby!" Angie finally spoke.

Derek closed and locked the door behind him. When he turned around, the sight of his wife's radiant face, lodged a dagger into his heart. He'd been suffering with guilt all day. His flight got in at Reagan National Airport at 2pm then he headed straight to his office at the National Harbor in Oxon Hill, Maryland for meetings for the rest of the day. But his thoughts were far from business. *How could I have cheated on this beautiful, loving and loyal woman?* He was still tripping over the fact that it had actually happened – he was waiting to be awakened from the nightmare he was hoping he was in.

All day he'd been wrecking his brain trying to pinpoint when he had that moment of weakness where he gave into sexual desires for another woman. Angie was his world – she and their kids meant everything to him. *So how in the world did I end up in bed with Breana for three days?*

Angie walked over to her husband and kissed him deeply. "I've missed you so much!" She hugged him, stepping into his welcoming arms. The masculine scent of his cologne comforted her. "I love you!"

Derek swallowed the lump in his throat. The dagger to his heart was deepening. "I love you too baby and I missed you." He squeezed his eyes shut, the pain of it was going to kill him – he just knew it. *You're an idiot! You have the world and may have lost it.*

"Are you hungry? I did barbecue salmon, wild rice and vegetables." Angie stepped back, out of his embrace. She looked up into her husband's face. "You look beat, how about you take a shower and I warm dinner up for you."

"Thanks, babe!" He averted his eyes. He couldn't look into her beautiful hazel eyes with his deceit looming over his head. He was beyond disgusted with himself. "I'll like that."

****

"I didn't think I'll ever get the kids to settle down and go to bed," Derek said to Angie as he walked into their bedroom.

"They missed you, we've never went a whole week without being together as a family." Angie flipped onto her hands and knees on the bed and crawled toward Derek as he walked toward the edge of the bed. She frowned.

"What's wrong?" His heart started to gallop in his chest. *Does she suspect anything?*

"I was hoping my period would hold off for a day or two, but she showed up," Angie pouted. She leaned up on her knees and placed her hands on his bare chest. "It's been a while since we've had sex. And I was hoping we'll be able to rekindle things tonight." She was referring to the fact that she'd had fibroids surgically removed which placed a temporary hold on their sex life – which she was eager to resume.

Derek breathed a mental sigh of relief. "It's okay babe. Flo is only here for five days." He was thankful for the out. He'd made an appointment to get some blood work done tomorrow. He knew he was dumb to cheat and stupid enough to do it with a woman he only knew on a professional level. The fact that Breana had mentioned he wasn't her first fling added to his turmoil. He didn't want to bring any of his mess home. He'd never cheated on his wife – ever! Their marriage was built on trust – and in three days he'd crushed it to hell.

"Well, I can do other things…" She licked her lips.

Derek stifled a groan. His woman was irresistible and the fact that she wanted to please him while she was out of commission, proved how in love and devoted she was to him. He felt like a complete fool. *How could I have betrayed my wife?* "I can wait for Flo to leave." Shame. He was drowning in shame at that point. He pecked her sweetly on the nose. Then picked her up into his arms, Angie automatically wrapped her legs around his waist. He carried her to the other side of the bed and sat. "Tell me about your day?"

Angie climbed out of his lap and got comfortable on her side of the bed. "It was okay. Though I did have one student that divulged a little too much about the happenings at home during language arts." She waited for him to get comfortable on his side of the bed so she could snuggle up with him.

Derek smiled. "Uh oh, do tell."

"Well she said that she caught her mommy and daddy playing hide and seek late at night – naked!" They both busted out laughing. "Oh my gosh! I was so shocked. All the other kids started saying 'ewww' and laughing. I had to quickly change the subject, but of course my curious fourth graders wanted to know more of what happened."

"Oh come on, you didn't let the child finish the story?" Derek joked.

"Of course not. I can only imagine the letters I may receive from the other students' parents tomorrow."

"Well at least her parents are together and apparently still enjoy each other. How many other children can say that?" *Yeah, and your kids may be a part of that group when your wife finds out what you did.* Guilt squeezed at his heart.

"Yeah, you're right," Angie yawned.

"Let's go to sleep." Derek reached for the light switch for the lamp on the nightstand and clicked it off. He then leaned in and kissed Angie on the forehead. "I love you!"

"I love you too baby. I'm so glad you're home."

Sleep evaded Derek that night, his mind was in too much turmoil. He held on tightly to Angie as she slept – he asked God for forgiveness and hoped that he would survive the secret he held from his wife.

Four

"Mr. Monroe so you're here to get blood work done to check for any diseases?" Dr. Taylor asked quizzically after he stepped into the examination room.

"Yes, and I would like to get the results back as soon as possible," Derek stated earnestly.

"Is there any reason why you believe you may have contracted anything?" The doctor asked. He pushed his glasses further up on his face.

Dr. Taylor had been Derek's doctor for years and he even knew Angie. Derek considered going somewhere else for the blood work, but he knew Dr. Taylor would adhere to his wishes of getting the results back ASAP. Plus there was the doctor/patient privacy rule Dr. Taylor had to abide by – which made Derek's decision of coming in easier.

"I just want to know." Derek wasn't in the mood for the drilling. He sat impatiently on the examination table. *I hope that chick didn't get me sick.*

"Okay, after I give you a physical exam I will have the nurse come in to get blood samples."

"Cool!"

Less than an hour later.

"I placed a rush on the results so you should hear back from my office before end of business tomorrow," Dr. Taylor informed Derek.

"Thank you!" Derek replied anxiously. He headed for the exit. Tomorrow evening couldn't get there fast enough. Last night trying to sleep next to his wife was complete torture. He kept berating himself for what he'd done. Breana had condoms, which they used, but he didn't want to take any chances. Had she planned on them having sex? Angie was his world. He wouldn't be the successful man he was today without her help. He knew he screwed up big time, but in his mind getting checked out for any diseases was his way of trying to right his wrong.

****

"Damn man you look like hell," Brian, Derek's college buddy said after taking a seat at the table in Buffalo Wild Wings restaurant.

Derek swallowed a swig of beer. After his doctor's appointment that morning he spent a few hours in his office then left to meet Brian. He needed to clear his mind and ease his conscious a bit.

"I feel like it."

"What up? You just got back from your week long business trip. I figured you'd be hung over from some welcome back sex with wifey."

Derek hung his head low in shame. "I messed up man." He needed to talk to his buddy and get some perspective on the situation. He and Brian had been the best of friends since their first year at University of Maryland. He knew he could count on Brian for some sound advice.

"Damn dawg, what is it?" Brian placed his forearms on the table and leaned forward. "Is it some business issues?"

"Worse!" Derek hesitated for a moment. "I...I cheated on Angie." He looked up to see his friend's reaction.

Brian laughed. "Man, quit playing. I know you'd never do some mess like that. So what is it?"

"Dude, I messed up while in the Bahamas."

Brian was stunned silent. He just looked at Derek with wide eyes. "The f–"

"Hi Sir, can I get you anything?" A waitress asked Brian.

Brian turned his attention from Derek to the waitress. "Yeah, get me the strongest drink you've got."

"The only type of alcohol beverage we have is beer Sir."

"Bring me the strongest one!" Brian stated.

The waitress scurried away sensing the seriousness between the two men.

Brian shook his head. "Derek, you playing me right, man? Angie is the best thing that happened to you. You treat her like a queen, you've been nothing but devoted to her since you guys met in college. And now you're telling me you cheated on her, with some random chick?" He was beyond shocked.

Brian was really rubbing salt in Derek's wounded heart. His friend was right, he'd been devoted to Angie since day one – and for him to have done what he did was mindboggling. He was still trying to figure out how and why. Temptation got the better of him. One minute he and Breana were chatting it up about business in the hotel bar, the next he was spending the rest of the trip in her room. Most of it was just a blur. And he wasn't even feeling Breana like that. He had absolutely no intentions for their business relationship to turn personal. Cheating wasn't something he did or thought about for that matter.

"I don't know what to do..." Derek started.

"Man, Derek. Quit playing. You punking me, right? You don't cheat, it's not in your blood. Single men like me do that type of shit, not you." Brian leaned back in his seat. He just knew his boy was pulling his leg. *No way this dude cheated on Angie. No way.*

Derek ran his hand over his bald head. "I'm serious Brian. I effed up. This whole thing has me tripping man. I love my wife. I don't understand how I did what I did."

"Bruh, you fa' real?" Brian was starting to trip.

"You know I wouldn't play about something like this. Angie and the kids mean everything to me. I can't lose them."

"Damn! No wonder you look like hell."

"Here you go Sir." The waitress placed Brian's drink on the table.

"Thanks!" Brian lifted the glass and took a long swig.

The waitress walked away.

"How do I tell Angie about this? Should I?" Derek asked earnestly.

"I never thought I would be having this type conversation with you – ever!" Brian placed his half empty glass of beer on the table.

"I don't like having this conversation at all."

"Was it just the time during your trip?"

"Yeah. And I still don't understand how I gave in to sleeping with her."

"Those Bahamian chicks are some good looking women. Once you go Bahamian those others aren't worth a damn..." Brian added, getting sidetracked.

"Well she's American. Breana Sutton, a real estate developer in PG County. We went down there for me to set her up with some contacts for some possible developments on the island."

"Ah, I've seen her picture on billboards around town. She's a looker. Yeah I can see how you fell for that. She got that brick house figure—"

"Come on man. I'm dying here."

"Sorry. So you just messed up during the trip?"

Derek nodded his head.

"Don't tell her. What she doesn't know won't hurt her," Brian said confidently.

"Not telling her is going to kill me. I can't keep this from my wife."

"If you tell her she's going to kill you. So either way you end up dead. At least this way you keep your family intact." Brian drank the last bit of his beer. "Do you think Breana may try to contact Angie?"

"No."

"Then don't say anything to Angie. I know you're tripping about it now, but you can handle it."

Derek shook his head. "How could I have been so stupid, man?"

"It happens to the best of us. You ain't the first and you ain't gone be the last."

"I love Angie!"

"I know you do. And just seeing how messed up you are about this, I know you ain't trying to mess up again. So sit tight and chill. Homegirl isn't a threat to your marriage, so you're good."

"I don't know." Derek was really doubting his friend's advice. Cheating was bad enough, but he felt keeping it from Angie would be worse.

"Look bruh. You will only make matters worse by telling your wife."

"I won't feel right keeping this from Angie..."

"Derek, trust me. Don't tell her." Brian shook his head. "That's why dudes like you don't have any business cheating, you don't know how to handle it."

"Maybe you're right," Derek conceded.

"Everything's gonna be cool."

****

Angie flipped through pages of a bridal magazine during her lunch break. Her class assistant was watching her students on the playground so she had a few minutes of quiet to herself.

"You hiding out in here?" Pauline asked after closing the classroom door behind her. "I don't blame you. The other teachers in the staff lounge are talking school politics." She walked further into the classroom and pulled up one of the student's chair from a desk and sat next to Angie at her desk.

"I'm looking for some ideas for me and Derek's ten year anniversary next year. I'm thinking about us renewing our vows on a beach somewhere." Angie took a bite from the peanut butter and jelly sandwich she made for lunch.

"Nice! Benjamin and I would be there."

"Good, because you're my maid of honor."

Pauline squealed. "Yay! But what about your sister Page?"

Angie shook her head. "I'm sure my sister won't feel any type of way about it. We're more like strangers than family." Page was Angie's half-sister. Their father divorced Page's mother because she was young and said she didn't want to be married anymore. A few years later, he met and married Angie's mother. Page has had a vendetta against Angie because she felt their father loved her more. Which wasn't the case because he always tried to involve Page in all their family activities — but by the time she turned sixteen and Angie was thirteen, Page refused to come over to their house and to have anything to do with them. So it was as if she didn't have a sister.

"Hmmm."

"I'm going to talk to Derek and see what he thinks about a destination vow renewal ceremony."

"Speaking of whom, how did things go last night seeing your man for the first time in a week?"

Angie closed the magazine then placed it in her desk drawer. "Great! Though Aunt Flo reared her ugly head. So no welcome home nookie for us."

"That's Aunt Flo for ya. But I bet the kids were excited to see him."

"They were. We even let them stay up an hour later than usual just so they could catch up with their dad."

"I can't wait for Bengy and me to have kids. You guys have the model family. Devoted husband and wife and two beautiful and intelligent kids."

Angie smiled. "Thank you! I'm really thankful for my family. And I know you and Benjamin will make great parents. I can't wait to spoil my blue eyed godchild."

Pauline laughed. "Well, I have to get pregnant first. But we're having fun working on it." Pauline and her husband Benjamin had been married for five years and had been trying to get pregnant for almost a year.

"Don't rub it in when I've been on a drought," Angie laughed.

"Puleeease. In a few days you will be wearing that poor man out."

Angie snapped her fingers. "And you know this!"

Pauline tsk-ed. "And you call yourself a teacher. Fresh, fresh!"

"Takes one to know one."

They both busted out laughing.

Five

The next day, Derek lifted his head up from the notes he was reviewing when he heard the click of his office door opening.

"Mr. Monroe I just confirmed you a speaking engagement at the Ebony in Business Expo at the Gaylord in Texas for January." Latoya, Derek's assistant stated after stepping into his office. She handed him some papers which he graciously accepted.

"Perfect! I've been wanting to speak at that event for years."

"Yup so all you have to do is sign on the dotted line and I will send it back to the organizers. And they accepted your speaking fee, which is pretty sweet I might add."

Derek smiled. Years ago, running his own Business Consultant business was only a dream. With help from Angie, he mapped out a plan and the rest is history. He was speaking to and consulting people on a national level. He enjoyed assisting and encouraging others to fulfill their dreams – because in turn he was fulfilling his.

"Angie is going to ecstatic when I tell her. We've been to that expo several times and every time we we're there, we would envision me on stage giving people tips on how to start and run their own businesses."

Latoya sat in one of the visitors' chairs at the front of his large desk. "Perfect. Do you want me to make travel arrangements for her as well?"

Derek reviewed the document Latoya gave him. "Yes! But I will confirm with her first about the dates. I hope it's not during any testing for her students and she won't be able to make it."

Latoya smiled. "I doubt Mrs. Monroe would pass up being by your side, Sir."

"Yeah, but I want to confirm with her first." He signed his name on the signature page then handed the documents back to Latoya.

"Okay. I will wait for your okay on the travel arrangements." She stood up after accepting the documents from Derek. "In the meantime I will scan and send these back to the organizers." She started for the door.

"Thank you Miss Simms." Even though Derek considered Latoya like a little sisters, he still preferred keeping things professional in his business which was why they addressed each other formally. Plus working alongside a woman everyday as his assistant, he never wanted the lines to become blurred for any inappropriateness.

"You're welcome!" Latoya closed the door shut behind her.

A few moments later his cellphone rang. He reached for it on the edge of his desk.

"This is Derek," he spoke into the receiver.

"Hello Mr. Monroe. This is Nurse Smith from Dr. Taylor's office."

"Yes," he answered anxiously. He sat up straighter in the chair. He'd been waiting for this call all day.

"Dr. Taylor wanted to call you himself, but he is caught up with another patient. He knew how eager you are to receive the test results–"

"Yes!" He exclaimed, cutting her off. He desperately needed to know the results. He's nerves were haywire. He'd been great all day keeping it together, now he needed to know his fate.

Sensing his anxiety, Nurse Smith continued. "All the test results came back negative Mr. Monroe."

Derek exhaled deeply. The pressure around his chest loosened. *God I know I messed up, but thank you!* To say he was happy about the news would be an understatement. "Great! Thank you Nurse Smith."

"Absolutely, it's not a problem. But remember to come in to do a follow up checkup if you feel there may be reason for concern. You have a great day."

"Thanks, same to you!" Derek ended the call and leaned back in his chair with a huge sigh of relief. Though he was still struggling with enormous guilt, not bringing home any diseases to his wife was a consolation for his offense he was happy to take. 'Don't tell her, man.' Brian's words echoed in his head.

Derek reached for his cellphone again. He dialed Angie's number.

"Hey babe, you think the kids would like going to the skating rink after I take you all out to dinner tonight?" His finding out he didn't contract any diseases from sleeping with Breana wasn't exactly something he should be celebrating – but he wanted to treat his family to a night out. And the news he just received added to his jubilation.

"Hey babe, hold on a sec," Angie told him. She pulled her cellphone away from her ear. "Josiah, don't forget your homework in your desk," she told one of her students before he left the classroom for afternoon dismissal. Josiah ran back to his desk to retrieve his homework. She always had to remind him.

"What were you saying, babe?" She asked Derek, returning to his call.

"I'm taking you and the kids out to dinner tonight. Do you think Dena and Devon would like going to the roller skating rink afterwards?"

"Of course they would! And dinner, that would be a treat." She smiled into the phone.

"Perfect, it's a date sweetheart!" *I'm so in love with this woman.* He knew he was going to fall in love with her from the moment he saw her walk across the courtyard at the University of Maryland years ago when they were college freshmen. Building up the courage to walk over to her and ask for her number was one of the best decisions he'd ever made.

Of course she made him work for it. She was so shy, he could tell. There was an innocence about her – which only intrigued him more. So he went through all the hoops to get that first of many dates and even agreed to wait until marriage to have sex with her. And on their wedding day he realized just how innocent she was. He was her first – something he would cherish for the rest of his life. And probably add to his early demise for the guilt that would kill him, he just knew it.

"Aww, thanks! I look forward to it, and I'm going to wear something special just for you."

The thought of his wife's naked shapely size eight body flashed through his mind. Watching her get dressed this morning still had him hot and bothered. "I like those black lace panties you have on today. It's really sexy for someone having a visit from Aunt Flo."

"Well you know I still like to wear sexy underwear just for you during my monthly visits," she enticed.

"I can't wait for your aunt to leave so we can get reacquainted." His body shivered in anticipation of making love to his wife again.

"Good afternoon Ms. Monroe…"

"Babe, I've got to go. A parent just walked in," Angie whispered into the phone.

"Okay. I'll be home early tonight. See you soon, love."

****

"K, bye." Angie quickly ended her phone call with Derek. "Hi Mr. Taylor." Angie stood up and walked to meet him at the center of the classroom.

"I'm sorry if I interrupted you," Aron said, though he wasn't sorry at all.

"Oh no, it's okay."

"Arnold is out front waiting on me, but I wanted to ask you about something he brought up last night about playing hide and seek naked."

Angie's face was flushed with embarrassment. Two other parents brought up the same thing that morning. She'd typed a note that went home with her students that day to explain how the topic of *being naked and playing hide and seek* came up and to apologize for the matter.

"I actually sent a letter home with the students today regarding that. I had a student that divulged a little too much about the meaning of being shocked during language arts. Which in turn they explained on how seeing their parents naked playing hide and seek shocked them."

Aron stifled a laugh. "Oh, well that explains things." He couldn't hold back the laugh any longer.

Angie joined him. She was thankful he wasn't one of those prudish parents.

"Seems I have to add that to my 'to do' list," he stated.

Angie couldn't agree with him more. She only had a couple days left for her period. The thought of being in throes of passion with her hubby brought a wide smile to her face.

Aron noticed, but assumed that her smile was in response to what he'd just said. Wicked thoughts of her raced through his mind.

"Well, I'm happy you're not having a hiccup about the situation. Kids say things sometimes that's hard for me to censor."

"I understand. I was just curious, is all."

"Great. Well, I'm sorry I have to rush, but I have a staff meeting."

"Okay cool. I hope you have a great weekend Ms. Monroe." He flashed her a million dollar smile.

"Thanks, same to you!" Angie went to her desk to retrieve her purse and messenger bag. She assumed Mr. Taylor had left. She turned around and saw him standing at the door.

"I'm always a gentleman, so I wanted to wait for you," Aron told her. He looked into her hazel eyes as she approached where he was standing. The innocent aura about her was like an aphrodisiac for him. The fact that she seemed completely unaware of his attraction for her kept him seeking her out every chance he got. He knew he was playing with fire. *She's married man.* But like a lion after a prey he had to keep watch, waiting for that perfect moment.

"That's nice, but you didn't have to." She walked out of the classroom with her bags over her shoulders.

Aron closed the door shut behind them. "Not a problem. See you on Monday."

"You too." She gave him a wave before walking away.

Angie went left down the hallway and Aron went right. Of course he couldn't help himself. He turned and got a great view of her shapely behind in a red pencil skirt as she walked away.

My, my, my!

Six

A couple days later. Angie stood in the door frame of her master bath. She had on a sheer white robe that easily revealed the matching white corset and lace panties underneath.

"I meant to ask you sooner, but I've been thinking about us renewing our vows for our ten year anniversary on the beach somewhere next year," Angie said.

Derek was lying in bed with the TV remote in hand, flipping through the channels. The vision of his wife in the doorway captivated his attention. His eyes seductively roamed over her perfectly imperfect body. She hated the straight marks she'd gotten from two pregnancies, but he found them sexy. It showed how much of a woman she really was. His woman. His queen. A queen he was going to surrender to every which way sexually that he could think of. His body instantly responded.

His mouth went dry. "Wh...What?" He didn't hear what she'd said. He was mesmerized by her beauty.

Angie trotted seductively over to him. Derek clicked off on the remote and flung it to the side.

"I said I want us to renew our vows on the beach for our ten year anniversary."

"Baby, we can do whatever you want." His brain went to mush. The scent of her lavender perfume was driving him wild. When she got close enough for him to touch, he reached out and cupped her ample behind. Squeezing her cheeks and filling his palms.

"Really?" She asked with sparkle in her eyes.

Derek gently pulled her down to him on the bed. He shifted and hovered over her. He kissed her full lips then slid down to her neck and shoulder.

"How about the Bahamas?" She asked in between moans.

Derek's body went cold, like a bucket of water was doused over him. He stopped his sensual assault on her neck then leaned away from her.

Sensing his change in mood, Angie opened her eyes and looked up at her husband. She watched a series of emotions crossover his handsome, mahogany face.

"What, did I say something wrong?" She became alarmed.

He rolled over and laid on his back, staring at the ceiling. His lust was replaced with regret and shame.

"Are you okay?" Angie leaned forward on her elbows.

Don't tell your wife! Brian's words echoed again in Derek's head. "It's nothing babe. The Bahamas is nice, but what about Bermuda? We've never been there." He hoped his cover worked.

Angie sensed that there was something more, but pushed it to the side. Her hormones were getting the better of her. "Bermuda? Yeah that would be nice." She shifted to where she was straddling him. She lifted his t-shirt up his belly and chest. "So that means you're cool with us renewing our vows?"

"Hmmmm."

Angie was kissing and licking his chest.

Derek pulled his t-shirt over his head to give her better access.

"Baby I love you so much!" Angie said while enjoying her feast on his body. "Marrying you was one of the best decisions I've made in my life." She sat up and started to undo her corset.

Derek's emotions were fighting between: need, hunger, desire and regret and shame. The instant Angie's breast broke free from the corset – need, hunger and desire conquered all.

It was his time to feast on his wife. Every crevice of her body got his full attention. She was his own personal playground. Her moans and cries of passion was music to his ears.

"Derek, baby...I need you...now!" Her body was on fire, she couldn't take the appetizer anymore, she needed the main dish – the meat – his meat.

Derek obliged. With her legs hung over his shoulders, he pushed purposely into her essence. The wet heat of her snug entryway caused his eyes to roll in the back of his head. *There's nothing or no one better than this!*

The moment their bodies connected in their lovemaking, it almost felt like the first time. After the restriction of sex from her doctor and Derek being away for a week, they'd both craved that intimacy that only lovemaking could bring. It set them on a high. Being with his wife confirmed that only she had and would ever make him feel as close to Heaven he could ever reach on Earth.

"I love you Angie Monroe," he declared as they both climaxed in ecstasy.

"I love you! Always and forever."

****

Their lovemaking continued until the sun came up. They enjoyed making up for lost time. However when Angie reluctantly climbed out of the bed to quickly shower so they could make Dena and Devon's soccer game – shame overwhelmed Derek as if he was just struck by a freight train.

He lay there with his eyes shut, listening to the sound of the shower running. Usually he would join his wife – but he felt like scum. *God I messed up!* He squeezed his eyes tight. Not telling Angie about his indiscretion had him feeling terrible. He hated to continue his deception. *I would want to know. He reasoned. I would kill the dude, whoever it may be, if she messed around on me, but I would want to know.* He opened his eyes. Could he forgive his wife if she ever did what he'd done? He swallowed hard. He wouldn't like being on the other side, that's for sure. But he would want to know.

"Derek, are you coming in?" Angie shouted from the shower.

He rolled off the bed, stark naked. "Of course!" he replied while walking toward the bathroom.

Not telling her is going to protect her and keep your family together, the devil on his shoulder advised. *You won't be able to move forward and have a happy marriage by trying to keep this a secret. Lies have a way of showing themselves*, the angel on his other shoulder warned. Derek mentally battled with right and wrong in his mind. He slid the shower door open and joined his wife. His woes temporarily forgotten.

I'm protecting my family.

****

Later that evening, Derek and Angie were dressed to impress. Derek wore a custom fitted navy blue suit and Angie wore a complimenting navy, knee length gown. Her face was beat to perfection and her bob hairstyle was laid expertly. Derek slid his hand down from the small of her back to her butt and gently squeezed it, filling his palm.

"I can't wait to get you out of this dress," he whispered huskily into her ear. Ever since their *reunion* last night, he'd been like a dog on heat. All day during their kids' soccer games he'd been feeling on her like a horny teenager. Angie was equally giving and receiving.

She blushed. "Behave Mr. Monroe."

They were making their way into the ballroom of a prestigious hotel in Washington, DC. Derek had been invited to the charity event which helped to raise funds for literacy. It was a great way to give back and also expand his business by schmoozing with the elite.

"We're not staying here long, so you know." His hand moved from her butt to her hand.

"I didn't get all dressed up like this just to stay here for five minutes," she said, turning to look at him with a smile on her face.

"You got all dressed up like that to torture me to death. But trust me, I'll make up for all the work you put into getting dolled up." He winked at her which sent a shiver of desire of what's to come down her spine.

After grabbing two glasses of wine from a passing waiter, they made their way to their reserved table.

"Mr. and Mrs. Monroe, y'all sure do clean up nicely," a familiar voice said from behind them.

Derek and Angie turned around to see the face to the voice.

"What up Brian, I didn't know you were coming to this shindig." Brian and Derek gave each other a bro-hug. "When did you start running in these circles, I thought it was too bougie for you?"

Brian owned and operated several urban clothing stores in DC, Maryland, Virginia and New York and was the first to admit he wasn't a suit and tie type of guy. But here he was dressed to the nines in a tailor made suit.

Brian laughed. "Well when you trying to impress a bougie chick, a dude got to do what a dude got to do."

"Well you do clean up nicely, yourself Brian." Angie remarked. She accepted a warm hug from him. "You should wear suits more often."

"And you look beautiful, as always," Brian complimented her.

"So where's the poor lady at? I need to warn her about you," Derek said, looking around to see if he could identify Brian's date.

"Come on now, you know I'm a good guy," Brian said with a laugh.

The MC for the evening took to the microphone and asked everyone to get to their seats so the program could begin.

"Well, you'll have to meet the lucky lady later," Brian said before walking away toward his table.

Seven

"Baby I won't be able to wait until we get home to have you again," Derek said as they quickly made a beeline toward the exit to leave the charity event. As he'd told Angie when they'd arrived, he didn't want to stay there long.

"Good thing I didn't wear any underwear tonight," Angie smiled wickedly.

He mouthed a cuss word as he envisioned her naked underneath her dress. His hand went down from her waist as they walked, to squeeze her butt. "If I had known that sooner we wouldn't have made it here."

"I know." She turned her head to look at him, then winked.

They rounded a corner, fully engaged in one another.

"Oops, sorry I wasn't paying attention," a female voice spoke. She'd walked smack dab into Derek's shoulder. She squeezed her arm from the impact to relieve some of the pain.

"It's okay. I'm sorry, we weren't paying attention either," Derek told her. He looked the Hispanic woman over to make sure she was okay after asking the same. She assured him she was, and it was then he noticed her companion. And in that instance his life literally flashed before his eyes. Breana.

"Derek Monroe," she said, finding herself lost in his eyes.

She quickly looked away though hoping not to send off any "we slept together" vibes. She meant what she'd told him in the Bahamas about not wanting to mess up his happy home. She shifted her eyes over to his wife. She felt a brief tug of jealousy when she took in how beautiful Angie was. But then she remembered she slept with the woman's husband, so she figured she had no reason to be jealous. They both had their delicious taste of him.

Recognition of Derek's name had the Hispanic woman gawking at him now, even more than she was before. "Oh, you're the guy Breana went on the business trip with to the Bahamas."

Angie watched the exchange. Her antennae was on high alert. She took both women in suspiciously.

Derek pulled himself together and said, "Yes, Ms. Sutton is my client and I was able to setup a few business deals for her there." He was anxious to get away. But he didn't want it to be obvious enough to cause Angie to become suspicious. His heart was beating quadruple times its normal rate. Brian was right, he isn't cut out to be a cheater – not that he'd intended to. He refused to do the politeness and introduce his wife to the woman he cheated on her wife with. He wasn't that trifling or at least he wasn't going to be.

"Damn girl, I see why you couldn't stop talking about him after you came back," the Hispanic woman said to Breana in a loud whisper.

If looks could kill Breana's friend would have died from a double assassination from the looks of death both Breana and Derek were giving her.

Derek gripped Angie's hand and tugged her away towards the exit. He felt like he was about to die from a heart attack. His body was sweating profusely from the onset of stress that now controlled his body. His mind was frantically trying to find the perfect lie to tell his wife to explain what just happened. *I can't go out like this. Not now, not like this.* He was cursing himself out for being such an idiot. How could he have let this happen?

Angie remained quiet the full ten minutes it took for them to wait for valet to pull up with their luxury car and for them to get into it. Her silence had Derek on edge. He was tripping the hell out. But it did give him time to come up with the perfect lie. He believed Brian to be true. *Don't tell her!*

"What. The. F..." HONK, HONK!!!

Derek allowed the impatient driver behind him to go ahead.

"...Was that?" Angie continued. She was pissed and trying desperately to keep calm which was why it took her until now to respond to the exchange which occurred.

Derek was sweating bullets. He had never been more afraid of anything than at this moment. His life, his family was at stake and it was all his fault. He had his eyes trained on the road as he maneuvered through DC's Saturday night traffic to make the forty-five minute drive home in Waldorf.

"That was Breana Sutton, the real estate developer I told you I was arranging some business for in the Bahamas."

Angie shifted her body in the passenger seat so she could look directly at her husband. Anger along with fear were about to choke the life out of her. Never in their nine years of marriage had she ever felt that her husband was deceiving her, that their marriage was at jeopardy. But something just wasn't right. The vibes she picked up from Breana and Derek's nervous reaction to their encounter told her something was up. *If he cheated on me he won't have to worry about using his hot dog ever again because it will be sliced to shreds.* But she didn't want to believe that. *Derek wouldn't cheat on me and destroy our family.*

"You know what the hell I'm asking you Derek," she gritted through her teeth. *Please God, let him say he didn't sleep with her.* The anticipation of his answer was going to kill her.

He knew she was pissed because she hardly ever cussed. He refused to look at her though. She would be able to see the lie he was about to tell all over his face.

"Baby, you don't think I would do something stupid and cheat on you? The Bahamas was strictly business." He swallowed the lump in his throat. He felt like the scum of the earth. "I don't know what her friend was talking about."

Angie started to breathe easier as she accepted his lie. She didn't know what she would have done if he had confessed to sleeping with another woman. She knew no one could stop a person from cheating, but she believed her marriage to be solid enough for Derek to not want to step out. She was a great wife.

She took care of her man emotionally and physically. Any man would be lucky to call her his wife. No she wasn't perfect and no she wasn't blowing her own horn - but she knew she was a great wife to Derek. So it would be hard for her to believe that he would ruin the wonderful thing he had. Plus he was the only man she ever loved. She saved her virginity just for him - her husband. They had two beautiful children and had made an awesome life for themselves. She couldn't imagine growing old with anyone else. So there had to be another explanation to what the Hispanic woman was talking about.

"You know I'm good at what I do babe. My clients talk about me all the time." He answered as if he was reading her mind. *Damn, you're getting too good at this.* He shook his head in disgust. His guilt was going to send him to an early grave.

"Hmmm." Angie considered his explanation. *I guess he's right.* She knew firsthand how wonderful Derek's clients thought he was. He'd made many people very successful in their business ventures from taking his advice.

Minutes later they were home. The kids were asleep. Derek paid the babysitter while Angie went upstairs to peek into the kids' rooms.

He and Angie weren't kissing and hugging on each like before they bumped into Breana and her friend. But his marriage wasn't over. He blew a mental sigh of relief. After letting the sitter out and locking the door behind him, his cell buzzed in his suit jacket pocket.

It was a text from Breana Sutton: **Derek I'm so sorry about my friend. Please tell me it didn't create any problems between you and your wife.**

Instead of replying to her text he quickly deleted her number from his phone. He didn't want to have anything to do with her ever again. His life would forever be tarnished because of his infidelity with her.

Derek walked up the stairs towards his bedroom like it was the eighth mile. His feet felt like led. When he'd said his wedding vows to Angie nine years ago he'd meant every single word. He'd vowed to be a faithful partner. And the fact that he wasn't had him dying inside. He couldn't continue to lie to her. He loved her too much to continue to deceive her. She was everything he ever wanted in a wife and mother of his children. She deserved the truth.

He stepped into the master bedroom. Angie was already out of her evening gown. And like she'd said, she was completely naked underneath. His breath caught at the luscious sight of his nude wife. Her back was to him as she hung her dress back up in the walk-in closet. He admired her nice shapely butt. His groin twitched from knowing how wonderful she felt from behind.

She turned around when she heard him walk into the room. The sight of her full breast, small belly pouch with stretch marks, her wide hips and thick thighs with a little bit of cellulite had him hard as granite. He lost his train of thought as he watched her kick off her heels and bend over to neatly place them in the closet aligned with her other shoes. He stifled a groan.

Angie enjoyed giving him a little show. She was eager more than ever to be connected as one with her husband after the little drama leaving the charity event. She needed the possible thought of his infidelity far away from her mind. And making love and reassuring her man and herself that they were solid was exactly what she needed.

"So what was all that talk you had earlier about making up to me for getting all dressed up?" She asked seductively as she walked out of the closet towards him.

'Don't tell her,' Brian's words echoed in his mind.

Angie cupped the back of his head with her hands and pulled his head down towards hers as she tiptoed, then she buried her tongue into his mouth, savoring the delicious taste of him. Derek's brain went to mush – the affect Angie had on his mind and body was amazing – especially after so many years of marriage. *And you cheated on her with Breana?* His conscious taunted him.

"Mmmm, baby," Derek tried to speak. If he was going to relieve his conscious, he had to do it now before his head below took over completely.

Angie nibbled on his bottom lip then started kissing his neck and moving her lips down to his chest, sliding his suit jacket off of him as she went and starting to unbutton his dress shirt after she'd successful slipped off his necktie.

"Angie, sweetheart, I need..." He couldn't speak any longer as she was starting to unbutton his pants with one hand while the other was massaging his tool. Her tongue was wickedly caressing his now bare chest as well. He closed his eyes in intense pleasure.

If he was going to do this, he had to stop her. Oh snap she had his pants at his ankles now. Derek's entire body was inflamed with passion and desire. But he found some strength to step away from her reach.

"What are you doing?" Angie asked bewildered by his action. Her brows furrowed.

Derek turned away from her. Looking at her completely naked wasn't going to help the situation – at least the situation in which he wanted to talk to her about Breana. Running into Breana tonight convicted him further, he knew he had to tell his wife the truth. She deserved the truth from him and not to find out in some other scandalous way.

"Baby, put a robe on, I really need to talk to you about something." Derek pulled his pants up and refastened them. His heart started to gallop violently in his chest.

Angie stood in the middle of their bedroom stunned for moment. The fact that he'd stopped her in her quest to start an intense lovemaking session meant whatever it was he wanted to talk to her about was serious. She snapped out of her trance and went to put her robe on which was hanging on the bathroom door.

When she turned around to face her husband, he was still standing in the middle of the room, bare chested, but his pants were back on. Anxiety and fear gripped her intensely, she sat on the edge of their king sized bed anticipating what he had to say.

Derek struggled internally with what he knew he had to say. He never thought he would be one of those men that succumbed to temptation and ate the forbidden fruit which wasn't their wife. Angie had always been, from the moment he saw her, the only woman he wanted in every which way. Breana however was able to breach his martial and moral contract in three days of passion on a tropical island. In that one moment of weakness, he realized he may have just loss everything that mattered most to him – his wife and children.

"What is it Derek?" Angie asked. She was so nervous she was starting to shake. She pulled the terrycloth robe tighter about her body.

Derek closed his eyes and exhaled deeply. *God I don't want to hurt my wife, how could I have cheated on her? She's the love of my life, I would die a thousand deaths for her. I never wanted to hurt her, and what I'm about to say would do just that.*

He slowly opened his eyes and looked at his wife sitting on the bed.

"WHAT IS IT DEREK!?" She was becoming hysterical awaiting what it was he had to say.

Derek's heart was breaking. "Angie…" He swallowed the lump in his throat. "I, the woman you saw tonight, Breana, we…I had sex with her while we were in the Bahamas." He couldn't believe he'd actually said what he said. The words left his mouth and each one left a bitter taste. Derek watched the array of emotions that crossed over his wife's beautiful face. The pain he was causing her crushed him immensely. He failed his wife. He failed their marriage. He betrayed her trust. But he hoped with everything possible, that she would somehow forgive him. He would do anything to make up for what he'd done. To rebuild her trust in him.

Angie sat on the edge of the bed completely numb. She replayed what Derek said in her mind multiply times. *I had sex with her. I had sex with her. I had sex with her.* Did she hear her husband right? Did he just admit to having sex with another woman? Did he just confess to cheating on her? Cheating on their nine years of marriage. Destroying their happy home?

Rage slowly formed within her, traveling from her toes then sped up quickly spreading throughout her entire body. "Your trifling ASS cheated on me?" She spat. She sprung from the edge of the bed and pounced on him. Hitting him about his body with lightning speed and strength. Tears covered her face. No way was this happening. No way did her husband, the love of her life, the man she trusted second to God, cheat on her. Was she not a good wife? Did she not please him sexually and emotionally like she thought? What did she do to cause him to cheat? "How could you? HOW COULD YOU?" She screamed. Tired of trying to hit him, because he'd caught her arms to stop her. She collapsed to the carpeted floor. Hurt and pain like she'd never known before took residence within her.

Tears welled in Derek's eyes. He was so sorry for what he'd done. He never meant to intentionally hurt her. He loved her. He only wanted her. "Baby I'm so sorry," he pleaded with great remorse. His heart was bleeding in sorrow. He reached down to help her up off the floor.

"DON"T TOUCH ME!" She shouted, swatting his hands away from her. "GET OUT!"

"What?" He wanted them to talk things out, he knew it wouldn't be easy, but he wanted them to work through and get past this. Breana was a huge mistake, a mistake he didn't want or have a desire to make ever again. With her or any other woman.

"Get your shit and LEAVE!" Angie spat. She hardly ever cursed. But tonight Derek was pulling it out of her. She weakly fought back the tears as best she could. She didn't want him to see her crying. She didn't want him to see how much he'd broken her. Finding some strength she got up off of the floor.

"Baby, please I want us to talk —"

"The only thing we need to talk about is how fast you can get your junk and leave! Or I'll help you by throwing it out." Her hazel eyes turned black with hate.

"You can't just throw me out Angie. Let's talk about this," he tried to reason.

"Oh, like you were talking with your bitch when you were screwing her?" Breana probably wasn't a bitch, but she couldn't give a damn at that point.

Derek was stunned silent. He'd never heard Angie talk like this — ever. The few curse words she spewed tonight were the most he'd ever heard her say in the entire time they'd knew each other. To keep the peace, and because he was the offender, he conceded. "Okay, I'll leave tonight and be back tomorrow –"

"I'll have the locks changed by then."

In disbelief he asked, "You're kicking me out of our house?"

Angie picked his dress shirt up off the floor and threw it at him. "No you did when you decided that sleeping with Breana was better than being faithful to your WIFE!" She was done with him. The sight of him, a face she once adored, sickened her. She wanted to throw up.

"Baby, I'm sorry. I'm so sorry. It was a mistake that should have never happened. It meant absolutely nothing. NOTHING!"

"First off, you're not allowed to call me *baby*. Secondly you can take your *sorry* along with my, I don't give a shit, and leave!"

Derek looked into Dena and Devon's rooms before he left, kissing them both on their foreheads. He was sickened with the fact that he was the cause of Angie's pain and ultimately the pain his children will have when they woke up tomorrow morning.

After grabbing a few of his things and throwing them into a duffle bag, he left.

Angie threw herself atop her king sized bed and cried until the sun came up. Life as she'd known it was over. She was heartbroken, angry, revengeful and saddened. Having to face her children when they asked 'where's Daddy' made her hate Derek even more.

Eight

Five o'clock the next morning, Angie still lay in the same spot from the night before. She barely got any sleep. She'd dozed off a few times during the night exhausted from crying her heart out, but would wake up a few minutes later to start another crying fit. She could barely open her eyes because they were so puffy from crying. She cursed Derek repeatedly throughout the night for ruining her and the kids' lives. How could he have been so selfish? Thinking only about his dick when he cheated on her, instead of thinking about his loving and faithful wife and two beautiful kids waiting for him at home? *Was it even one time? Only in the Bahamas? Had the affair been going on for a while?*

Angie rolled to her side and reached for the cordless phone on the nightstand. "Do you know a good locksmith?" she groggily asked into the phone. Her throat was extremely dry and it hurt her to talk.

"Angie?" Pauline asked before yawning deeply. "Oh my God, is everything alright?" Pauline turned her head and noticed that the clock on her nightstand read five-ten in the morning. She began to panic. Angie never called that early, and she didn't sound good.

"Do you know a locksmith?" Angie asked again. She laid her head back against the pillow and closed her eyes. She wanted all the locks changed before Derek had the bright idea of showing up this morning. She didn't want to see him, and she was afraid that if he did come today – the scene would be deadly. And she didn't want to scare Dena and Devon. Finding out that their parents were splitting up would be traumatic enough. And she would leave the job of telling the kids to her cheating husband. No way was she going to be the one to tell the kids that they were getting a divorce – because as sure as the grass is green – she would be divorcing Derek's two-timing behind. She deserved better than an unfaithful spouse.

Pauline sat up in her bed, and adjusted the covers, as to not awake her sleeping husband. She was always a light sleeper and picked the phone up after the second ring. "Angie, what the hell are you asking for a locksmith for at five in the morning?" She whispered into the phone.

"Do you or Benjamin know someone that can come here right now to change my locks?"

"Angie, I swear to God you better stop asking about the locksmith and tell me what is going on?" She could hear in Angie's voice that she'd been crying and wanted answers now. Pauline quietly climbed out of the bed and walked towards her bedroom door to better talk to her friend in the living room.

Angie's heart started to beat rapidly in her chest. The scene from last night of Derek's confession came flooding back to the forefront of her mind, which it wasn't far to begin with. She wished last night was just some horrible nightmare. But the pain in her chest told her otherwise.

"Derek confessed to cheating on me last night while he was away in the Bahamas. I kicked him out. Now I want the locks changed before his trifling ass shows up here today and I end up in jail for committing murder in front of my kids," Angie told her friend. She said it so calmly, she surprised her own self.

Pauline froze on the steps leading down to the main floor of her home. "Angie, are you serious?" she asked in complete disbelief. Hurt and sorrow for her friend caused her to stop her descend and sit on the step.

"You know me better than to lie about something like that."

Tears welled up in Pauline's eyes. She knew if she was shocked and experiencing emotional pain over what Angie just told her, she knew her friend must be in terrible shape. "Oh, Angie. I'm so sorry..."

"Do you or Benjamin know someone that can change my locks right now?"

Pauline wiped the tears from her eyes. "Benjy's brother is a contractor, I'm sure he knows someone. I'll call him and have someone over there ASAP. And I'll be there in ten minutes. I'll use my key."

Angie remained silent for a moment. The hurt and pain of Derek's betrayal was really taking its toll on her. She wanted to scream. She wanted to hurl something across the room. But she restrained herself because she didn't want to wake and scare the kids. "How could he Pauline?" she wept into the phone. "How could he do this to me, to us?" She cried. The tears bulldozed from her eyes.

Pauline couldn't help it, she cried with her friend. "Sweetie I don't know. People do crazy things sometimes. I'll be over in ten minutes, okay." Pauline got up from the step and turned around to return to her bedroom to get dressed. "I'll take care of the locksmith."

"Thank you!" Angie breathed into the phone. She wouldn't be able to make it through this devastating part of her life without her best friend.

Twelve minutes later, Pauline was walking into Angie's bedroom. She lived right around the corner in the upscale neighborhood in Waldorf, Maryland, so getting there quickly wasn't a problem. She'd called her brother-in-law and was able to get him to send a locksmith over. He said the guy would be there in about thirty minutes, after Pauline stressed the urgency.

"Dena and Devon are still asleep," Pauline said walking toward Angie still lying on the bed. "I told Benjamin to come and pick them up and take them to church and perhaps lunch afterwards. That way it will give you some time to face them." Pauline toed off her flats and climbed in the bed next to her best friend. She'd NEVER seen her so broken.

Angie still had her terry robe on from the night before. She managed to climb under the covers after relieving herself in the bathroom after her call with Pauline. "Thanks. That would be great."

"I got water on to make tea. I figured it's too early to get drunk." Pauline tried to ease the mood a little bit.

Angie smiled, happy for the mental distraction. "Girl you know your virgin drinking behind ain't getting drunker than a lil tipsy. But I'll hold you to that later on."

"Just one teaspoon and I'm drunk."

They both busted out laughing.

"Well after all this drama, I'll get you used to hard liquor. Because I'm going to need something to numb the pain." Angie fought the tears that wanted to escape. She was so sick of crying.

Pauline pulled her in for a hug. Angie's head rested on her shoulder. "It's going to be okay Angie. This will soon be in the past."

"I'm so tired of crying over him, especially when he didn't consider my feelings when he screwed Breana Sutton."

"Breana Sutton?" The name rang a bell for Pauline. "You mean the real estate developer? The one with those billboards all around town?"

Angie told her all about last night.

"Do you think they've been having an affair for a while, or was it just the Bahamas?" Pauline was in complete shock. Shocked that she was actually there consoling her best friend. Shocked as to why – *Derek cheated.* Not that she knew a type, but Derek just didn't seem like the type of man that would cheat on his wife. Angie was his world. He treated the woman like a queen – the way any man should his wife. So the fact that Derek stepped out on his marriage was baffling. He just seemed like such the doting, loving and faithful spouse. *Damn!*

"You know what, I don't know and I don't care at this point. Once was enough! No marriage is perfect – but I sure as hell thought ours was close. Never, ever had I felt disrespected by Derek. Never have I felt that he may have been cheating or ogling other women. And last night, when we bumped into Breana and her friend, that's when I knew something was up. Even when he made up some excuse in the car on the way home I believed him, because again, he never gave me a reason to not trust him." Angie pushed the tears from her eyes. "I don't know if he confessed last night because we bumped into her and she threatened to reveal things or something, or if he did because he was so remorseful. He's been back from the Bahamas for over a week. He'd kept this from me for over a week, made love to me, and knew he cheated."

Angie was beginning to hate Derek with a royal passion. Every ounce of love she once felt for him was replaced with bitter hatred.

"What am I going to tell Dena and Devon?" Having to face her kids about this was what burned her the most.

"We'll figure something out." Pauline heard the kettle whistling. "Let me make our tea. I will also bring up some fruit and muffins." She honestly didn't know how to comfort Angie other than being there for her friend. How do you console a woman that just found out her husband trampled all over her heart?

****

By seven-thirty all the locks to the outdoor entrances on the house were changed. Angie even instructed Pauline to change the garage door code. While the kids were still sleeping, she pulled out all of Derek's clothes and personal items out of the closet and drawers and threw them in large trash bags and placed them on the front porch. She thought putting them in trash bags was too generous, but Pauline talked her out of burning them in the fireplace. Or better yet, putting them in the tub and dousing them with bleach. *Gawd that would've felt so good.*

She crawled back into bed, exhausted from the activity. Derek had called on the house and her cell phone several times wanting to talk to her, but she ignored all. His sorry meant nothing to her, absolutely nothing. Especially since he wasn't sorry enough to not commit the act in the first place.

"I'm going to make breakfast for the kids before I wake them up to get dressed for church," Pauline said, heading toward the bedroom door. "You get some sleep, okay."

Angie nodded her head under the covers. La la land of dreams was calling her name. "Thank you for being here Pauline."

"Of course!" Pauline stepped out of the room and closed the door behind her.

****

Ten o'clock, Derek pulled up into his driveway. He waited this long because he wanted to respect Angie's wishes and give her some time to – *what? Get over what I've done?* He didn't know. But he just wanted to give her time to at least cool off a bit, so maybe now they could talk.

He didn't get any sleep last night because he was so worried about Angie. After leaving his house, he got a room at a local hotel. He was happy to see Pauline's car parked in his driveway. That made him feel a little bit better that she had her best friend with her. But also shameful for yet another person knowing about his indiscretion. He wasn't a perfect man – but cheating on his wife was something he thought he would've never done. But he prayed to God that she would forgive him. He'd made a huge mistake. Breana was only sex, nothing more, nothing less. And he hoped Angie wouldn't throw their marriage away over it. He knew she would need time and at this point, he was willing to wait it out. Divorce wasn't an option. *I can't lose my wife.*

Derek got out of the car. He was curious about the numerous trash bags on his porch. Suspicion of what was inside them caused his anxiety to spike. He inserted his house key into the lock of the front door. It didn't turn. He tried it again. *She changed the locks?* His thoughts were confirmed when the lock still didn't turn.

Fear coursed through his body of what it all meant. He frantically rang the doorbell. "Angie! Angie, baby!"

He heard footsteps coming toward the front door. "Go away!" Pauline snapped peeking out the narrow window framing the door. Her pale, cream face was becoming red with anger. She and Derek had developed a great friendship over the years and it pained her to be mean toward him, but Angie had been her girl from day one. So her loyalty lie with her friend. "She's finally sleeping."

"Pauline, please let me in. I need to talk to her and see the kids," he pleaded. He didn't care if it was making him out to be some type of punk. His heart was on the line.

"The kids are at church. And Angie just went to sleep a while ago. She's devastated, Derek! Devastated!"

Derek hung his head in shame. "I know. That's why I need to talk to my wife. We need to talk."

"Look, she's not in any condition to face you right now. Trust me, I'm telling you this for your own good. You cheated on her Derek, dammit how could you? You guys had the model marriage and you went ahead and shot that to hell." She bit down on her bottom lip, stopping herself from wanting to use every cuss word known to man to tell him about his behind.

"You don't think I know I messed up?" Derek slammed his hand against the front door, causing Pauline to jump back in fear. "I effed the hell up. I know that. And you telling me that isn't going to change it. So I need to talk to my wife. I need her to know how sorry I am. How terrible I feel about what happened and for hurting her. I need to grovel at her feet. I need..." Tears rolled down his face. He was losing it. Just a couple weeks ago his family was perfectly intact. Now? Now it was ruined because of him.

Pauline felt his pain. She knew he'd messed up tremendously. But seeing him like this – she believed he was sorry for what he'd done. But that still didn't change things. "Derek I can see this is hard for you too. But this is a lot for her right now.

You can't expect her to just be okay after you dropping the bomb on her just last night. Give her time, you owe her at least that."

He nodded his head in agreement. She was right. He was being selfish in wanting Angie to talk to him right away. "I want to see Dena and Devon."

"I'm sure that won't be a problem. When Angie gets up I will talk to her about making arrangements for you to see the kids, okay?"

"Please Pauline. I know she may not be ready to see me, but I need to see my children. Today."

"I will call you," she assured him. "And you may want to take your things with you before she puts them in the trash."

"Thanks." Derek reluctantly turned away from the front door and picked up as many trash bags of his things and carried them to his car. He made two more trips before he got them all in his car. He resigned himself to the fact that he may be staying at the hotel for a while. He could stay with Brian for a bit until Angie was ready to let him back in, but he wasn't into living the bachelor lifestyle again. Brian's place was a revolving door for women. And the last thing Derek needed or wanted was to be around any of that. He could also look into getting a month to month lease for a small apartment or condo. But he didn't want to think about his separation from Angie lasting long enough for that to be necessary.

Nine

Pauline tried to convince Angie to take at least a week off from teaching, but she refused. She got herself together to wake up at six am Monday morning to get her kids up for school and get herself dressed as well. She wouldn't allow Derek's affair to cause her to be stuck in a constant funk. Though it wasn't easy looking at her reflection in the mirror as she brushed her teeth. Her eyes were still a little puffy and red. But eye drops and makeup would remedy that. Her heart on the other hand was a different matter. But she knew she would make it through it. Someway, somehow.

"Mommy, when is Daddy coming home?" Devon asked after Angie placed a plate of hot pancakes in front of him.

Yesterday she'd agreed for Derek to pick up the kids after they got in from church. She relayed to Pauline, that he was to tell the children that they were separating or else she would tell them the ugly truth as to why. Supposedly he just told the kids that he was going to be away from them for a few days. She was expecting them to have a barrage of questions when they returned from being with Derek, but they didn't. To them it was as if he was just going on another business trip.

"Baby." She swallowed the lump in her throat. This was the question she didn't want to answer, because as far as she was concerned the answer was *never*. She didn't know why Derek didn't tell them the truth — which was he was moving out permanently. All he did was gave them false hope. "Daddy's..." Should she tell them? Should she too prolong the inevitable? "...Mommy and Daddy are breaking up sweetie. That means Daddy and Mommy will still be your parents, but we won't all live together anymore." Never in the nine years of her marriage did she think she would ever have to say these words to her children.

"What, why!?" Dena cried. "Daddy said that he was just going to be gone for a few days."

I hate you Derek!

"Well it will be more than a few days. It will be all the time."

Angie watched as tears welled up in Dena and Devon's eyes. Her heart broke at the sight. All of this because Derek couldn't stay faithful. She clutched her children to her bosom, to comfort them. Tears of her own descended down her face, ridding her of her disguise.

"I'm so sorry. I'm so sorry. Sometimes Mommies and Daddies break up. But that doesn't mean we don't love you, because we love you very, *very* much."

"Are you getting a divorce?" Dena asked, sniffling on Angie's blouse.

Divorce? Well isn't that the result of an extended separation? "Ah, yes. We're getting a divorce."

"What's a divorce?" Devon asked.

"It's when your parents are no longer married." Dena broke out of Angie's embrace then ran out of the kitchen. Angie watched her daughter go, feeling completely helpless.

She stayed to comfort Devon some more. He finally stopped crying and reached for his apple juice on the counter. "You think you can finish up your breakfast, sweetheart?" she asked him.

Devon solemnly nodded his head.

It was settled. They weren't going to school today. She made sure her six year old son Devon was okay before going in search of her eight year old daughter to console her as well.

Angie desperately needed to get away. How she thought she was ready to get back to work, after her world was destroyed just two days ago, she didn't know. It was a hopeful feeling. She didn't want to succumb to depression because she seriously felt it coming on. She needed to be strong not just for herself but also for her children.

After what Angie told Pauline about breakfast this morning with the kids, Pauline called their school and informed the principal that she and Angie would be out for at least a week. She didn't care if her job may be in jeopardy. Her best friend needed her. After discussing it with her husband Benjamin, she booked a stay at Great Wolf Lodge in Williamsburg, VA for the rest of the week, for her, Angie, Devon and Dena.

She figured the kids would have fun at the waterpark, and it would allow Angie to grieve the end of her marriage in peace.

****

Brian burst into Derek's office with Latoya, Derek's assistant, on his trail. "Mr. Monroe, I told him not to come in until I notified you—"

"It's okay Miss Simms," Derek told her. He was sitting with his back to them. He was staring aimlessly out the window overlooking the huge Capital Wheel and the Potomac River.

When he got into the office this morning, he looked like hell. The proof of that was written all over Latoya's face when she saw him after he stepped off the elevator into the office suite. His face was scruffy from not shaving. His eyes were a little bloodshot from a hangover he got after trying to drown his sorrows. His clothes were wrinkled and disheveled. Thankfully he didn't smell like he looked. He did manage to get in the shower before heading in today. He'd informed Latoya that he didn't want to be disturbed unless it was Angie or something relating to his children.

"Okay," Latoya said and backed out of the office closing it shut behind her.

"Shit!" Brian said walking over to where Derek sat behind his desk. "You told her didn't you?" He looked his friend over. *Damn.* "I told you to keep your mouth shut, man." Brian leaned against the wall, studying his boy some more. He looked like he'd died and came back as a zombie.

Derek didn't answer. He just continued to stare out of the large window.

"I knew something was up when I peeped you and Angie bump into Breana Saturday night. I've been blowing up your cell. Even called the house yesterday and Pauline told me that Angie wasn't taking any calls and she didn't know where you were."

Derek had forgotten that Brian was at the charity event that night. But he still remained silent. All he wanted was for his wife to just pick up at least one of his calls so he could hear her voice, even if she cussed him out, he just wanted to hear her voice. The pain he was feeling over what he'd done was like no other he'd ever experienced in his life.

"Derek, man. You've got to talk to me." Brian nudged him on the shoulder.

"She kicked me out of the house. I haven't seen or spoken to her since that night." Derek blinked, then continued to stare into nothing.

Brian ran his hand over his bald head. He felt his boy's pain. Angie was as great a woman a man would ever want. The type of woman men would give the world for. Secretly he was always a bit envious of his friend's marriage. But seeing Derek all torn up like this had him feeling bad for him.

"Have you tried calling her, going over to the house?"

Derek turned his attention from the window and looked at Brian as if he was stupid. "Of course. But she doesn't want anything to do with me." He huffed. "Yesterday when she told Pauline it was okay for me to get the kids for a while, she said I had to tell them that we are getting a d...divorce."

"Damn bro." Brian had to sit down for that one. He knew things would be bad if Angie found out. But the d word?

"She wants a divorce." Derek fought back the tears. "Damn, I know I jacked up, but she could at least let us talk about things before she started throwing out getting a divorce. I couldn't tell Dena and Devon that. So I just told them I would be away for a few days. I hope like hell Angie is ready to talk to me by then."

Brian felt a twinge of hope of his own. "Give her some time, man. Finding out you cheated had to be a major blow. Hopefully in a few days she'd be ready to talk."

"I hope so man. I don't know what I'll do if I lose my family over this mess."

The intercom on Derek's office phone chirped. He turned around in his chair then pressed a button on the phone. "Yes."

"Ah, Ms. Breana Sutton here to see you Sir. I told her you weren't accepting any visitors but she's insisting on waiting."

Derek groaned. She was the last person he wanted to see.

"I thought you ended things with her," Brian said.

"I thought I did too." Derek cursed under his breath. He hit the intercom button. "Send her in."

"You need to handle that." Brian stood to his feet. "Where are you staying until things die down?"

"Aloft."

"You know you could stay at my place," Brian offered.

"Naw, thanks though. I need time alone." Derek stood up.

"Hit me up later man. Drinks on me." Brian started for the office door. Just then Breana walked in. His steps halted as he overtly checked her out in a tight dark blue pencil skirt, vertical white with blue striped blouse and six inch heels. He stifled a groan. *Dayum, I see why my boy slipped.* Her body was banging, and her face was the cherry on top. He nodded his head in acknowledgement of her and continued for the door, not before turning around to check out her, assets.

"What do you want?" Derek asked. His patience with her was past expired. Yeah they both were to blame for his current dilemma, but he thought when they were in the Bahamas they agreed to cut ties.

"Good morning to you too," she snapped. She was there to check on him to make sure the little incident Saturday night didn't cause any drama to his *happy* home, and he had the nerve to give her attitude. But when she surveyed him closely, she realized things didn't turn out favorably. He looked like a bum. *A sexy bum though*, she had to admit.

"Cut the shit Breana. What do you want?"

"Excuse me?" She placed her well-manicured hand on her hip and struck a diva pose. "Watch your tone and language with me. I only came here because you didn't answer any of my text messages of phone calls. After running into you and your wife on Saturday I just wanted to make sure everything was alright."

He sat down, forgetting his manners to offer her a seat. "And it never occurred to you that perhaps I didn't need nor want you feeling the need to check up on me? We're not friends. We were barely business associates, what's going on in my life is none of your concern."

For some reason that hurt. But perhaps he was right, why did she care? *Because he turned you out in three long days of the best sex of your life. And because...* "Well forgive me for having a heart. Like I told you in the Bahamas, I don't want to mess things up with you and your wife because of what happened between us."

Derek groaned internally. *If only I can go back in time, I would have never went on that trip.* "Okay. That's well noted. Please do me a favor and delete my number from your phone. I've recommended someone else as your business consultant, whom I'm sure would assist you well with your future endeavors." He wanted this woman as far away from him as possible. Being in her presence felt as if he was cheating on his wife all over again, and he didn't like it one bit.

Breana swallowed deeply the lump in her throat, from the hurt of him dismissing her like she was nothing. *Get it together chick, this isn't your first rodeo, you know the rules to the game. Keep it moving.* "Okay, well." She stumbled with her words. She really didn't know what to expect when she came there, but being rushed out like this wasn't a factor. "I guess I'll see you around."

God I hope not. Watching her turn to leave, he felt a little bad for his tone with her. "Take care of yourself Breana." He added as pleasantly as he could.

"You do the same." She threw over her shoulder then walked out of his office. And hopefully out of his life, Derek prayed.

Ten

"It's been three days and I haven't heard anything from Angie or Pauline. Where the hell are they?" Derek slammed his hand on Brian's kitchen counter. He had come over because he was about to lose his mind worrying about where his wife and kids were at. He needed someone to help calm his nerves.

"You haven't heard anything since Pauline's text message to you Tuesday morning?" Brian opened the fridge to retrieve two bottled beers.

"NO! I even went to Benjamin to get him to tell me where they were, but all he said was that they were safe and they would be back soon. I guess I should be thankful for at least that tidbit of information." He accepted the beer from Brian and took a long swig.

"Think she went to her folks in Florida?"

"Naw, I called as if I was checking in on them and they didn't lead on to anything."

"Bruh, I think if you want things to eventually work in your favor you need to relax a bit and give Angie her time. When she's ready she will reach out to you man. But if you're blowing up her and Pauline's phones every ten minutes, you ain't helping the situation."

"How can I relax? For all I know she's having divorce papers drawn up."

"Angie's hurting man. But I don't think she's talking to a lawyer. She probably just took the kids away to give her some time to process everything." Brian sat on one of the high back stools at the counter.

"Okay, maybe you're right."

"I know I am. Plus Benjy knows where they're at and they're safe. You know he would tell you if something was up."

Pauline's husband Benjamin wasn't as tight to them as Derek and Brian were to each other, but all three men had built a bond over the years. So Benjamin was cool, Derek knew he could trust that his boy would be straight up with him.

"So chill. Angie will call you soon," Brian continued.

＊＊＊＊

The following Monday, a week after finding out her husband cheated, Angie made her way back to work. The time away to Great Wolf Lodge was beneficial. She was still struggling though, there was no way she could get over the hurt, over the doom of nine years of marriage, in a week. But she had to get back to work. She had to get back to her students. And she and her kids needed to resume some semblance of normalcy in their lives.

Her cellphone buzzed annoyingly in her desk drawer, like a mosquito buzzing around your ear. She looked at the name and picture of her husband displayed on the phone. *I seriously need to delete his picture and number.* She wanted to ignore the call. Her students were starting to stroll into the classroom for the day, with there being about fifteen minutes before the bell rang.

"What!" she snapped into the phone.

There was brief silence. Derek was stunned that she actually answered his call. It had been a week since he'd heard her voice. "Angie," he breathed. "It's so nice to hear your voice."

She rolled her eyes. "I'm about to hang up."

"Wait! Baby –"

"Don't you dare." She gritted through her teeth.

"Can I take you out to lunch, I really want us to talk?"

"No!"

"Angie we need to talk."

"Whatever you need to say to me from now on will be done through Pauline or my lawyer."

That was a sucker punch to his heart. "Lawyer?"

"Yes. My lawyer. We're getting a divorce. But in the meantime arrangements will be made regarding the children."

"Bab...Angie, we don't need to get a divorce. I love you! I made a stupid mistake, yes. But we can work through this. We can't tell the children we're getting a divorce, it–"

"I already told them since you punked out." She scoffed. "You are the cause of this Derek, not me. You were the one that cheated, not me. So stop calling me. And don't you dare try to come and see me. I'm done with you, DONE!" She had to remember to keep her voice down because she was at work. Which was why she didn't want to answer his call in the first place. She had to remain strong. She sucked in her tears then wiped away the strays that had already escaped. "I hate you, I hate you so much! You're trifling...Ashley you dropped your book sweetie." She told one of her students that just walked into the classroom. She turned her attention back to the call. "Stop calling me Derek. You'll hear from Pauline later. Dena and Devon want to see you, so perhaps you can pick them up from her house when you can." She hated him, but she could never punish him by keeping their children from him.

"Angie..." Derek croaked. His worse fear was coming to fruition. His wife hated him and was divorcing him and it was all his fault. "I love you! Baby I love you so much. I was a fool Angie, I messed up and I will do whatever I have to, to make it up to you. Please give me, give us another chance. Please?" He couldn't just let her go. *No!* He didn't want to be with anyone else. She was his wife, the mother of his children, they were supposed to grow old together. "Baby please?"

Tears were streaming down Angie's face so fast she couldn't wipe them fast enough. "I've got to go." She ended the call. Her heart was painfully constricting in the cavity of her chest. She muted her phone then slid it back into her desk.

Angie stood up abruptly and headed toward her classroom door in hopes of seeking her classroom aide in the hallway. She needed a quick escape to get herself together.

"Good morning Ms. Monroe."

Not paying attention, because her head was down while she wiped tears from her eyes, Angie had walked right into the granite of Aron's chest. He reveled in the softness of her breast against his upper body. He took the opportunity to slide his hand down her arm to the small of her back to steady her. He itched to palm her round behind, but found a morsel of strength to refrain himself. The lavender scent of her perfume enticed his desire for her. Reluctantly he stepped back, he did not want her to notice his arousal forming an imprint in his pants.

"Oh, I'm sorry," Angie said.

Aron could sense something was off because of her demeanor. "Are you okay?"

She sniffled, then wiped at her eyes again before looking up at him. "Yes. I was just going to the door to find my aide."

Her students busied themselves with their early morning activities before the bell rang for the day, not paying the two adults much mind.

Angie stepped out of his way and made it to the door. She peeked down the hallway, seeing students walking leisurely toward their classrooms, however no sight of her classroom aide.

"I can stay here and wait while you go and do whatever it is you need to do," Aron offered. He desperately wanted to hug her. Perhaps that would take some of her unhappiness away. She wasn't as bright and cheerful as she usually was whenever he'd spoken to her. *I wonder what's up.* He missed seeing her last week while she was away. He wondered if her disposition this morning was related to her absence.

"No thank you! But thanks for offering." She looked down the hallway once more. "So how was your weekend?" she asked him as cheerfully as she could muster. Despite her desire to escape and cry her eyes out in the bathroom, she was still a teacher and had to remain professional.

Aron studied her face a bit longer, then looked into her hazel eyes. "It was great, what about yours?" He noticed the dimness that appeared in her eyes at his question. *Yeah, something is definitely up. Could there be trouble in paradise?*

"Mrs. Monroe, look what I made?" Veronica, one of her students chimed in, twirling around in front of her.

Angie scrunched her face in confusion. "What did you make Veronica?"

"This skirt, see?" Veronica ran her hand down the yellow plaid skirt she had on.

By closer inspection, Angie could tell it was homemade. "Oh wow, that is wonderful. You did that all by yourself?"

"Yes ma'am. Well with a little help from my Grandma."

"You did a great job!" Angie patted Veronica on the head. "Maybe you can make me one next time."

"Oh yeah! I can do that Mrs. Monroe. I just need your measurements."

"Okay, I will give it to you later, okay."

"Okay." Veronica twirled away to show her skirt to her classmates.

The school bell rang.

Angie looked up at Aron who was still studying her. She started to feel a bit uncomfortable under his eyes. Uncomfortable with the fact that he probably could see distress written all over her face. *You can do this. Just take one day at a time. The pain has to eventually go away, right?*

"Well it's time to start class."

"Are you sure you're alright?" He needed assurance for some reason.

"Yes, I'm fine, thank you for your concern. You just caught me at a bad moment, but I'm good now."

He hesitated, but eventually said, "Okay. Hope the rest of your day is better."

"Thanks!"

****

By ten o'clock that morning Angie had a huge boutique of sunflowers on her desk. The note read:

Hope this brightens up your day as you always do mine.

Best regards,

Aron Taylor

It certainly did place a huge smile on Angie's face. She thought his gift was very thoughtful and what she needed to help bring her out of her funk for today. She however didn't realize his *secondary* meaning with the gesture.

Eleven

A month had passed. Derek finally gave in to having to lease a temporary condo. Actually he leased a condo a week ago because staying at the hotel was ridiculously expensive – but he was holding on to hope that Angie would come around and allow him to move back home. Fat chance so far. Thankfully though, no divorce papers yet. But her lawyer did contact him, so he knew she was serious about it.

They did make arrangements for him to get the kids Thursday to Friday and every other weekend. So far it had been working out. He hated it though. Hated having to pick up and drop of his children at Pauline's house. Angie refused to see him. So, it had been a month since he'd actually seen his wife. Though when he made his daily drive by the house, just to check things out; he caught a glimpse of her once going through the front door.

To say he was barely surviving was an understatement. Getting out of bed each day without his wife lying next to him was a daily stab to his heart and a constant reminder of the mess he'd made.

"This sure is a true bachelor's pad," Benjamin said, sitting down on one of the four beanbag chairs Derek had in the small living room. He didn't want to invest in better furniture because he wouldn't be staying there long. He was determined to get his wife back – to stay married.

"This place is only temporary," he informed Benjamin. That had become his mantra. His separation from his wife and kids was *only temporary*.

"Thanks for coming to hang out though. I know Pauline probably hates my guts."

They both focused on the flat screen TV ahead, to play each other in a video game.

"Naw, she doesn't hate you. She just hates what you did. Angie's her best friend – you know how that is."

"Yeah, I know."

"So what's your plan?" Benjamin asked before taking a swig of beer.

Derek knew exactly what he was referring to. "First, I need to find a way to get her to at least talk to me. It's been three weeks since I spoke to her. All of our communication has been through Pauline or the lawyer she got."

"She won't even reply to a text message?"

Derek shook his head. "Nope, nothing."

"Damn!"

"Exactly. I keep trying to figure out a way, but I just don't know what."

"How about suggesting going to counseling? Has her lawyer brought that up?"

"Naw, not from the fees they will get from representing us in divorce, they trying to get paid. And since I cheated, she doesn't have to wait for us to be separated a year to file."

"When do you guys meet with the lawyers?"

"Tuesday."

"I say bring up counseling. Grovel, do whatever you can to show them that you want to try to work things out, even if Angie isn't budging. Maybe her lawyer would encourage her to at least give it a try, at least for the kids' sake."

A light bulb went on in Derek's head. "Yeah, that just may work."

"At least give it a try. I know you love her man." Benjamin patted him on the back. "I'm feeling your pain dude. I don't know what I would do if Pauline wanted to get rid of my white butt."

"Trust me Benjy; you don't ever want to find out."

Twelve

"Did he send you here?"

"No. I came to check up on you on my own. I wanted to give you some time first, so I've been keeping tabs on you through Pauline."

Angie held the door ajar, still unsure of whether to let him in or not. After taking a deep breath, she stepped aside to let him into her house.

"You look good," Brian said, stepping into the home.

"Thanks, I guess." She shut the door behind him, then walked ahead of him back into the family room where she was indulging in reality TV to keep her mind distracted from the chaos of her own life. Dena and Devon were over at their friends' house for a few hours. She was happy for the reprieve.

Brian watched her walk away, dressed in black yoga pants and a pink tank top. Her bare feet padded lightly against the hardwood floor.

"So how have you been?" Brian took a seat opposite her in an arm chair.

"Honestly Brian, I don't know how I feel talking to you about what's going on between me and Derek. You probably knew he was cheating—"

"Don't put that on me Ang," he was the only person that shortened her name. "When he told me what happened, I told him he had to tell you right away." Brian lied easily through his teeth. "I told him he was stupid for what he did. He went and messed up a good thing."

That took Angie by surprise, but she was happy to have him in her corner. "Really?" She was still doubtful that Brian didn't stick up or try to cover for Derek.

"Derek's my boy, but I have to admit when a person messed up, and he messed up big time. You deserve better than that. I know how faithful and loving you've been to him and he just screwed some random chick and broke up his happy home."

Brian was laying it on thick. Thing was – he'd always had a thing for Angie, something he'd never admitted to anyone. He always wished he'd saw her first when they were in college, before Derek did that fateful day. Angie was the type of woman he wanted to retire his player card for. And Derek's dilemma gave him a window of opportunity he'd wanted for years. No, before today he'd never done anything to separate the two — but hell, if Derek was about to lose her, he was the best replacement. And if he got her, he wouldn't do something as stupid as cheat on her.

"I do deserve better, which is why we're getting a divorce. I don't think I could ever forgive, let alone forget, what he's done," Angie bit out. She was doing great emotionally before he showed up, watching reality TV, and allowing the reality stars drama to deflate her own. She had her good days and bad days, but today was one of the good ones. She hadn't cried at all today, but talking about Derek now wasn't helping.

"You've got to do what's best for you. Start fresh and new. The next man you get with I'm sure would know what a great thing they have and won't do anything to mess that up." He admired her beautiful mocha face and hazel eyes. He shifted his gaze down to her lips. He'd dreamt of kissing her lips for years and the thought of that possibly becoming a reality caused his groin to twitch. "Derek's a fool for what he's done to you."

Angie stared at him, wide eyed by his admission. His words encouraged her a bit with the internal struggle she had about wanting a divorce. No she didn't want to be with her husband anymore, not after his betrayal, but divorce was so final, like putting the last nail in the coffin and she wasn't sure she was ready for that just yet. How could she just flush nine years of marriage down the drain? How could Derek?

"Thank you for understanding. I thought you would be pleading Derek's case, telling me how sorry he was, blah, blah, blah. I just can't take him saying sorry anymore. He's left me a sorry voice message every day. I'm sick of it!" She slumped back against the couch. She mentally fought the onset of a headache that was threatening to come on. She rubbed the temples on the side of her face. *I was doing so good until he showed up talking about this.*

"I'm here for you Angie, anything you need just let me know." He sat back comfortably against the chair. He knew he should be feeling terrible about stepping to his best friend's wife – but Angie, Angie was finally going to be single and that gave him all the green light he needed.

"Thank you Brian."

"Where's Dena and Devon?"

"At their friends' house. I have to run and pick them up later." She yawned.

Brian reluctantly took that as his cue to leave. He'd laid good foundation for Angie to believe he was on her side in all this. *You're a dirt bag.* His conscious admonished him. *Derek's loss, all's fair in love and war.* He stood to his feet.

"I'm not gonna hold you up any longer. Go take a nap while the kids are gone," he offered.

Angie stood and stretched. Brian took the opportunity to check her out openly without her noticing, as her head went back while her hands went up in the air. He got a little glimpse of her stomach from her tank pulling up while she stretched. Her full breast pushed up as she did.

He imagined all of the things he wanted to do to her sexy size eight frame. His mind hadn't gone there in years, since they were in college, out of some respect to his friendship with Derek. But, *my, my, my.* He murmured under his breath. *Derek you're a damn fool!*

"Yeah, I'm going to soak in a bubble bath then afterwards take a long nap." Angie started toward the front door. She was suddenly feeling very fatigued. All the crying, mourning and worrying she'd been doing was draining on her body.

Brian followed her butt as she walked ahead of him. No ounce of shame had yet to announce itself within him. Angie opened the door to let him out.

"Call me *anytime* if you need *anything*," he offered.

Derek slowed his car down as he approached his house. The sight of a car other than Angie's or Pauline's in his driveway caught his attention. He crept closer to the house. He recognized Brian's Range Rover. *What is he doing there?* His eyes darted from Brian's car up to his front steps. There he saw Brian and Angie talking. He eyes took her in. Brief sightings like this was the only opportunity he'd had of seeing her. His eyes travelled from her bare feet up her entire luscious body. His own body warmed at the sight of his wife. He longed to go closer, but had been keeping his distance out of respect for her wishes. He'd messed up enough, he didn't want to force his presence on her. But he wasn't sure how much more of not seeing her up close and hearing her beautiful voice, he could take. What was crazy was, he was looking forward to seeing her on Tuesday for their meeting with their lawyers. How crazy was that? But he was gonna take whatever he could get, it was a chance to see his wife face to face, up close, the first since *that* night.

Angie's bright smile looking up at Brian kicked in a predator instinct within Derek. They didn't notice him because of several eight foot evergreen plants that lined the front portion of the property. But he had a good view from his angle though. He stopped the car at a discreet distance. Angie leaned in and hugged Brian. That didn't alarm Derek as much, but what did was when he noticed Brian leaning in and - *did he just take a whiff of her?* He'd seen his friend do it to women he was *involved* with, countless times to recognize the maneuver. Then his best friend's hand glided down a little lower than *respectful*, almost touching Angie's butt. He was seeing red. His nostrils flared in anger. He was about to charge out of his car toward the house, just when Angie broke free of their hug. *What the hell was that? Am I tripping?*

Derek watched as they said their goodbyes and Angie closed the door behind her. Brian then walked to his car. Derek took a moment to calm his nerves and get his rage under control. *I'm tripping. I'm straight tripping.*

He pulled out his cell phone and dialed Brian's number. "Where you at?" He asked in a neutral tone.

"Hey what up?" Brian chimed from his Bluetooth. Derek watched as Brian backed out of his driveway. He'd backed up himself and parked behind a car to stay out of view.

"Nothing man, just hitting you up."

"I was gonna call you man. I'm just leaving your house, I went to check in on Angie for you."

"Yeah, I didn't know you we're going over there."

"Yeah, I wanted to give her some time before showing up. Since she doesn't want to see you, I figured I'll go and check in on her for you. She's still struggling with everything that went down. Bruh, she's real serious about divorcing you." Brian maneuvered down the street away from the house.

"Hmmm." Derek was fighting with wanting to ask Brian if he was trying to make a pass at his wife. He and Brian had been friends for a long time, he'd never disrespected him in that way. But he didn't have a good feeling about seeing Brian and Angie *hugging.* They've hugged before over the years, but today... He shook the thought out of his head. *My boy wouldn't do anything like that.* He reasoned being separated from Angie for the past month had his mind playing tricks on him. *But still...*

"I don't know how you're going to be able to fix things, man. She's dead-set on drawing up those papers."

"We'll see," Derek answered noncommittally. A battle was going on within him to not check Brian. "I've got to go, I'll hit you up later." He ended the call not waiting for a response. He would hate to have to bury his friend – but he would if the small feeling of betrayal within him bloomed. For now, he parked the thought to the side. He had bigger matters at hand – winning his wife back.

Thirteen

Ten-thirty Tuesday morning, Derek waited impatiently in the conference room of Angie's lawyer's office. His lawyer, Samuel Rivers, sat next to him, reviewing some documents. Angie's lawyer, Regina Flowers, had escorted them to the room ten minutes ago, informing them that she would return once Angie had arrived.

Derek was anxious to see his wife. It had been thirty-five days since he looked up-close into her beautiful mocha face. His stalkerish glimpses of her were no comparison, though it helped him from going crazy.

The conference room door creaked open. Derek sat up straighter in his seat. The moment Angie stepped into the room his mouth went dry. His love, his life, his wife, was beautiful as ever. The hunter green wrap dress she wore hugged her body to perfection, and brought out her hazel eyes, which couldn't be missed if you tried. Her bob hair cut was perfect as always, and her minimal makeup highlighted her natural beauty. He was in awe. He wanted to leap out of his seat and crush her to his chest. He ached to hold her in his arms and kiss her soft lips.

He stood up in respect of her presence. "Good morning." He greeted her.

Angie barely looked in his direction as she made her way to the opposite side of the massive oak desk to take a seat. To her surprise, her heart was beating like a freight train in her chest. It had been more than thirty days since she'd kicked him out. And just the sight of him, reminded her of all the love she still had for him which was now hidden under the layers of hate that was cemented into her heart.

Instead of replying to Derek, Angie did say good morning to his lawyer in return to his own greeting to her.

"Okay, let's get started shall we," Mrs. Flowers stated. "My client is seeking divorce on the grounds of infidelity. Which means, she doesn't have to wait for you all to be separated for one year..."

"Angie," Derek called out. "Do you really want to get a divorce?" He was still hopeful despite the reason they were in the room in the first place.

Angie turned a deathly glare in his direction. "No, I don't!"

Derek breathed a sigh of relief.

"But I don't want to remain married to a cheater either. So I want a divorce and I don't want you holding things up during the process."

"Baby, I made a mistake. It was only in the Bahamas, I swear to you." He couldn't go out like this. "I have no intentions of doing anything like that ever again. We've been separated for a month, can you give us a chance to talk things through?" He asked desperately.

"Mr. Monroe, my client is ready to move forward—" Mrs. Flowers started.

"Isn't the point of mediation to come to a resolve which is favorable for both parties?" Mr. Rivers asked mockingly to Mrs. Flowers.

"Baby, please. We can go to counseling..." Derek spoke up.

"Counseling for what Derek? For you to learn how to keep you dick out of other women's pu—"

"Mrs. Monroe!" Mrs. Flowers admonished. "There's no need to go there."

"What!" Angie snapped. "I'm not the one that destroyed our marriage, he did! I don't want to go to counseling, I want a divorce. I was a great wife to you Derek, I was faithful, I loved you! And what you did..." Angie bit back the tears. "What you did, I can't forgive. I barely want to look at you, much less stay married to you. I can care less of how many times you slept with her because all it took was one time for you to rip my heart out of my chest." She covered her face with hands. She hated that she was crying in front of him. But the pain of it all gripped her at her core.

A bullet could have just blown his brains out and it still wouldn't have felt worse than what he felt at that moment watching his wife cry all because of what he'd done. His heart bled for her. He was immensely sorry for sleeping with Breana. He couldn't change what happened. No matter how many times he wished, begged, prayed to God that he could, he couldn't change what happened those three days in the Bahamas. But he was willing to find a way, he wasn't quite sure what it was, but he would find a way to make it up to Angie.

"I'm sor–"

"Enough with your damn sorry!" She snapped.

He tried a different approach. "I love you Angie Diana Monroe. I love you!" He didn't care that their lawyers were in the room with them, he needed to plead his case. "I don't want a divorce. Yes I know what I did is grounds for one, but I don't want to lose you. I want us to work things out. I made a terrible mistake, it was stupid and selfish. But I don't want our family to be separated. I want to rebuild your trust in me, sweetheart. I love you!"

His words played a tug-of-war on Angie's heart. Hearing him say he loved her did penetrate her heart just a little. She had removed her hands from her face and wiped the tears from her eyes, she forced herself to look at his face to gauge his sincerity. She didn't know what to think, what to believe. She loved him but now hated him just as much or probably even more.

She shook her head 'no'. She wished things could go back to the way they were before she found out he cheated. From the time he approached her in college, she knew he was the one for her. She knew she would be the mother of his children. She knew they would grow old together and see their grand and great grandchildren. But... "I want a divorce."

Derek's heart was shattered once again. Tears stung the back of his eyelids.

Mrs. Flowers turned to Angie and conversed with her quietly. "I know you were dead-set on filing divorce papers, but I think perhaps you should consider trying counseling first. Even if it's just one session, at least give it a try to ensure divorce is what you really want." She felt a bit of sympathy for Derek.

"I just want this over and done with, the sooner the better. I want a divorce," Angie stated affirmably.

Derek struggled to hear what they were whispering to each other about as he watched them across from him at the large desk.

"Mrs. Monroe, my client will be willing to sign divorce papers without contesting them if you agree to go to counseling first," Mr. Rivers stated.

Derek shot his attention to his lawyer. "What the hell, no!"

"I'm just strategizing. She's obviously struggling with her decision," Mr. Rivers informed his client.

Derek turned his attention back to Angie and her lawyer.

Angie looked at Mr. Rivers then shifted her gaze to Derek. "If I agree to counseling, you'll sign the divorce papers without any issues, once we ensure all our assets and finances are squared away?"

Derek swallowed visibly. Could he agree to that, to just sign away his life with his wife and children? "Yes," he answered softly. He'd wanted a chance to gain her trust back, if this was it, he'd take it. And he hoped like hell it would work.

Angie stared at him across the table, stunned by his response. "Okay, I'll agree to go to at least one session."

"No! To make it fair, we would need at least six months of counseling for any change to come about," Derek asserted.

"Hell no! I said I would go, but not for six months. As far as I'm concerned we can begin the process of filing."

"Mrs. Monroe, Derek is only trying to ensure you both do everything possible to save your marriage. Six months of counseling isn't unreasonable. You have your two children to consider in all this as well." Mr. Rivers knew throwing in the kids would be a soft spot for Angie.

Angie bit down on her bottom lip not to hurl obscenities out at Derek again, really she was getting tired of it. And quite frankly she didn't like the person his affair had turned her into. She was cussing like a sailor. So not ladylike, so not Christian-like, so not teacher-like, so not mother-like and so not Angie-like.

"Fine!" she replied tersely. At least when the ink is dried on the divorce papers she would have the little comfort of knowing that she at least made an effort. But she and Derek were DONE as far as she was concerned. Being with Derek again would only remind her of him being with Breana. Him kissing her, touching her, having sex with her. She abruptly shook her head in hope that it helped to erase the disgusting images from her mind. She'd been battling with them for a month.

He is tainted. What we had could never be again.

A huge smile spread brightly across Derek's handsome mahogany face. She agreed to counseling. *Thank you God!* "Thank you Angie. I will research some marriage counselors and forward them to you so we can choose the best person for us." This was his chance. *I'm going to win you back baby. I'm going to regain your trust.*

"I've got to get back to work." She was done with this meeting. It didn't turn out like she'd thought. They should have been discussing how they would split their assets. Prolonging the divorce would only torture her more. Angie stood up after pushing her chair back. She picked her purse up off of the table. She said her goodbyes to the lawyers, then headed for the door.

"Angie," Derek called out.

The baritone in his voice caressed her hearing. She missed the way he called her name, it was like no other. She actually shivered when he did, but it was quickly covered with disgust. She ignored him and continued out of the conference room, down the hallway toward the exit.

"Angie please." He reached out and got a hold of her soft delicate hand. The contact shot electricity through both of their veins. Angie tugged out of his grip. But halted in her hasty retreat. Derek stepped in front of her so he could admire her face, his hand itched to reach out and caress it. "Can I take you out for lunch?" He looked into her mesmerizing hazel eyes.

Derek's closeness was wreaking havoc on her senses and she despised it *very* much. She believed he shouldn't still have this effect on her after his betrayal. She cursed her body for reacting in anything but hatred toward him. She wanted to stew in her animosity for a long time and him being close wasn't helping.

"No thank you!" She moved to step around him, but he put up his arm to stop her. "I've got a class to teach."

"You are also allotted a lunch break, and it is lunch time."

"Derek." She lowered her voice when she saw a woman walking down the hallway in their direction. She didn't want more people in their business. "I agreed to counseling, not to have lunch or to partake in any other activity with you."

"A part of counseling is us being able to communicate and get along, having lunch would be a start."

Angie snapped her neck with attitude turning her head to face him. "Why don't you ask Breana for lunch, what happen, your bedmate isn't available?" She stepped out of his way and began walking toward the exit again.

"There's nothing going on between me and her," Derek said walking alongside her.

"Ask me if I give a damn, because that would pretty much cover whatever else you have to say to me." She pushed the glass door open and walked out of the law office.

Derek stopped walking and watched her leave. He was consoled with the fact that she at least agreed to counseling.

Fourteen

A week later, Derek found a Marriage Counselor, Dr. Sydney Williams. She came highly recommended and had a great success rate with helping couples resolve their issues. Angie had no interest in reviewing the list of counselors he had found, everyone one of his emails, text messages and calls to her went unanswered. She did, however, reply to his text message about the date, time and address for their first counseling session.

It was seven-fifteen in the evening. Derek was anxiously checking the time on his watch. Angie was fifteen minutes late. He knew he gave her the correct info for meeting Dr. Williams in her office in Waldorf, Maryland. Their house was only five minutes away so he didn't see any reason for her to be tardy. He had called Angie five minutes ago, but like usual, his call went unanswered and sent to voicemail. He hoped she hadn't stood him up.

Sensing his unease, Dr. Williams asked again if he would like something to drink. She was sitting comfortably in one of the three high back chairs in the middle of the room, Derek was sitting in one as well. The space resembled a living room, with two couches, a coffee table with a large area rug underneath it, a huge bookshelf filled with books was against the wall and house plants were positioned perfectly in the space. The walls were painted in a warm calming color which complimented the welcoming décor. If she was going for creating a comfortable atmosphere – she'd achieved it.

"No thank you." He was fighting like hell to remain calm. This was his shot to work things out with Angie – her not showing up wouldn't help.

Being great at what she does, Dr. Williams knew he was worried his wife wouldn't show up, and from her experience, that was a great possibility. She'd witnessed a lot as a marriage counselor over her seventeen years of practice so nothing really surprised her in her line of work.

Twenty-two minutes late, Angie was escorted by Dr. Williams's assistant to the room where Derek and Dr. Williams were already awaiting her arrival.

"Sorry I'm late," she said, stepping into the room. The assistant closed the door behind her. Really she wasn't sorry, but she wouldn't be a bitch and say that to Dr. Williams.

Derek breathed a sigh of relief when Angie stepped into the room. He didn't want to get started until she arrived, but by her late arrival, he was preparing to just leave.

"Oh, it's not a problem. Waldorf traffic can get a bit hectic sometimes," Dr. Williams said, feigning an excuse for her. She stood to greet Angie with a handshake. "It's a pleasure to meet you Mrs. Monroe." They shook hands.

"Yeah," Angie mumbled under her breath. She turned and instead of sitting in the third high back chair, similar to the ones Dr. Williams and Derek were sitting in, in the middle of the room, Angie walked over and sat on one of the couches. She had no desire to sit near Derek. She barely made it to the counseling session tonight. This was a complete waste of her time as far as she was concerned. Since Derek confessed to his affair – he was dead to her. So she would rather take her chances swimming naked in the Atlantic with sharks during her monthly cycle, than go to counseling to try to revive their marriage. Even Jesus couldn't bring her marriage back from the dead, she believed, and if He could – she wouldn't want Him to.

Angie listened as Derek explained to Dr. Williams as to why they were there. The whole time he talked, she envisioned wrapping her hands around this neck and using all her might to squeeze all ounce of life out of him. Then she would drag his body into the parking lot, start her car and roll over every inch of him. And when she was done with that, she would douse him with lighter fluid and set him on fire. She would marvel at the reds, oranges and blues of the flame as his body burned to ashes. His ashes would then be released into a sewer to be with all the other shits like him. She hated him, *hated* him with a royal passion and hearing his voice right now, created fury in her gut. She was there on a school night, away from her kids, away from her bed, because of *his* infidelity.

"Mrs. Monroe?" Dr. Williams asked for the third time, breaking Angie from her mental vengeance.

She shook her head, blinked, then looked in Dr. Williams direction. "Huh?"

"I asked if you have anything to add to what Mr. Monroe said regarding your needs for counseling."

Angie shook her head "no." She didn't want to be there, but if coming would help move their divorce along smoothly, she figured it was worth it. But that didn't mean she had to participate. And it would probably be best that she kept quiet –

the callous side of her which she'd adopted since his confession, would only make her say and do things that would have her escorted off the premises in handcuffs. She sat back comfortably against the couch and pulled a file out of her purse to file her nails. *Nothing this woman says is going to change the fact that Derek cheated and I want out.* She made a mental note to bring her Kindle for the next session so she could kill time reading a novel.

Derek looked over at his wife, it was obvious she didn't want to be there. Her showing up late was fact enough. But this was his chance to redeem himself so he needed her to mentally be there with them during the session. "Angie, can you come and sit over here with us?"

Angie cut her eyes at him. "I'm comfortable where I am," she spat.

Derek got up, walked over to where she sat on the couch and took a seat next to her. Their legs touched as he sat. Angie's body recoiled at his touch which caused her to flinch away from him on the couch, but he grabbed her gently by the arm halting her from putting much space between them. Angie's body started to shiver from his hand on her, but quickly she masked the sudden desire by yanking her arm out of his grip.

Dr. Williams watched the exchange. *At least they're not physically and verbally fighting.* She got up and sat in a chair closer to the couch so she could face them both.

Angie scooted away from him leaving a wide gap between them on the couch, she resumed filing her nails, unbothered.

Dr. Williams noted Angie's demeanor. "Mrs. Monroe, it's pretty obvious that you don't want to be here, and perhaps coming won't change things between you and Mr. Monroe, but I hope you will give it a good effort." Dr. Williams paused to ensure she had Angie's full attention. Angie's hazel eyes focused on her which prompted her to continue. "If you only take one thing away from our upcoming sessions, I hope it's that you shouldn't allow what Mr. Monroe did to change the beautiful person that I sense that you are. I understand that he may have damaged your trust, but it was of his fault and not your own that he cheated, so you shouldn't project that onto yourself. Don't allow his infidelity to turn you into someone you're not."

Angie blinked rapidly. Dr. Williams's words hit her to the core. Derek's affair and betrayal had changed her. She wore a cloak of bitterness and anger. Unconsciously at times she was inflicting her anger for him onto anyone that crossed her the wrong way. Before, she used great restraint in her actions, now it didn't faze her. He broke her, the confident, joyous, amicable woman she once was – was becoming extinct.

Derek was still watching Angie. His affair had changed her, he could tell – and not for the better. Her whole demeanor had changed. She seemed angry all the time, not just at him, but with everything and everyone. Knowing that he did that to her added another huge weight on his heart. *She deserves to be happy. Am I selfish for making her come to counseling, for my affair? To want to save our marriage when I'm the one that screwed up?*

"So Mrs. Monroe, I want to ask you again, is there anything you want to add to what your husband said about you both seeking counseling?" Dr. Williams asked.

Angie shifted on the couch to get a little more comfortable. "After what he's done I don't want to be married to him anymore." Angie lifted her eyes from her lap up to Dr. Williams's face. "And I don't want to allow his affair to turn me into a bitter, angry person. Our marriage is pretty much over as far as I'm concerned, but I want the old me back," Angie confessed.

Dr. Williams masked the smile that threatened to spread across her face. Her job was to remain neutral and give her best advice to both parties. "A great way to get the old you back, is to forgive your husband for cheating on you."

Angie turned deathly eyes toward Derek. *Forgive him? I want to kill him!*

"The Bible speaks greatly about the power of forgiveness. It's more for your benefit than the offending party," Dr. Williams was very forthcoming with her biblical beliefs. She had a doctorate degree in counseling and psychology, but she also had great knowledge of the Bible and it worked perfectly in her counseling sessions. "Releasing Mr. Monroe—"

"Please call me Derek," he interjected. The formality was becoming annoying.

Dr. Williams nodded. "Do you prefer I address you by your first name as well?" She directed her question to Angie.

Angie nodded.

"Okay. Like I was saying Angie, releasing Derek from his offense would help you to heal and not allow the anger to destroy you."

Angie was quiet for a moment, then she laughed hysterically. "You say that like it's the easiest thing to do." She shook her head. "He..." she pointed an accusing finger toward Derek. "...My husband of nine years, I mean for goodness sake we just celebrated our anniversary a few months ago. I was planning for us to renew our vows next year. And he goes and cheats on me. He slept with another woman. He gave himself willingly to another woman. All the while I was home with our two children being a loving and devoted wife. I loved him the way the Bible speaks about how a woman ought to love her husband. I supported his dreams, I stood by his side through thick and thin, I gave birth to his two children. I made sure our marriage stayed exciting – planning monthly dates, and weekend getaways. And I made myself available for sex whenever possible because I enjoyed it as much as he did. But he CHEATS ON ME! I CANNOT forgive that!" She refused to cry, but the tears were burning the back of her eyelids begging to be released.

"Baby, I'm so sorry. You are a great wife, I can't imagine my life without you. What I did was stupid and selfish, but I love you! I love you so much Angie. I made a huge mistake and I will pay for that every day of my life knowing how much I've hurt you." Derek reached for her hand but she snatched it away.

"I'm sick of your sorry Derek! I wished you'd never done it. What did or didn't I do to make you cheat?" She knew she shouldn't blame herself for his affair, but it was a nagging question in the back of her mind.

Derek shook his head while scooting a little closer to her on the couch. "You didn't do anything wrong. I did. I'm to blame, not you." He wanted to hug her and hold her to his chest, but he knew he couldn't – not now at least.

The flood gates broke. Angie's face was wet with tears. She wondered if she would ever feel *normal* again. Whenever the pain was numbed, something caused it to be inflamed all over again.

"Angie, like I said earlier – do not allow what he did to negatively be projected onto you. You cannot control anyone's actions. We all make up our own minds to do the things that we want to do. So even if you were a terrible wife, which clearly you weren't, you didn't make Derek cheat."

Angie nodded her head to Dr. Williams while wiping her face with her hands.

Dr. Williams closed her notebook and uncrossed her pants clad legs. "Until we meet again next week, Angie I want you to work on not allowing Derek's affair to have so much power over you. Things certainly won't change in just a week, but I want you to start trying now to have that burden lifted off of you. Okay?"

"Okay," Angie responded weakly.

"Derek, respect her healing process and give her time to warm up to you. You can initiate contact, but don't push if she's not ready."

"I will," Derek said.

"Good. We'll meet next week at seven." Dr. Williams stood. Angie picked up her purse and followed suit and Derek stood up after her. They followed Dr. Williams to the door.

Remaining quiet, Derek walked behind Angie to her car in the brightly lit parking lot. The cool night temperature of autumn hung in the air. Angie pulled her leather jacket tightly against her body. "Thank you for coming tonight." He told her while reaching for her door handle to open it for her after she deactivated the car alarm and unlocked the doors.

She said nothing as she allowed him to open her car door. She slid into the comfortable leather seat. She shoved the key into the ignition and started the car.

"Can I take you out to lunch or dinner sometime this week?" He continued. Remembering her words to Dr. Williams minutes ago about their marriage being over had him beyond anxious to have some type of connection with her. He needed her to remember how great they are together.

Angie pulled on the door to close it. She just wanted to get home to their kids and crawl into her warm bed.

"Baby, please talk to me."

Instead of cussing him out like she really wanted to, she said. "Goodbye Derek." She yanked on the door a little harder. He released his hand off the door and allowed her to close it shut. Angie reversed out of the parking space, not even bothering to see if he was in her way, then drove off.

She came. He took solace in that fact. He walked toward his car deciding to head over to the gym. He was already dressed in a designer tracksuit. He'd been working out religiously since their separation. It kept him from going out of his mind for not being home with his family where he belonged, and it also helped suppress his sexual appetite for his wife. He was determined the next time he had sex it would be with Angie. *She's all the woman I need.*

Fifteen

Derek and Angie had been going to marriage counseling for a month and she had yet to warm up to him. The thought of it was driving him crazy. He felt like he was losing her and it was nothing he could do about it. He'd thought by now with their weekly sessions with Dr. Williams that Angie would at least be open to sitting down and having a conversation with him outside of Dr. Williams's office – but he had no such luck. All arrangements for him picking up and dropping of the kids were still through Pauline and Benjamin. So the only time he saw or spoke to her was during their counseling sessions.

"I'm heading out for the day," Latoya, his assistant said poking her head inside his office.

Derek pulled his attention away from his computer screen and looked up at her. "Alright, have a good evening."

"Thanks, and everything is set for your dinner meeting with the Smiths tonight."

"Perfect." He nodded in her direction. She turned and left, closing the door behind her. He had a dinner meeting in an hour with a young couple that were interested in starting their own home improvement business, they sought his advice on how to get it up and running successfully.

He leaned back in his chair, running his hand over his smooth bald head. He missed his family. This whole living like a bachelor mess was not for him. Derek reached for his cellphone on the corner of his desk and dialed Angie's number.

"Hey," he said when she picked up the call. She rarely did when he called, so he was thankful.

He could hear her hesitate, but then she said, "What do you want Derek?" like it pained her to talk to him.

"I'm just calling to check in on you, how are you?"

"I'm of no concern to you anymore, so why bother?"

Still she hadn't hung, so he was happy despite the cold shoulder. "You're always my concern Angie. I love you," he confessed sincerely.

There was a long pregnant pause. "I'm busy right now with parent teacher conferences..."

"Oh, yeah, I got the email from the kids' teachers about theirs being later this week."

"Yup."

"I can bring you guys' dinner so you won't have to worry about that tonight."

"We'll be okay, I have leftovers in the fridge."

That's something else he missed too, Angie's home cooking.

"Can I at least come over later and hang out with you all for a bit?"

She huffed loudly, clearly annoyed with the conversation, but he didn't care. He was fighting here. Fighting to get a chance in any way he could. He was desperate to get his family back.

He could hear a male voice on the other end of the call, it seemed Angie covered the phone to talk to the other person.

"I've got to go," she said into the phone.

"Okay, but what about later?" he pressed. He was curious about the male voice, but figured it was a parent of one of her students.

"Bye Derek." She hung up.

He exhaled deeply. Dr. Williams told him not to press her, but Angie wasn't giving him any type of leeway. But at least divorce papers hadn't been filed, so there was still hope. He finished prepping for his dinner meeting, then made his way out of his office.

****

Every time Aron laid eyes on Angie, she found a way to take his breath away. To say that he wanted her badly would be an understatement. He felt like a freaking school boy always trying to find an opportunity to be in her presence. His son Arnold didn't need him to walk him to class every day, but he did just so he could see Angie. Plus it also made him look even more of a devoted father – which he was. Women eat that stuff up. And he was hoping that along with his charm, and good looks Angie would start to warm up to him.

Tonight was parent teacher conferences and he chose the last time slot for his meeting with Angie. He'd walked into the classroom when she was on her cellphone, but she quickly got rid of whomever she was talking to. She probably did it because it was the professional thing to do, but he wanted to believe that she found him more important than the person on the phone.

"So I'm you're last for today," he stated, sitting on the hard plastic desk chair.

"Yes you are," she replied with a smile. He watched as she looked through a manila folder pulling out some sheets of paper. "Arnold is doing very well in fourth grade. He has an A average and gets along very well with his classmates." She slid over a few of Arnold's graded papers for him to review.

Aron looked over the papers. His son made him very proud. He was a stickler for making sure Arnold had a well-balanced life. He helped his son with his homework and studying for tests and also had him playing sports to keep him active. And he made sure his only child had time for fun too. It seemed it was paying off.

"I really enjoy having Arnold in my class. When he's done with his work, he assists his classmates that may be having a little trouble finishing up theirs. And it's really been helping those students that struggle in some areas. So along with some other students, I would like Arnold to be a part of a peer tutoring session I'd like to start for one day a week, if you're interested."

"Of course! That would be great. Will it be right after school?"

"Yes, I'm thinking of Wednesdays for forty-five minutes. So he would have to be picked up at three-thirty."

"Yeah, that won't be a problem," Aron replied.

"Good. Helping others is beneficial to him as well as his classmates."

"I agree." Aron flashed a sexy smile that for the first time caught Angie's attention sending a warm current throughout her body.

She fidgeted in her seat at the feeling his presence suddenly aroused within her body. His midnight dark eyes were fixated squarely on her. His handsomeness was greatly pronounced to her at that moment. She had never really recognized his low haircut and smooth chocolate skin. And lips women would probably pay millions just to kiss.

"Ms. Monroe?" Aron spoke, but Angie was still caught up in her new awareness of him. Her mouth suddenly became dry. "Angie..."

"Huh?" she snapped out of her reverie at the sound of her first name.

"What were you daydreaming about Ms. Monroe?" He asked seductively, drawing her eyes to his mouth.

Angie shook her head, then quickly retrieved the papers on her desk shoving them back into the manila folder. "Sorry, it was nothing." She had her head down, embarrassed by where her thoughts had taken her.

"Looked like you were thinking about something very *interesting*, care to share?"

She looked up at his handsome face. She watched him lick his lips, and damn if she didn't get moist from the act. She clamped her thighs together to suppress the urge.

She cleared her throat. "So, I will send a letter home about the peer tutoring once I have it all set up."

Aron smirked, knowing that she was purposely changing the subject. Not to be arrogant, but he just knew her daydream had to have been about him. He saw how her hazel eyes suddenly turned a darker green.

"How about I take you out to dinner, to...talk more about the peer tutoring?"

"Thanks, but no thank you, I have to get home to my kids."

He waited for her to add husband, but no mention. *Bingo!*

"And husband?" He arched a curious brow.

"Just *kids*."

He heard the emphasis on *kids*. If he wanted a green light, he just got one. "Maybe next time. And then you can tell me about your daydream."

Watching her get flustered confirmed to him that it had something to do with him.

"I can give you more to daydream about." *But reality is better.*

"And how do you know it was about you?" She finally found some confidence to speak and look up at him.

He stood up after she did. "The body doesn't lie Ms. Monroe."

She stepped around the desk and headed for the classroom door. He admired her as she walked away. When she got to the door, she turned back to look at him still standing by her desk.

He walked toward her, like a lion about to pounce on its prey. Angie watched him lustfully. This was the first time since falling in love with Derek, that another man had this power over her. The forbidden thoughts in her mind of Aron was taking her on a high of desperate need. Want. Desire. When Aron stood next to her at the classroom door, her heart was beating rapidly in her chest as if it was about to bust out.

"Good evening Ms. Monroe," he said, looking down at her. Her hazel eyes had turned a dark green. He wanted to kiss her. Her whole body was screaming at him to do it. But he felt now wasn't the time. He groaned internally stepping away from her and reaching to turn the classroom door handle.

"Good evening Mr. Taylor," Angie said after swallowing a giant lump in her throat. She watched him leave, admiring his swagger. *Good gawd!*

****

"Meet me at the house!" Angie barked the order then ended the call. She shifted the car in drive then sped out of the school parking lot.

Derek knocked on the front door of the home he had built for his family. Angie had all the locks changed when she forced him to leave so he couldn't use a key. *I've got to figure out a way to move back home.* The door swung open moments later. Derek stared awestruck at the sight of Angie in her short, thigh-high silk red robe. It was his favorite and instantly his soldier rose from the sight of her.

He swallowed deeply. "I came right over after you called." He never knew what to expect from her. Justifiably so, she had been nothing but hostile toward him since she found out he cheated.

"Come inside." She stepped to the side to let him in.

Derek stepped in and looked around the house from the entryway, everything looked the same since he left two months ago. Family photos were still intact, even the ones with him in it. "Where are the kids?"

"Asleep. Since I had conferences this evening Tina fed and had them in bed by the time I got in," she said, referring to the babysitter. She locked the door.

She was surprisingly polite and forthcoming, which gave him an eerie feeling. *Is she planning to kill me?* He looked around again looking for a gun, knife or some other type of weapon she might use on him.

"So..."

Not giving him a chance to finish his sentence, Angie pounced on him, locking her lips with his. He groaned deeply, completely surprised and aroused by her actions. She broke the kiss and started to unbutton his dress shirt. He helped her by anxiously pulling it over his head. He had so many questions but didn't dare utter a word in fear the fantasy he was experiencing would end. Angie, satisfied that he was free from upper body clothing frantically tried to unbuckle his belt. Her apparent need for him had him literally busting at the seams. It had been two months since he had sex with his wife. Two months since he'd had sex period.

Derek watched as she freed him from his pants. The sexy sight of her nude body, which he could now see from the opening of her robe, and the scent of her arousal was about to drive him mad. He needed to be buried deep inside of her folds. He lifted her up and she automatically locked her legs around his waist. Forget about making it to the bedroom, his first feast of her was on the steps. They enjoyed each other multiple times on the steps and in the master bedroom.

Fully satisfied and sated, Angie rolled over to her stomach pulling the sheet with her to hide her nakedness. "You can leave now," she uttered drowsily.

WHAT!? Derek knew he didn't hear her right. "What did you say?" He was starting to get comfortable in his own bed which he hadn't slept in for so long.

"You need to leave before the kids wake up and see you and get the wrong idea."

"What wrong idea? I'm your husband!"

"Soon to be ex! So get your stuff and go." She was tired and just wanted to sleep. "Lock the door on your way out." She yawned widely.

Derek sat up in the bed. "So what was that we just did, multiple times?"

"That was me allowing you to scratch an itch I had. Unlike you I don't sleep around and I don't like toys. You are the only man I've been with, remember?"

He turned to look at her, but her back was to him. "I don't sleep around..." he started.

"Derek you did what I needed you to do, so just go!" She yawned. "I probably do need to explore other options for when the itch arises again."

He went from zero to one hundred in a second. The vein in his neck was bulging. "What the hell does that mean?" The thought of her being with another man was going to cause him to have a nervous breakdown. He hopped off of the bed as if he'd just got burnt.

"Exactly what you think it means. I saved myself for your trifling behind, wanting to give the ultimate gift to my husband and what did it get me?" She leaned forward on her elbows. "You cheating on me with some random chick."

"I messed up baby, I'm sorry and I want to make things right." *I can't lose you.*

"Start by leaving and locking up on your way out." She turned and fluffed her pillow then laid her head back down.

"Angie, you're not sleeping with anyone else!" He gritted through his teeth. He knew that he probably had no right saying that considering the situation, but *dammit she's still my wife!*

"Goodbye Derek." She dismissed him. She silently prayed for him to just leave. Having sex with him was just that – sex. It wasn't the way it was before his affair. The only way she got through it and allowed it to fulfill her sexual need, was to not think much about it while enjoying the act void of any emotions. Tears stung her eyelids. *It will never be the same again.*

He huffed, frustrated by how the night was ending, but decided to just leave. It was late and he didn't want to argue. He knew he'd done enough damage already and the last thing he wanted was to add fuel to the fire. He left the bedroom and dressed on his way downstairs as his clothing was discarded about the house.

Sixteen

"She threw your ass out again?" Brian stated. He extended his arm forward and tried to grab the basketball out of Derek's hand. They were playing one on one at a rec center not far from the home he shared with Angie in Waldorf.

They were both shirtless, exposing their sculptured upper bodies, wearing basketball shorts. Each eager to one up the other.

Derek swiped around Brian, jumped and was able to dunk the ball into the basketball rim. "I win!" He shouted triumphantly doing a happy dance. He'd won two out of three games.

"Damn, I'm seriously off my game." Brian headed toward the bleacher to get something to drink. Derek followed behind with the basketball in hand.

"But yeah man, she kicked me out my own house, *again*. When she called me I didn't know what to expect and I sure as hell didn't expect to end up having sex with my wife again but I for damn sure didn't see it coming when she told me lock the door on my way out." He grabbed his bottle of Gatorade out of the cooler that was sitting on the bleacher and took a long swig.

"Maybe you didn't give it to her like she wanted," Brian teased. He took a seat on the bleacher and started to wipe the sweat off of his body with a towel.

"I know how to satisfy my wife," Derek stated confidently. Just remembering days ago how she was clawing at his back, screaming his name and how her womanly folds clamped around his manhood so tightly when she came repeatedly, had him getting hot and bothered. But he wasn't going into details about his sex life with his boy. Bedroom details were strictly off limits when it concerned Angie. No way was he sharing how great his wife was in bed, only he would have the knowledge of that fact.

"So she just used you for sex?" Brian laughed despite himself. "Dudes do that all the time to women, so that's funny as hell."

Actually she pretty much did use him for sex, and he enjoyed every moment of it. But what was pissing him off was her statement of finding *other options* to quench her thirst.

"Man are you alright?" Brian watched his friend zone out.

Derek had a death grip on the Gatorade bottle and had it crushed in his hand. What was left of the liquid was dripping from his hand onto the floor. He shook his head out of his thoughts. "Yeah man, I need to get my wife back, before I end up doing some crazy shit."

"Dude I don't know how you managed going two months without sex. So even though I was tripping over you cheating on Angie, I won't blame you if you went and got you some temporary *kitty*." Brian changed his phrase when he noticed a group of teenage girls walking into the gym. They looked like they were there for cheerleading practice or something. Brian stood up and swung his towel over his bare shoulder.

"That's not what I'm talking about. I cheated on my wife once, I sure as hell not doing that again." They started for the exit, Derek carried the small cooler with him.

"Well, I'm just saying, if she ain't trying to work things out, you can't be in the wrong for getting some tail."

Derek shook his head.

****

"You had sex with him, so that means you still love him," Pauline said right before pushing a spoonful of black eyed pea soup into her mouth. She was hanging out at Angie's house on this Friday evening while Benjamin was away for business.

Dena and Devon, along with their friends, were steps away from the kitchen in the family room, playing board games.

"It means I was horny and he's the only man that I've slept with." She swallowed the soup in her mouth and continued, "And of course I still love him, but I hate him just as much," she admitted.

"It's been two months, you've had time to cool off, so why not try to work things out with him?"

The friends were sitting at the kitchen table while keeping their eyes and ears on the kids.

"He cheated on me Pauline. Some women can look past that, I sure can't and probably won't," Angie stated adamantly.

"Then why did you call him for sex if you hate him so much?"

She called him because Aron had started a fire within that she desperately needed to put out. But the moment she locked lips with her husband, Aron was the furthest thing from her mind. No sex with Derek wasn't like it was before, but she'd be lying if she said he didn't make her want to run down stairs and cook him some steaks afterwards. He knew her body probably better than she knew it herself so he knew all the places she liked to be touched.

"It was a mistake that won't happen again...it's time for me to move on."

"What about the marriage counseling?"

"You know I'm only going because he said that he won't protest the divorce if I did. But I'm at the point where I just want to get it over and done with. It's not fair to me or the kids. We could probably be divorced in the five months that I'll be wasting going to marriage counseling for a marriage I no longer want. I wasn't committed to him for nine years for him to cheat on me and I stay with him like some fool."

Pauline had no words for that. Because she honestly didn't know what she would do if she were in Angie's shoes. But despite Derek's wrong – she knew he loved Angie and felt that they could find a way to mend their marriage. She hated seeing her friends go through this.

"So what are you going to do the next time you get that *itch*?"

"Find someone else that can scratch it," Angie said with a serious tone.

Pauline rested her spoon down on the placemat under her bowl of soup. "You're still married Angie."

"Derek is too and that didn't stop him from stepping out. Besides we're separated."

"*Separated* but not divorced," Pauline countered.

Just then Angie's cellphone started to ring. She reached for it sitting on the table where they sat. Pauline noticed the caller's name displayed on the phone.

"You've been talking to him a lot lately." Pauline arched her brow.

"Hi Brian."

****

"Hey you, just calling to check in on you and my niece and nephew." Brian was lying back against his headboard with the flat screen TV, ahead of him on his bedroom wall, on mute. He'd just taken a shower, pulled on boxers and crashed on his large custom sized bed.

Unbeknownst to Derek, Brian had been checking up on Angie and the kids regularly and making biweekly or more visits at their house, mainly when the kids weren't around, to his pleasure. He didn't know how he would explain his way out of that if Dena and Devon were to tell Derek about his frequent visits. He didn't worry about Angie saying anything because she pretty much didn't want Derek around.

He was becoming her confidant during this difficult time in her life, which he figured was his best way of getting a chance with his best friend's wife.

"We're good. Sitting here with Pauline and watching the kids with their friends," Angie told him.

"I can catch up with you la—" Brian started.

"No. Hold on a sec."

He heard her telling Pauline to give her a few minutes. He smiled with the knowledge of her finding a few minutes just to talk to him.

"I want to ask you something," Angie said getting back on the line. She was making her way up the stairs to her bedroom.

"Go for it." He pulled one arm up behind his head and relaxed further on the bed.

"Is Derek still seeing Breana?" She cringed, anticipating his answer. But the question had been bugging her, she didn't want to give Derek the satisfaction of asking him herself, to make him think she was giving him much thought. But she didn't believe him when he said he wasn't with Breana anymore during their meeting with their divorce lawyers.

Angie walked into her bedroom and closed the door behind her.

"No he's not seeing her anymore," Brian admitted, though he was tempted to say otherwise.

She breathed a sigh of relief. She sat on the bed with the phone clutched to her ear.

"But, as a man, we can only go so long without sex before we fix it. And with you telling him you want a *divorce...*" he purposely let that linger. "...If you're wondering if there's another woman, I don't think so. But, he's a man..."

The thought of Derek finding another woman to replace her made her sick to her stomach. Yeah he cheated on her with Breana, but for him to get another to *permanently* replace her was something she just didn't want to think about. *He was supposed to be my forever.* Her whole mood took a nosedive. She knew marriages weren't perfect because people weren't, but never did she think divorce would be something she and Derek would face, they were supposed to be until death do we part.

"Did he tell you we had sex a few days ago?"

Not that I want to think about it, since I have plans of getting you in my bed. "Yeah he did. And the fact that you threw him out afterwards." He was telling on his boy like a bitch, but he would play the game if it meant her as a reward afterwards. "Maybe it's time you move on since you've told me repeatedly that you're done with the marriage. The back and forth really isn't good for any of you."

Angie was silent for a few moments, Brian would have thought she'd disconnected, if he didn't hear the faint sound of her breathing on the other end of the line. "I do think it's time we just end the marriage now and move on with our lives." She laid back on the bed with her eyes closed. A series of great memories of her and Derek's relationship flashed through her mind bringing tears to her eyes. She could feel the onset of a headache between her temples.

"I know it hurts, but hanging on to something that's dead isn't healthy." Being a serial manipulator with women most of his adult life, allowed the words to flow through his mouth with ease and no trace of remorse.

Angie nodded her head, forgetting he couldn't see her. She allowed the tears to slowly roll from her eyes. "I know," she croaked.

"I'm sorry things turned out this way for you and Derek, but life goes on and you're going to be okay during the process of healing."

"Yeah," she responded weakly.

"Mommy..." she heard Dena's voice calling out for her.

"Thanks for the chat Brian, I've got to go." She sat up and wiped the tears from her eyes.

"Alright, I'll check in on you later." After ending the call he placed his cellphone on the nightstand.

"Dinner's ready sweetheart." A half-naked woman sashayed into Brian's bedroom carrying a tray filled with hot steaming food.

"Thank you baby." When his flavor of the day got close and placed the tray next to him on the bed, he palmed her round behind as she bent over. "I'm gonna take care of this delicious food so I can move on to my *dessert* next." He pulled her to him then stuck his tongue deep into her mouth.

Seventeen

Derek hadn't attended church in weeks, but today he found himself in the lobby of Praise Tabernacle, the church he, Angie and the kids attended for the past six years. He was being warmly greeted by church members that had the impression his absence from church was because he was away on extensive business travel. *Must have been something Angie made up.* He got hopeful considering the fact that she hadn't told them that they were separated.

"It's great to see you too Miss Adderley. How is that cat Simon of yours doing?" He asked the sixty-nine year old. He bent over to hug her, being careful not to knock the large rimmed purple hat she had on off of her head. She never went a Sunday without wearing one of her many church hats that coordinated with her outfits. Even though most members dressed casually, she was always decked out. 'I grew up having to always wear my Sunday best to church', she'd told him on many occasions.

"That old kitty cat is doing better than me. He's fat as ever," she told him with a smile. Though sixty-nine, she could easily pass for fifty. She was single, never married and no kids.

"You're looking handsome today, like always. And looks like you been working out too." She openly checked him out admiring him in dark trousers and a vertical striped shirt tucked neatly into his pants, he wore a light weight dark jacket as well. He'd shaved his bald head that morning and neatly trimmed up his goatee. "If you weren't married, I'd try to snatch you up to make you my boy toy," she flirted.

Derek laughed. She never failed to express her attraction for him. She'd even done it in front of Angie, but they never took her serious enough to give it much thought.

"Stop flirting with Mr. Monroe, Miss Adderley. He's a married man," Delores admonished. She was an usher and ten years younger than Miss Adderley, but based on their friendship one would think the age difference was reversed. She joined them where they stood in the large lobby of the church. "For a woman that flirts as much as you it's a mystery you never married."

Derek and Delores exchanged a friendly hug. "How are you Mrs. Delores?" He asked.

"I'm good. Busy keeping this fast tail in check though," she answered, mentioning Miss Adderley.

"Cock-blocker," Miss Adderley mumbled under her breath.

Derek almost choked when he heard it.

Delores shook her head. "In the church and still can't act right." She tugged on her friend's arm. "Come, let me escort you to your seat. I hope Pastor Clark got a good word for you today."

Derek shook his head as he watched the women walk toward the entrance of the sanctuary and disappeared behind the doors.

"Dadddddddyyyy!!!!" Derek turned toward the sound of his son's voice. He watched as his wife and two children walked into the church lobby. Devon broke off running toward him and Dena wasn't far behind. He got down on his haunches and hugged his children then gave them both a kiss on their cheeks.

"How are you guys?" Derek asked. His heart filled with so much love for his family.

"Daddy are you staying to go to church with us?" Dena asked ignoring his question.

Derek stood up and faced Angie. She had a blank look on her face so he couldn't tell if she was happy to see him. But he sure was happy to see her. She was dressed nice, like always in his opinion, in a multi-colored maxi skirt, yellow blouse and leather jacket. A pair of ankle boots completed her ensemble. She had red lipstick on that beckoned him to kiss her lips.

"Yes I'm staying for church," he told Dena.

"Yay! Can we all go to Olive Garden afterwards Daddy?" Devon asked enthusiastically. He was hopping up and down in excitement from seeing his father.

Derek brought his eyes back toward Angie's face. She still hadn't said anything, so he used that to his advantage. "Sure, you, me, Dena and Mommy will go to Olive Garden after church."

"Thank you Daddy," both kids said hugging him.

"Dena and Devon, go to Children's Church, I'll be there in a sec to sign you in," Angie finally spoke.

"Okay," Dena and Devon said before obeying their mother. They loved Children's Church so they were eager to go.

"What are you doing here?" Angie asked Derek once the kids were out of earshot.

"I'm attending church with my family." He was done with keeping his distance. Calling him over and having sex a few days ago, gave him the green light he'd been waiting for. Even though she did ask him to leave afterwards, and she was still giving him the cold-shoulder whenever he'd called her, telling him that night won't happen again and that she still wanted a divorce.

"We're getting a divorce Derek." She told him flatly, but kept her voice low so people around them entering the church won't add them to the church gossip.

He stepped closer to her, her beauty and the tantalizing scent of her perfume was drawing him nearer. "We're *still* married now. I'm fighting for you, for my family, I love you and I'm determined to keep you as my wife." he said in her ear. He moved his lips closer touching her right ear before backing away.

The act sent a shiver down her spine. Angie's knees almost gave out underneath her. The heat of his nearness, the minty scent of his breath and his declaration, made her weak with need for her husband. The feeling shocked her, she didn't think she would ever feel that for him after his betrayal.

"I'll sign the kids in Children's Church and I'll meet you in the sanctuary." Derek walked off before she could say anything against it.

She bit down on her bottom lip as she watched her husband walk away. His presence and authoritative tone had her swooning. She didn't think she'd ever been this turned on in her life.

****

"Are you going to stay over at our house too Daddy?" Devon asked as the family made their way out of the restaurant. To Derek's surprise, Angie didn't put up a fight about joining them for lunch after church. They'd actually had a good meal, it was as if things were back to normal and the feeling was making him very optimistic.

However not to push things too far, he looked at Angie and asked, "Would that be okay with you?"

She hesitated for a moment, but nodded her head. "Yeah that would be fine, they want you to come."

A megawatt smile brightened his handsome face.

"Can I ride with you home Daddy?" Devon asked.

"Me too!" Dena added.

"Yup you both can."

Derek walked Angie to her car, opening the door for her. "See you in a bit, beautiful." He winked at her before closing the car door for her. The kids trailed behind him toward his car.

"Pauline, Derek's coming over to the house." Angie spoke into her Bluetooth as she maneuvered her car out of the parking lot. Pauline didn't attend church today because she was picking Benjamin up from the airport.

"I thought his visitation is next week. Benjamin and I aren't home yet for him to pick up Dena and Devon."

"No, he's coming to our house."

"Oh."

"He showed up at church today, we sat together during service and we all just left from having lunch at Olive Garden, now he's driving with the kids back to our house."

"Is that a bad thing?" Pauline wanted clarification before she responded. Angie didn't sound pissed, but she'd been pro divorce and hating Derek's guts for weeks.

Angie sighed deeply. "Pauline girl, I'm so confused."

"You're in love with your husband, that's all that is."

"He cheated on me."

"Yes he made a stupid mistake. But don't you think you both have suffered enough?"

"He slept with another woman!" Angie said as if her friend didn't understand the magnitude of that fact.

"Look, I would probably slice Benjamin to pieces if he ever did that to me..."

"And I won't ever do that!" Angie heard Benjamin protest in the background.

"...But Angie, Derek seems very remorseful for what he's done. He loves you and the kids and is fighting to keep his family. Maybe you should try to meet him half way. Things won't change overnight, but it's worth a try before you go ahead with divorce," Pauline advised.

"I don't know." The tug of war of love and hate for Derek was becoming too much for her.

"Take it one day at a time, at your own pace. You've already agreed to counseling, try to take it a little further by allowing him slowly back into your life."

"This is why I hate him sometimes, he's made our lives a mess. We shouldn't be going through this right now."

"I agree. Just take baby steps Angie and follow your heart."

"Alright, I'm home and they're pulling up behind me. Tell Benjamin welcome back home for me, and I'll talk to you later."

"Okay. And Angie, just let go and allow God to lead you. You're so focused on what Derek did to hurt you that you're not seeing all that he's doing to make things right."

"I know. Bye chica." Angie ended the call just before Derek walked up to her car door to open it for her.

"Mommy, Daddy said we can have a movie night and eat popcorn," Dena said with a huge smile on her face.

Angie smiled, she hadn't seen her kids this happy in a long time and it was a refreshing sight. "Oh cool. Now we have to vote on the movies we're gonna watch." Angie got out of the car.

"I want to watch *Transformers*," Devon chimed as they all walked to the front door.

"I want to watch a Disney movie," Dena threw in.

Angie unlocked the front door.

"You two go and change and I'll get the popcorn ready to watch the movie." Derek closed then locked the door after his family was inside.

Angie walked behind the kids as they made their way up the stairs.

"Baby, you wouldn't still have some of my clothes around that I can change into, would you?" He stopped her retreat by placing his hand on her shoulder.

She turned to face him. "I think you'll be able to find something upstairs." She turned back around and continued up the steps. Derek didn't hesitate to follow her.

Walking into the bedroom he once shared with his wife, was like déjà vu. What he wouldn't do for a repeat of what they did on their king sized bed a few days ago. His whole body ached to make love to his wife again.

"You may be able to find some clothes in the drawer I didn't get rid of, *yet*." Angie walked into the master bathroom and closed the door behind her.

There wasn't much of his clothes left, since she'd bagged everything and had them on the doorstep months ago, but he was able to find an old t-shirt and basketball shorts to change into so he could be more comfortable.

Angie stepped back out of the bathroom right when he'd stepped out of his dress pants. He stood near the walk-in closet only wearing boxer shorts. Gone was the little belly he'd had months ago, replaced with washboard abs. Angie swallowed visibly, as she admired her husband. She saw how toned he was a few days ago when they had sex, but now she was actually able to fully appreciate it. She always found him sexy, even when he had the little bit of a gut he'd gained over the years. But he was always muscular everywhere else, but seeing his physique like it was when they were in college caused her to almost swallow her tongue.

"I'm sorry," she said shyly. She reluctantly turned her back to him to give him privacy.

He smirked, happy with the fact that she was checking him out. "Sorry about what?"

She didn't answer.

"We've seen each other naked many times, no need to be shy now." He walked up behind her and pressed his hard body against the softness of hers. His hands trailed down her arms. He sniffed her neck, then placed his lips on the spot that he knew would make her weak. Sure enough, she collapsed against him, her breathing ragged.

"I've missed you so much." He breathed on her neck. He gently turned her around and kissed her as if he would die if his lips weren't on hers. Angie's arms snaked around his neck, pulling him closer to her. Her soft breasts crushed against the steel of his mahogany chest. There was urgency in their embrace, it was as if they were kissing each other for the very first time – and it sure felt great. It felt like home.

"Daddy..." Dena called out nearing their bedroom.

The sound of her daughter's voice snapped Angie out of the haze of ecstasy she was in. She struggled out of his embrace and backed away from him just as the bedroom door swung open.

She caught her breath, then said, "Knock before you walk into my room, Dena," Angie admonished.

"Sorry Mommy, I'm just excited Daddy's here."

"Okay, we'll be down in a bit."

"Okay." Dena turned around and left the bedroom closing the door behind her.

Derek was looking at Angie with hunger in his eyes. It was a good thing his back was to the bedroom door because his erection was prominently at attention. Angie lost her train of thought just looking at it. She gulped.

"We'll finish this later," he promised her.

She brought her eyes up to his face. "No we won't!" She bypassed him and went to the walk-in closet to change out of her clothes from church. "After the movie you're leaving."

"I want to be back home Angie, with you and my kids. This is a start, but I need more opportunities with all of us together...and you and me *alone*."

"Derek..."

"Give me a chance, please."

Angie shook her head. Her back was to him as she stood at the entrance of the walk-in closet. "I'm...I don't...I'm not ready," she admitted. "You hurt me really bad and I just can't put that aside so easily."

"I understand."

She turned to face him. "No you *don't* understand!" She spat. "You weren't the one cheated on, I was." She stabbed a finger at her chest. "You weren't the one that had their heart ripped out of their chest hearing the love of their life admit to being unfaithful, so NO, you do not UNDERSTAND!"

Derek remained quiet. What could he say? Saying sorry just wouldn't cut it. He walked over to her and pulled her gently to him for a hug. He held her snuggly to his chest. She was resistant at first, but he soon felt her defenses break and she started to melt into him.

They stood there holding each other, saying nothing, all the pain, hurt and love they had for one another spoke volumes in their embrace.

"Mommy, Daddy!" They heard both Dena and Devon call out for them from downstairs.

Derek and Angie slowly pulled away from each other, still remaining verbally mute, however their eyes spoke for them when they made eye contact. Angie turned and went about changing out of her clothes from church into something more comfortable, and Derek put on the clothes he was able to find out of the drawer. He soon left out of the room, leaving Angie to continue changing.

Eighteen

True to her statement – Derek left after watching three movies with his family yesterday. He didn't want to push Angie beyond what she was ready for by insisting he spend the night, and to perhaps finish up what had started in their bedroom. So when Angie told him it was time for him to leave after he helped with getting the kids to bed, he did as she asked without a fight.

He'd felt her warming up to him the entire day – which was a huge accomplishment, so no way did he want to risk her emotionally closing back in on him by insisting that he stay longer.

Angie's face lit up with a huge smile when she walked into her classroom this Monday morning and found a beautiful arrangement of red roses on her desk. She walked briskly over to her desk, resting her purse and messenger bag on it. She quickly snapped the card that was attached to the vase and red it:

Thank you for a wonderful day yesterday.

I hope you have a great week baby.

I love you!

Derek

Angie couldn't help but sigh after reading Derek's note, she smiled brighter just thinking about them being together yesterday – as a family. She wouldn't admit it to him, but she really enjoyed having him spend the day with her and the kids. The whole day she tried to be aloof because of his presence, but deep down inside he was breaking down all her defenses. And when he wanted to stay longer after the kids went to sleep – had he pushed, she had no doubt they would've ended up in bed, or wherever they got to first, making love until the wee hours of the morning. Her body craved her husband like an addict needing its next fix. Derek was her one and only lover, and he'd certainly left his name tattooed on every inch of body, claiming her as his. And damn if she wasn't. Which made his affair and their separation so difficult for her to cope with.

"Oooh, looks like someone had a *great* night," Pauline said eyeing the roses on Angie's desk and seeing the goofy grin on her friend's face. She stepped into the classroom and closed the door behind her. "Did Mister and Missus have some *adult* time after the kids were put to bed?" Pauline asked with a mischievous grin on her vanilla face. She came and stood at the front of Angie's desk.

Angie still clinging to the note, sat down in her comfy desk chair. "Let's just say the day wasn't as bad as I thought it would be. It was...actually nice having us all together again as a family," she admitted. She tucked the note into her purse, then stored the purse away in one of her desk drawers.

"So does that mean you're going to give Derek another chance?" Pauline asked, hopeful. She leaned against the edge of desk.

"Having one good day in his presence doesn't change things."

"No, but the fact that you did says a lot. You do recall I had to talk you out of buying a gun to go sniper on his behind."

Angie huffed. She pulled out a file filled with papers she'd graded over the weekend out of her messenger page and placed it on the desk. "Okay so I don't want to kill him anymore but I still want a divorce."

Angie's cellphone started ringing in her purse. She quickly retrieved it. She smiled, despite herself, when she saw Derek's name on the screen.

"Hmmm, that smile says otherwise," Pauline noted.

Angie ignored her friend and answered the call. "Hey," she sang.

Derek chuckled, hearing the excitement in her voice. *God I've missed hearing that.* "Good morning beautiful."

Pauline turned and started for the classroom door to leave, giving Angie some privacy. She smiled to herself on her way out the door. She didn't have to ask who Angie was talking to on the phone, it was written all over her face.

"Good morning. Thank you for the roses, they look and smell beautiful." She couldn't help the girlie voice she suddenly had while talking to him.

"I'm happy you like them."

"How were you able to have them delivered so early?"

"Because I did it myself before heading into the office. I tipped the security guard twenty bucks to put it on your desk for me."

Angie laughed. "Thanks, they definitely were a pleasant surprise." She sat back comfortably in her chair, spinning it back and forth playfully as she spoke to him.

Then there was an awkward pause, both unsure of where to take the conversation next.

Not wanting to end the call now and looking at the clock on his desk, Derek knew Angie had about fifteen minutes before her students started scrolling into the classroom for the day. He initiated small talk, which they engaged in contently. All thoughts of his affair, the separation and possible divorce were placed on the back burner, as they chatted seamlessly with each other.

They talked until Angie told him she had to go because her students were making their way into the classroom.

For the next couple days, Derek made it a point to give Angie a good morning call, which she began to look forward to. She still knocked down his invites for them to have lunch or dinner together, but had no problem with also chatting with him before bed after he'd spoken with the kids.

****

Dr. Williams arched her brow peculiarly, she sat quietly as she watched Derek and Angie walk into her office, *together*.

Usually, they came minutes apart. But that wasn't what surprisingly caught her attention, it was the way the couple was, *flirting* with each other.

After the greetings were exchanged, Dr. Williams watched as Derek waited for Angie to get comfortable on the couch, then he sat down right next to her. Shoulders and legs touching, and Angie didn't – flinch. The couple was chatting away about each other's day, it seemed they'd forgotten Dr. Williams was even in the office with them.

She cleared her throat, bringing the attention to herself, where she sat in front of them. She smiled, "I take it there's been some changes in your communication with each other since last we met." Her eyes studied Angie's mocha face which was free of makeup, however, her eyes shone brighter than they had the last times she'd met with her. Dr. Williams then allowed her eyes to dart over to Derek's mahogany face. *They are a beautiful looking couple.* She saw how much more relaxed Derek's composure was and he held a smile that couldn't go unnoticed.

She prompted a response from them with her eyes, waiting expectantly.

"We spent the day together as a family on Sunday and Angie and I have been talking frequently since," Derek told her.

Dr. Williams was very pleased. She turned her attention to Angie, since she was the one dead-set on not having anything to do with her husband. "So you're warming up to *really* mending your marriage?"

Angie hesitated for a moment, but replied, "I'm...I just want to take things slow and see what happens."

Dr. Williams nodded her head. She closed her notebook that was on her lap. "For tonight's session, I want you two to go on a date."

"What?" Angie asked sitting upright.

"A great way for you two to rekindle your love for one another is to date each other, like you did when you first met." Dr. Williams stood up. "So you're going on a date, doctor's orders. I'll see you next week." She headed to the door of her office, signifying the fact that she meant what she said and hoped that they would abide by it.

****

Keeping it simple, Derek and Angie decided to have dinner at a local restaurant. Angie was a bit skittish which was weird to her since Derek was legally her husband, but since his betrayal things were just *different*. She wasn't sure if she should or could trust him. He'd massacred her heart which was slowly coming back to life and she didn't want to risk putting it into his hands again. Even though they knew each other well – it did feel as if they were just getting to know each other all over again. Which made Angie feel like her twenty year old self when she and Derek first started dating. She had nervous butterflies swarming around in her stomach every time he looked at her with his piercing dark eyes or whenever his body brushed up against hers.

Derek was a little perplexed with Angie's shyness around him, it was arousing, but unsettling at the same time, because she shouldn't be shy when it came to her husband of nine years. But it was his fault, he reminded himself.

Dinner went well, however. They gradually started to laugh and have fun with each like they did before. Angie's timidity slowly subsided to Derek's relief.

They had sat and enjoyed each other's company for several hours. It was definitely needed and they were both thankful for Dr. Williams pushing them to do so. "You didn't have to follow me home," Angie told him after he opened up her car door for her.

"What kind of date would I be if I didn't make sure you got home safely?" He teased her, but his voice also carried a serious undertone. He was a gentleman if nothing else, and she knew that.

The butterflies returned again as Angie unlocked the front door. "Do...do you want to come in for a bit?" She asked over her shoulder.

Like I would say no. "Yes." He responded coolly. He followed her into the house and locked the door behind him.

He walked behind Angie as she made her way into the family room, she took off her jacket as she went. "Hey Tina," she said, seeing the babysitter on the couch, fully engrossed in her text book.

"Hey Mrs. Angie...Mr. Derek." She added in surprise when she saw Derek walk into the family room behind her.

"Good night Tina," he responded with a nod.

"Thank you for staying later." Angie handed Tina a few bills after the babysitter had gotten up and retrieved her text book.

"Oh it wasn't a problem. The kids went to bed forty minutes ago."

Moments later, Angie stood nervously at the front door after seeing Tina off. She wiped her sweaty palms along her thighs that were covered in jeans that hugged her figure like a glove. Derek stood a few feet away, leaning leisurely against one of the columns in the entryway, his eyes swept seductively over her body. He loved when she wore those jeans, but hated when other men checked her out in them, but he couldn't blame them – his wife was HOT!

The sexual tension was crackling between them. They'd been flirting with each other all night. But neither took it beyond that.

Angie walked toward him. "I'm going to take a shower," she announced, passing him and heading for stairs. He looked at her back in disbelief as she walked away. "You're more than welcome to join me," she added seductively over her shoulder.

Hell yeah!

Quietly, they undressed in the master bathroom, teasing each other with each layer of clothing that was removed. When Angie got to just her ruby red panties and bra, Derek thought he would die from anticipation of seeing her completely naked. He licked his lips while his eyes hungrily roamed over her curvaceous body. He wanted to step closer to her and touch her soft skin, but waited for her to give him the okay. He was leaving the ball in her court, *for now*. But his patience was waning.

Angie lusted over her husband's naked body. Her head tilted to the side as her eyes traveled up his strong, tone legs, to the deliciously thick rod of his sex. She bit down on her bottom lip, already tasting the chocolate in her mouth. Hesitantly her eyes continued upward to his flat stomach and broad chest. She felt herself melting. When her eyes got to his, the hunger she saw there, was almost her undoing.

She undid then flung her bra to the floor, her full mocha breasts with Hershey kiss nipples stood erect. She wiggled seductively out of her panties, then kicked them to the side.

Derek didn't know his tool could get any harder, but yup, it just did. He needed her so badly it was painful. "Baby, I don't think I can take this strip tease much longer," he breathed out hoarsely.

"Then come and get what you want." She turned around, giving him full view of her plump mound, turned the water on in the walk-in shower and got in.

Derek had her up against the tile wall in seconds. His mouth and hands greedily assaulted her sexy body. Which Angie surrendered to him without a fight.

They filled themselves with each other until they were exhausted prunes breathing heavily on the shower floor. Finding a little bit of strength, Derek shut the shower off and carried Angie out. He dried her off, then tucked her into bed. He didn't even know if he could find the strength to drive home. But after the last time they had sex, he figured he'll save her the spiel of him having to leave.

"Where are you going?" She asked him after he kissed her on the forehead and started toward the bathroom to retrieve his clothes. She could barely keep her eyes open. "Come here." She pulled the cover back to welcome him into the bed.

Derek stood there looking at her, unsure of if she knew what she was asking him. But he was too tired to figure it out. He climbed into bed with his wife and instantly Angie snuggled up against him. Within seconds they both succumbed to peaceful sleep.

Nineteen

"Daddy?" Dena asked with surprise. She stood still at the entrance of the kitchen. Derek was in there wearing the jeans and long sleeve t-shirt he wore the night before. He was busy scrambling eggs and flipping pancakes.

"Good morning sweetheart." He turned to greet his daughter with a smile.

"Daddy!" Dena ran to him, he stepped away from the stove and effortlessly picked her up into a bear hug.

"How are you doing this morning baby?"

"Daddy!" Devon yelled joining them. Derek scooped him up to into his big strong arms. He kissed both of them on their cheeks, then placed them back on their feet.

"Are you living with us again now Daddy?" Dena asked expectantly. Her eyes were lit up with hope.

"No, Daddy was just a little tired last night and spent the night," Angie said to the kids and Derek's disappointment. She walked into the kitchen, fully dressed for work, in a navy blue pencil skirt, burgundy sweater, dark tights and stylish brown boots that reached her calves. Her hair which got wet last night in the shower, was freshly pressed and styled in her signature bob hair style.

Derek boldly checked her out, admiring her outfit choice for the day, though anything she wore would still make him want to rip it off of her and have his way with her enticing body.

Dena and Devon groaned in displeasure by what their mother said.

"Are you guys hungry for pancakes?" Derek asked in hopes of cheering them up. He would've been kidding himself if he thought because Angie didn't kick him out last night meant that she was ready for him to move back home – though he had some hope that perhaps that would be the case.

"Yes!" They sang in unison.

Derek went about finishing breakfast, afterwards they all ate together. After Angie told the kids to go upstairs to get the book bags, she used the opportunity to talk to Derek. "Thank you for cooking breakfast." She watched as he placed the dirty dishes in the dish washer.

"It's the least I could do after working you so hard last night." He couldn't help it. He winked at her.

Angie smiled bashfully. She was surprised she was able to get up this morning, her whole body ached, especially between her thighs. A reminder she would have for days to come of their lovemaking. "Yes and I have the aches as proof."

His face fell into concern. "I'm sorry baby..."

She flipped her wrist. "It's okay, I'm not complaining."

He grinned. *That's my girl.* She knew how to take her man's girth and insatiable appetite.

"I shouldn't have asked you to stay last night."

His grin turned into a frown. "Why not?"

"Because I don't want the kids getting confused or getting their hopes up."

He didn't expect for things to change overnight, but damn, was it just him that sensed things between them were turning around for the good? "Of us never getting back together?" He asked with a pang in his voice.

"I need more time Derek."

He closed the dishwasher door securely shut, then walked over to where she sat at the kitchen table. He saw uncertainty in her eyes. He needed to reassure her that he wanted her and *only* her, his mistake was one he had no desire of repeating – ever!

Derek extended his hand to her, which she reluctantly accepted. He cupped the back of neck after she stood, then possessively claimed her mouth. He poured every bit of his love for her into the kiss. His tongue mated vigorously with hers – sucking, biting, licking. He needed her to know that he was hers and hers alone. He felt her resolve breaking, her fingernails were digging into the flesh of his arms as she gripped him tightly, using him as an anchor because of her now limp legs. He hugged her tightly to him, not breaking the kiss, afraid the spell that was surrendered upon them may break. He needed her to know that they were meant for each other – God created her *specifically* for him. She was his rib.

The sounds of Dena and Devon making their way down the steps broke the incantation Angie fell under. Her eyes popped open, Derek still held her tightly, kissing her passionately. She pulled back, using the little bit of strength her weakened body had left. Derek's eyes opened, he too was brought back to reality.

Their eyes held each other's, they both felt the power that was transpired in the kiss.

"I love you! And I will give you the time you need, but know we *will* get back together," he promised.

Angie slipped back into the chair, she didn't have the strength to stand. At that moment, she hated and loved the power he had over her. Enough to destroy her or take her to unexplainable heights.

"We're ready!" Dena announced when she walked into the kitchen, Devon was on her heels.

Derek turned toward the counter to hide the effects of the kiss to his body.

"Okay, give me a minute to grab my things," Angie told them after regaining her composure.

"I know you'll go to the same location, but I'd like to take them to school this morning." Derek turned around, after getting the beast under control.

Dena and Devon were pleased with that idea, Angie gave him the okay. Minutes later they were all filing out of the house.

Twenty

"You can put the cupcakes over there," Angie told Aron, pointing to a cleared table in the back of the large classroom. He'd entered the classroom carrying a tray of cupcakes and bags filled with utensils and goodies to celebrate his son Arnold's tenth birthday. It was early November and the classroom was nicely decorated in fall theme with leaves and pumpkins.

Ever since the night of the parent-teacher conference, every time Angie laid eyes on Aron, an electric jolt shot through her veins. She'd never experienced that with a man other than Derek. But unlike Derek, she was able to control this new feeling she was experiencing with the parent of one of her students. It felt entirely unethical, adulterous, a feeling she didn't like. Thankfully, neither one of them spoke a word about that night – the night she saw him for the first time, the night he had her hot and bothered. She felt very ashamed, but it seemed they were able to push past that awkward night and resume their parent-teacher relationship.

Angie was able to wrap up today's lessons forty-five minutes early to give Arnold the opportunity to celebrate his tenth birthday with his classmates. Angie along with her aide and Aron passed out plates and utensils to the students. Moments later, a knock on the classroom door indicated the arrival of the pizza Aron said he'd ordered.

Twenty-five minutes later, the classroom was filled with laughter and fun banter from the students enjoying the celebratory occasion.

"Thank you for allowing us to celebrate his birthday in class," Aron said coming to stand near Angie at the rear of the classroom as she observed her students.

She shifted her gaze to him with a smile. She was still at awe at how she never noticed how strikingly handsome he was until the night of the parent-teacher conference. "You're welcome, I try to accommodate birthdays as much as I can." She turned back to observe her class. They were a great bunch of students, she lucked out this school year and was very thankful for that.

"So…" She could hear the timidity in his voice. Aron cleared his throat. "I wanted to ask, would you go out to dinner with me sometime?"

She turned shocked eyes toward him. This was the first time a man, other than her husband, had asked her out on a date since she was in college. The moment she and Derek became exclusive, she'd turned off any signs that she as *single and ready to mingle*, but up until recently, it seemed the sign was turned on. *Was it?*

She honestly at that moment didn't know how to answer him. Could she say yes? She and Derek were separated, but she was starting to become lukewarm to the prospect of trying to work things out with him.

"Uhmm…" She bit down on her bottom lip, confusion fogged her brain. She was tempted, oh so tempted to say yes, but she couldn't. "I appreciate that you would want to take me out for dinner, but things with me are a bit *complicated* right now." Did she reveal too much? *Dammit I just should have said no thank you.* But she didn't want to overtly reject him. His attraction to her, which she recently realized, was refreshing, to say the least.

She saw the disappointment in his alluring eyes. "Perhaps when things become, uncomplicated?" He hit her with his megawatt smile.

She couldn't help the smile that tugged at the corners of her mouth. "Perhaps." She didn't want to make any promises, however just because she and Derek were going through a rough patch, which could lead to divorce, didn't mean she wanted to be single for the rest of her life.

Derek watched the exchange between Angie and Aron from the small rectangular window in her classroom door. His heart almost stopped when he witnessed his wife openly flirting with the guy. To others it may not be detected, but he knew his wife and knew when she was flirting. He'd come to the school early to pick Devon and Dena up to take them to their dental appointments. Angie had told him three-fifteen was the best available time the dentist had today for their cleaning and asked if he could pick them up and take them because she had staff meeting after school.

He narrowed deathly eyes at Aron, he could read all the inappropriate things the man wanted to do to his wife. He'd had that look on his face many times when he looked at Angie – so he knew. His fists instinctively clenched at his sides. He took a few deep breaths to cool his temper, he didn't want to walk into the classroom and traumatize the students by crucifying this dude. But with the mess of things he'd made with his wife, her reluctance to fully allow him back into her life, had him jealous beyond measure. The last thing he needed was this sucker dude sniffing around his wife.

He pushed the door open to the classroom and walked in with confident strides. He greeted Angie's aide who was sitting at the front of the classroom then made his way to the back where Angie stood wide-eyed watching him approach like she'd been caught with her hands in the cookie jar. *Something's definitely up between these two.* But he also knew he was in no position right now to question Angie on it, at least not outright.

"Derek," Angie spoke his name, recovering quickly from the shock of seeing him at that moment.

Derek walked directly to her, invading her personal space, and captured her mouth with a kiss before she had time to reject him. He probably shouldn't have in front of her students, but he didn't give a damn. Dude needed to know that she was off limits – point, blank, period!

"Just wanted to say hello before I scooped the kids up for their dental appointment," he told Angie after releasing her lips.

She blushed. Then looked around frantically making sure her students hadn't witnessed what just happened. It seemed they didn't because they were still too busy chatting and eating to pay the adults in the back of the room any mind. At least she hoped.

Derek mean mugged Aron as he looked him over, letting him know with his eyes he better not approach his wife ever with his BS.

Aron mean mugged him back letting him know he didn't give a shit. *The fact that you had to come in here to stake your claim partna means it's a fair game.* Aron walked away, not wanting Angie to feel obligated to introduce her to her soon to be ex. *'Cause that's what he will be with me in the picture.* He went to light the candles on Arnold's birthday cake.

"You shouldn't have done that Derek," Angie snapped at him once Aron was out of earshot.

"But you liked it," he teased with a disarming smile.

"Go and get the kids so they're not late for their appointment," she replied tersely, cutting her eyes away from him.

He wasn't feeling her vibe. Yeah their relationship was really rocky right now, thanks to him, but why was she *really* mad with him at this moment? "Is something going on between you and that dude?" He asked in a harsh whisper.

If looks could kill he would've died a thousand deaths with the look she just shot him. "I'm *not* like you Derek," she snapped.

Yeah, he knew he deserved that, but he was also relieved by her response. "I'm sorry Angie."

"Just go and get the kids. I'll see you when you drop them off." She walked away from him and went to assist with passing out slices of birthday cake.

Derek left the classroom, but not before whispering another apology in Angie's ear and giving Aron a promise with his eyes that he would eff him up royally if he crossed the line with his wife.

****

During the next couple weeks, Angie eased into allowing Derek to spend more time with her and the kids, plus she didn't want to keep bringing Pauline and Benjamin in the middle of their marital woes. They ate dinner together at least four times a week, sat together in church and on the nights that Angie had the kids, Derek came over to assist with their homework as best he could with his work schedule. Things were *almost* feeling like normal – with the exception of him not living back home or any physical intimacy between Angie and Derek.

After putting the kids to bed on a Wednesday night, Derek made his way back downstairs where Angie was sitting on the couch with her legs stretched out grading papers. He sat down next to her and rested her bare feet into his lap. He went to massage them, but she snatched them out of his reach.

"What are you doing?" She peered at him over her reading glasses.

"I was going to massage your feet like I always did when you're stretched out on the couch grading papers or on your period."

"Things aren't like that between us anymore," she reasoned. She curled her feet underneath her and went back to making notations on a student's test paper.

Derek blew a frustrated breath. "Baby, I've been trying really hard for things to get back that way between us, please meet me halfway."

Angie's hand halted from writing. She looked up at Derek and studied him for a moment. "Tell me Derek, how long would it take for you to forgive me for cheating on you with another man?" She pinned him with her eyes, and watched the flash of fury that illuminated in his irises at just the thought of her being with somebody else.

"Have you?" He asked, trying to remain calm.

She shook her head "no", holding back from wanting to verbally say more.

He blew a mental sigh of relief. "Honestly baby, I don't know. Something like that would really mess me up, I'd want to kill dude," he admitted. He shook his head of the painful thought. "But I hope like hell that I would see how sorry you are and how much you're trying, and I would give you another chance."

Angie continued to study him, measuring his words. "You and I both know that's BS! You wouldn't want to have anything to do with me. You men do your mess and expect us women to just forgive and move past it, but if the table is turned, all hell breaks loose."

"I'm not most men Angie, that you have to give me credit for. I effed up royally – yes, it was stupid as hell, but I love you! And if the table was turned, I hope my love for you would help me be able to move past it."

She shook her head unconvincingly. "Whatever Derek." She flicked her wrist and went back to grading.

"Look, if you cheated on me and fell in love with the dude, then yeah, there's no way we would probably be together after that. But if it was purely physical, we could work it out," he answered honestly. It would take him a minute to get over that mess, but he could move past it.

Derek leaned forward and took the pen, then papers out of Angie's hands, then placed them on the floor. "Baby, please see how much I'm trying to get things back to the way they were. You, Dena and Devon are my life. I want to come back home to my family. I want to sleep in my bed, next to my wife. I want to make love to my wife."

Angie's body hummed with desire. For the past weeks her resolve was chipping away slowly but surely. She missed her husband. She loved him. The sting of his affair was still there, but it was no longer debilitating. She took Dr. Williams advice and had forgiven Derek for what he'd done, which allowed her to be open to him coming around so often. But she still wasn't ready to go all in. She still didn't feel she could trust him – and that was the most heartbreaking thing of all.

Derek scooted closer to her on the couch and brought his lips inches away from hers, their breaths mingled. He could see the desire highlighted in her hazel eyes. Her breathing had become rapid from his nearness. His hands caressed her pajama clad legs, up to her thick thighs. It had been two weeks since he'd had her, two weeks since he was between her luscious thighs. He needed her like he needed his next breath. His hands reached the junction of her thighs, he could already feel her moist desire through the thin layers of pajama pants and panties. She hissed when his hand made contact with her treasure. His need rose evidently too.

"I need you baby."

"You...you need to leave and go home," she replied hoarsely and unconvincingly.

"Do you *really* want me to leave?" He fondled her through her clothing. Her head fell back which gave him the opportunity to latch his mouth and teeth onto her lean neck. He kissed her right on the spot she liked. *Bingo.* Her hands flew around his neck, drawing him closer.

"I need you too," she confessed.

That's all he needed to proceed. He had them both naked in rapid speed. She straddled him expertly and gave him a ride no other woman would be able to compete. He made sure that the neighbors heard her calling his name until the wee hours of the morning.

Twenty-One

It was five days until Thanksgiving and Derek was in a great mood. Things were looking up and he couldn't be more grateful. He and Angie were still living separately, but he was convinced it would be only a matter of time before he was sleeping comfortably in his own bed with his wife snuggled up next to him. Life was great! He had become very diligent with his daily prayers just praising and thanking God that his family would be mended soon. He smiled to himself, slightly distracted as he drafted up an email to one of his clients about a few business prospects.

Angie, to his relief, was fine with him coming along on their planned trip, from months prior, to her parents in Florida for Thanksgiving. Her parents knew they were living separately, but was overjoyed when told he would be joining his family for the trip.

"Mr. Monroe," Latoya said after given the okay to enter his office.

"Yes?" He looked up from his computer at his assistant.

"Breana Sutton is here to see you and is very insistent on it." From the last time Breana was there, Latoya knew the woman was bad news and wanted to give her boss the heads up.

The smile that Derek had engraved on his face suddenly turned into a frown. He hadn't spoken to or seen Breana since he threw her out of his office demanding that she never contacted him again. *The devil is always lurking.* He wanted to tell Latoya to tell Breana to leave, but he didn't want her doing his dirty work. "Send her in," he responded, agitated by the Breana's unwanted presence.

"How are you?" Breana asked walking coolly into the office. She went and claimed one of the visitor's seats in front of his large desk.

Derek rolled his eyes. His affair wasn't just her fault, but seeing her reminded him of the worst mistake he'd ever made. *How could I have been so weak?*

"You're looking better than the last time I saw you," she continued as if they were old friends catching up. And just like that, he remembered how easy it was to chat with Breana during their trip to the Bahamas. Besides his current distaste for her, she was a nice woman. Ambitious, funny and full of personality. She was able to assist him in doing the one thing he never thought he'd do to his wife. And for that he wanted to keep a huge distance away from her. No, he had no sexual desires for her, but no way on God's green earth could he work with her ever again.

"I remember correctly asking you *never* to contact me again." Derek sat back against his desk chair eyeing her suspiciously.

"And I haven't–"

"But today you're here. You and I have *nothing* that we need to talk about for you to be here interrupting my day."

"Actually we do." She gave him the same stare down he was giving her. Her beautiful face had a stubborn glare.

"Which is?" He arched an irritated brow.

"I'm three months pregnant." The words flew out of her mouth knocking the wind out of Derek. "I found out last month. I know this is the last thing you wanted to hear from me, but I had to let you know that we're having a baby."

"We used protection!" He tried his best to keep his cool.

"And we both know that they can break," she countered.

"How could I believe that I'm the father?" The sound of that had him sick to his stomach.

She arrested him with menacing eyes. "Because you were the *only* person I slept with at that time."

They stared each other down for what seemed like hours. Each processing the information in their minds and the ramification of it all.

"F@#K!" He roared like a vicious lion. He saw his whole world crumbling down around him. Breana jumped in her seat, terrified by his outburst. Within seconds everything on his desk was swiped off of it and slammed against the wall to the left of it. Laptop, papers, pens, files all disintegrated. Latoya raced into the office, frantic by what she heard from the outside. Horror was in her eyes at the scene of Derek kicking his desk chair against the floor to ceiling window, putting a huge crack into it.

"Mr. Monroe!" she shouted. But rage was still evident in his eyes. "Derek! Sir, please calm down," Latoya begged. She saw Derek not only as her boss but a big brother, he'd helped her out so much with this job and his kindness.

Getting his rage under control, he turned to face the window. Breathing heavily. He ran a frustrated hand over his smooth bald head, down his face, over his goatee, then shoved his hands in his pockets. "Thank you Miss Simms, I'm fine now," he answered with a false sense of calm.

Latoya watched him, with his back turned to her, she was reluctant to leave. Then she turned to look at Breana who looked like she was on the verge of tears. She slowly backed out of the office, closing the door shut behind her. *I knew she was bad news.* She went to her desk to start the process of ordering Derek a new laptop and calling maintenance to have the window fixed.

"I need a paternity test!"

Finding her ability to speak after recovering from the shock of Derek's outburst, Breana smooth her hands over her tweed pants. "Are you suggesting that I'm lying about you being the father of this child?"

Derek turned around slowly, eyes of contempt landed on hers. "Hearing that you're possibly pregnant with my child is the last thing I need in my life, so forgive me if I'm skeptical. You yourself told me that sleeping around is something that you engage in, *often.*"

"You think I'm some type of slut?" She jumped defensively to her feet. "Just because you don't want to mess up your *happy home*, doesn't mean *me*, who you willingly slept with, being pregnant with your child, is a slut. Because if I am that makes you no better, Mr. Happily Married Monroe!"

She hit him below the belt with that one. But hell this whole thing had him in a mental turmoil. *How am I supposed to tell Angie this? Dammit!*

"You are the father of this baby I'm carrying Derek, whether you want to believe it or not. And I will not risk *our* child's health by having a paternity test done while pregnant." She hated the fact that he doubted her, and she wasn't even sure if she should have told him about the pregnancy to begin with, but came to the resolve that he had a right to know.

Derek exhaled deeply. *God this can't be my life!* "Breana, I don't even know what to tell you right now." He was at a complete loss. He wanted to lash out at her, but their predicament wasn't entirely her fault. And if she was carrying his child he would do the right thing and be a daddy to him or her.

"You don't have to say anything about it right now. I know I laid a lot on your lap, so take some time to let it all sink in." She reached for her clutch on the chair she was sitting on. "I meant what I said when we were leaving the Bahamas, I don't want to mess things up with you and your family..."

The irony of that? He thought shaking his head.

"...All I want is for you to acknowledge and accept that we are having a child together and I want you to be a part of our baby's life." She turned and left the office leaving him standing completely at a loss of how in the world he was going to be able to figure everything out. *One mistake and I got the death sentence. Will Angie ever forgive me for this?*

Twenty-Two

Angie didn't like the fact that her family was torn apart, resulting in her separation from Derek, but she took advantage of the days he picked up the kids from school for them to spend their nights with him. She was able to catch a breather after teaching fourteen kids all day.

After leaving the school that afternoon, she and Pauline went and got manicures and pedicures at their favorite nail salon in St. Charles Mall. They were now back at Angie's place, freshly showered, wearing comfy clothes, about to catch up on their new favorite show, *Empire*. They were two episodes behind and wanted to get the shows in before the airing of a new episode tomorrow night.

Just before Angie was about to press the button to view the show recorded on DVR, they heard the front door chime, the door shut then footsteps sounded on the hardwood floor. That reminded her that she left the door unlocked. Seconds later Derek was in view. He walked toward them, where they sat on the couch, like he was the Angel of Death. Fear gripped Angie, causing her heart to gallop in her chest. *Did something happen to one or both of the kids?*

"Angie, we need to talk."

She could see anguish etched into his handsome mahogany face.

"Derek, is everything okay?" Pauline asked. She too was starting to freak out from the affliction in his demeanor.

"Pauline, please give me and Angie a chance to talk," he said nicely. It seemed the weight of the world was on his shoulders.

"Derek, did something happen to the kids?" Angie asked frantically.

He shook his head. "They're fine. Tina's watching them at my place."

Angie sighed loudly with relief. But she was still freaked out, something serious happened and she was afraid of finding out. She shifted her eyes to Pauline. "We'll catch up with *Empire* later," she told her friend.

Pauline unfolded her legs from underneath her then stood up. She looked from Angie to Derek, then back at Angie. "Call me later." She left the house quietly.

Derek stood in the same place, unmoved, like his legs were lead. *Maybe she doesn't deserve me as her husband after all, because all I've been doing lately his breaking her heart.* After Breana left his office, he felt his life completely went to hell. Funny how just before Breana walked in, life was looking pretty good to him, then the atomic bomb dropped.

"What is going on Derek?" She didn't know if she could handle what he had to say. The last time he had to talk to her, he admitted he cheated. She was visibly shaken. She placed her hands under her thighs to help still their shaking.

Finally he moved and took a seat in the arm chair next to where she sat on the couch. He closed his eyes, trying to find the right words. *But what they hell are the right words?* "Breana—"

"You're still sleeping with her?" she interrupted him.

"NO! Absolutely not!" He affirmed. "I promise you there is nothing going on between me and her."

She felt she was able to believe him on that. She waited for him to continue what he had to say.

"But, she told me today that she's...pregnant." He felt like he just took a bullet to the heart, the pain of uttering those words to his wife would stay with him forever.

Angie stared at him blankly. Hot tears pained the back of her eyelids. The hurt from his words ricocheted throughout her entire body.

He felt like crap. *How am I, her husband, the person that was to protect her from harm, be the one that hurt her the most?* He knew he wasn't a perfect man, but he thought he was better than this. Better than to take his wife's love and commitment for granted, and throw it away in three days of unadulterated selfish sex that was destroying his family. His family was suffering because of his unfaithfulness.

He didn't even know what to say to her. She was tired of hearing him say sorry, and honestly, he was tired of having to say it himself. Sorry wouldn't take away the ramifications of his actions.

"I hate that I keep hurting you Angie. I feel terrible about it. But I promise you, nothing is going on with me and Breana."

"You slept with her not even using protection?" She asked with disgust, coming out of a daze.

"We used protection." The conversation was making him feel more horrible by the second. But was it wrong for him to hope, that someway, somehow they could overcome this? *God help me*, he silently prayed.

There was deathly silence for a few moments.

"Not only did you cheat on me, which I was beginning to think, maybe I can get past it. I could learn to ignore the thoughts of you having sex, touching, kissing and being intimate with someone else. But a baby Derek? You got her pregnant! I just can't ignore a baby." Angie angrily pushed tears away from her face.

"Angie, sweetheart..." Derek started.

"I can't, God I can't do this Derek! I feel like such an idiot for even attempting to give our marriage a chance."

"We can still work this out," he pleaded desperately.

"How!? By Breana bringing your baby over to our house for me to play stepmom?" She asked with disgust.

Derek sat with his elbows on his knees, holding his head in his hand. He was defeated and completely disgusted with himself.

"I'm done Derek, DONE!" She didn't think her heart could ache more painfully than it was at that moment. She took deep breaths to help calm herself, she feared she was having a heart attack because the pain was so severe. *And I thought he couldn't hurt me more than he'd already had.*

Derek looked up, his eyes were red and filled with tears. He was holding them back, but hearing the finality in her words, which signified the end of his marriage, the end of his family being together, cut him deeply. It was all his fault.

"I want us to still go to your parents together for Thanksgiving."

Angie shook her head "no".

"I know I don't deserve it, but please give me this last opportunity for us to be together as a family during the holiday." He didn't want to give up on his wife, on his family. But he'd hurt her so much, if she wanted a divorce, he wasn't going to fight her.

It would be too selfish for him to, he thought. He loved her too much to intentionally invoke any more pain upon her. But this act of love, would be the hardest thing he'd ever have to do.

"Just go, leave me alone," she responded in a harsh whisper. She got up, not looking back, and started for the stairs.

"Angie please, just give me Thanksgiving and if you don't want anything else to do with me, I understand."

She said nothing, continuing her ascent up the stairs to her bedroom.

Twenty-Three

"Sit next to me Daddy!" Devon exclaimed as he slid into the narrow passageway to seat 7B on the airplane.

Derek placed his family's carryon luggage in the overhead compartment, then took his seat next to Devon. Dena and Angie sat across the aisle from them in their double seats. Angie made a point to sit in the window seat, so she wasn't next to Derek in the aisle seat. Thankfully Dena didn't have the fascination of wanting to see the clouds like her brother did.

Angie had grudgingly agreed for Derek to still accompany them to her parents in Delray Beach, Florida for Thanksgiving. She did it because she didn't want to disappoint Dena and Devon, they'd been hyped about the trip for weeks. Plus, it would make up, somehow, for what they would have to face once they returned to Maryland.

Angie had been a wreck since Derek told her Breana was pregnant – with his child. She didn't know if she would have any Thanksgiving cheer this holiday. *Thankful for what?* Thankful that her cheating dog of a husband wanted to spend the holiday with them? Thankful that her family will be torn apart? Thankful that soon she would be a divorced single mother? *No, your life isn't what you want it to be right now, but you're still alive and healthy, and you have two beautiful, healthy children. There's a lot for you to be thankful for and you would know that it if you not focus on the negatives.* Her conscious admonished her. But still she was salty, and fiercely fighting depression.

****

"I hate him Mommy," Angie said leaning against the kitchen sink while peeling sweet potatoes for their Thanksgiving dinner. The house smelled delicious. Angie and her mom had gotten up bright and early at five and started their yearly tradition of cooking a spread for their family. Both her parents came from a small family and with Angie being their only child together, her half-sister from her father's first marriage still refused to be a part of their lives, their family was smaller. But aunts, uncles and cousins from around the country would be there at three for dinner. The house would be filled with at least twenty-five people soon. Angie enjoyed these moments alone with her mother.

Cooking and chatting. During the last few months of chaos in her marriage, she wished her mother lived closer so she could've glean some of her motherly love often.

"Then why did you agree for him to come along with you and the kids?" Evelyn asked her only child. She was heartbroken when Angie called and told her that she and Derek were separated because he cheated. She sat on the phone for hours listening to her baby cry over her marriage. Angie begged her parents not to come to Maryland, because although she was going through a tough time, she felt she needed to be strong for her kids and get it together. Having her parents there would've slowed the process. James, Angie's father, wasn't too happy about it, but he wanted to respect his daughter's wish. He did, however, call and had a long chat with Derek, letting him know how disappointed he was in him for hurting his daughter.

"Because I didn't want to disappoint Dena and Devon. They idolize Derek, he's their hero. And with us living apart for the last few months, they were really excited about us all coming here together for Thanksgiving."

Evelyn placed three pans of pumpkin pies she'd made from scratch in one of the two ovens she had in her huge kitchen.

She wiped her hands on her apron, then went to pull out a pot to start making macaroni and cheese.

"What are your plans when you all return home?"

"I'm filing for divorce."

"Just like that?" Evelyn arched a brow. She placed the pot on the counter, then turned to face Angie. Her naturally long coarse hair was tied up in a messy bun on top of her head. At fifty-seven, she only had a small streak of gray hairs on the left side of her head. Her beautiful face was smooth like butterscotch. She stood at five-two with a demeanor as meek as a mouse.

"What do you mean just like that?"

"You're just going to file for divorce?"

"Mommy, he cheated on me and got another woman pregnant." *Wasn't that more than enough reason to divorce?*

"You told me that you had forgiven him and was beginning to heal from his betrayal."

"He got her pregnant. How would I look staying with my husband to help him raise a child he conceived outside of our marriage?"

"Are you worried about what people *may* think more than what is best for you and your family?" Evelyn filled the pot with water.

"He hurt me. I'm not going to be able to handle him having a baby with someone else. I wanted to die when I found out he cheated." Angie couldn't believe she was defending her reasons for wanting a divorce, to her mother.

"I know he hurt you sweetheart. I wanted to fly up to Maryland myself and go ghetto on his behind..."

Angie had to bite back the laugh that wanted to escape from her lips because of her mother's remark. *Ghetto? She been watching too much reality TV.*

"...But from what you've been telling me up until finding out about the pregnancy, Derek has really been trying to mend your marriage. I'm not telling you to divorce your husband, and I'm not telling to remain married to him either. But please don't base your decision on what you think you staying or not staying with him would make you look like. Honestly, I thought you would've filed for divorce right after you found out, so the fact that three months after his affair you're both here together – says a lot."

"It says I'm an idiot for trying to spare his feelings. I'm an idiot for continuing to bend to his will after he'd already ripped my heart out of my chest and stomped all over it." She threw the sweet potato she hand in her hand into the sink with a loud THUD.

"Do you still love him?"

Angie closed then squeezed her eyes tightly. "I do and God knows I hate that I do. But I love myself more, Mommy. I will not stay with a man that can so easily toss my love and loyalty aside."

"He made a stupid mistake, dear. And he's been trying to make amends."

Angie turned hurt eyes towards her mother. "You're defending him?"

Evelyn shook her head. "Of course not. Shoot I would've filed your divorce papers months ago myself. I'm just trying to give you things to think about before you sign on those dotted lines that would put an end to your nine years of marriage."

"You make it seem like I'm at fault. Like it's because of me that we're getting a divorce." Angie was hurt. The decision of splitting their family wasn't on her.

"No it's definitely not!" Evelyn wiped her hands on her apron then walked over to hug Angie. "Baby I want you to be happy. So whatever decision you make I'm with you. I just don't want you to make such a life changing decision based off of the wrong things. Do it because you're sure in your heart it's the best for you and my grandbabies. Pray about it sweetie. Get God's guidance. You have every right to divorce Derek if you want to, just make sure it's what you really want."

"What I really want is for my husband to have never cheated." Angie dissolved into her mother's loving arms.

Evelyn patted her on the back. "I know sweetheart, I know."

"I know a divorce is the best thing. I would not be able to stand by his side and help him raise his child with Breana. I can't and I won't. I would grow to despise him each and every day."

"Then that's it." Evelyn pulled away from their embrace. "It's not going to be easy in the beginning, but everything will work it's self out."

****

Hours later, everyone sat on the veranda with their stomachs filled to capacity. Angie loved visiting her parents in Florida, especially during the cold temps in Maryland. It felt great to be outside in eight-five degree weather, wearing a tank top and Bermuda khaki shorts. Most of the family left after dinner. But Angie's cousins on her mother's side: Ray and Veronica were still there, with their kids, and Angie's Aunt Leah on her father's side, remained. The adults sat back in the wicker chairs with comfortable padding while looking out in the well maintained tropical backyard, at the kids playing on the playset.

Ray had a seven year old daughter and Veronica had an eight year old son. She and Angie were pregnant with their first children at the same time.

"So how have you been big cousin?" Veronica asked. "I'm still trying to be like you cuz. Wonderful husband and kids, you got the whole package girl."

Angie rolled her eyes. Not at her cousin, but at her comment. *Wonderful husband? Yeah right.* Since their arrival at her parents' house two days ago, Angie had been avoiding Derek as much as humanly possible, which wasn't easy considering the fact that they were all sleeping under her parent's roof. Instead of sharing the second master bedroom with him, like they always did in the past, she slept in it alone and he slept in one of the other four spare rooms her parents had in their home. She wasn't one of those people that could fake that everything was peachy in her world. It wasn't, and to help maintain some peace during the holiday season, she limited her contact with him. But she still wasn't ready for everyone to know her business.

"Trust me Veronica, you don't want to be like me. But I'm sure you'll have your perfect package soon. How's things going with you and Steven?" Angie asked, turning the attention off of herself. She felt Derek's eyes on her, but refused to look his way.

Angie watched her cousin's eyes glaze over. Veronica scooted closer to her cousin to try and keep the conversation private. "Girl Angie, I think he is the one. But I haven't introduced him to Vance yet..." Vance is her eight year old son. His father died five years ago in a car accident.

"Don't go going all hush, hush on us. I want to know about this Steven too," Evelyn stated.

"It's nothing serious to talk about now, Aunt Evelyn."

"She lying. She be with that dude so much, they damn near married," Ray outed her.

Veronica rolled her eyes at her older brother. "Oh shut up! And how would you know, running around with all them hoodrats." She threw back jokingly at her brother. They were always trying to rile each other up. You would think at their ages it would've ended by now.

"Oh Lord, boy. When are you going to settle down and find a good mother for Kaley?" Leah asked. Even though Ray and Veronica were her nephew and niece in law, through her brother being married to their Aunt Evelyn, she still treated them like blood.

Ray shot daggers at his sister. "I'm in no rush to get married again Aunt Leah."

"Yeah, but your daughter need a mama," Leah stated. She was referencing the fact that Ray's ex-wife ran off years ago to live in France with some rich wealthy man she met online.

"Leave the man alone," James spoke up. "Let him find a good wife in his own pace."

"Plus I don't have a problem with being single. I tried marriage and we all know that didn't work. So I'm good," Ray said confidently. "I'll leave that happily ever after mess to you guys." He flicked his wrist toward Angie and Veronica.

Angie scoffed loudly, which caught everyone's attention.

Her parents: James and Evelyn already knew the deal. So curious eyes from Veronica, Ray and Leah turned towards her.

"Don't tell me there's trouble in paradise," Ray said shifting his gaze from Angie to Derek who sat next to him. He'd picked up on the distance between the couple that always were lovey-dovey whenever he was around them. Matter of fact, Derek had been mute most of the afternoon.

Angie was tempted to put her husband's dirty laundry out there for her family to see, but she held her tongue. Seeing him sitting across from her, and the topic on the floor, angered her. The holidays were always the best for her. She enjoyed getting into the festive mood, but it took everything ounce of grace she possessed to endure the last couple days being around him. *Only for my children's sake.* Their happiness meant more to her.

"We're going through a rough patch right now, but everything will work out," Derek said smoothly. His eyes caressed his wife's face. He was hoping that they would've survived Thanksgiving dinner without bringing up the obvious – things weren't going well with the Monroes. It killed him to keep his distance from her. So many times he wanted to reach out and hug, kiss her or hold her hand. But he'd forfeited his right and she made it obvious that he better not dare cross the line. He was thankful that he was there though. Dena and Devon really wanted him to come, so despite the uncomfortable situation, his kids were good, so he could deal with the rest.

The look of disgust Angie gave him pierced his already slaughtered heart. His wife was near him, but it felt like they were miles apart. That's how thick of a wall Angie had erected before him.

"I'm going to the beach." Angie stood up abruptly and started for the French doors that led back into the house. Her move killed anymore questions anyone may have had about the state of their marriage.

Veronica stood up. "I'm coming with you." She turned to Derek asking with her eyes 'what the hell did you do?' Before following behind Angie.

He felt like crap. How other men deal with this type of mess and survive, he didn't know. He didn't owe her family an explanation. And he'd already faced her parents, and dealt with their anger over how much he'd hurt their daughter. James chewed him out and even threatened him. He wasn't afraid of her father, but he respected him. He screwed up. But he'd be damned if he sat there and allow the rest of her family to beat him up about it. He got up and went to play with his children. He came for them anyway and despite everything – he was a great father to Dena and Devon and it would remain that way.

Twenty-Four

Days later, Derek was sitting on the edge of his bed. He picked up his cellphone from the nightstand and went to see who had texted him. It was Breana. Since returning from Angie's parents seven days ago, he hadn't made any contact with her. He was still trying to wrap his head around the fact that he had gotten her pregnant. He had all kinds of suspicions. Did she poke holes into the condoms she brought on the trip? Was the business deal in the Bahamas her plan to seduce him? Did she steal his sperm from the used condoms and got herself pregnant with his child?

He shook his head, this crap was going to drive him crazy. He looked at the picture she'd sent him. It was an ultrasound. He stared at it blankly. Well if he thought she was pulling his leg, she in fact was pregnant. He'd seen many over the course of Angie's pregnancies with Dena and Devon. But unlike the first ultrasound pictures he'd seen of Dena and Devon – he wasn't ecstatic. He felt nothing but dread. He threw the phone onto the bed, not evening bothering to send a reply. He planned to take care of his responsibilities, but pretending that he was happy about the situation was out of question.

He got up and went into the bathroom to relieve his bladder then wash his face and brush his teeth. After he was done taking care of his personal hygiene, he walked down the short hallway to the first spare bedroom.

"Dena, baby it's time to wake up." He gently nudged his daughter awake after pulling back her covers. "We have to find Jamie a birthday present before her party this afternoon." After a few more tries, Dena slowly opened up her eyes, then yawned widely.

"Okay Daddy," she said sleepily.

"Good girl. Get out of bed and get changed."

Derek left her room and went to Devon's. His son was already awake, still lying in bed playing a game on his tablet. "How long have you been up?"

"I don't know, ten minutes," Devon answered, fully engrossed in his game.

Derek took the tablet from him. "Get in the bathroom and wash your face and brush your teeth. We're eating breakfast at IHOP," he said to appease his son after taking away his tablet.

Minutes later Derek was back in his bedroom closet getting a pair of dark designer jeans to put on. His cellphone chimed indicating a text message. After pulling on the jeans, a V-neck brown sweater over his white t-shirt, and putting on tan Timberland boots, he picked up his cellphone to see who'd texted. It was Breana again. He groaned internally. She was going to piss him off quickly if she kept texting him.

Breana: **I saw that u read my last msg. U have nothing to say about seeing ur 3rd child's pic 4 the first time?**

Derek: **Yeah like how the hell their mama got pregnant!**

He threw the phone back on the bed and went to put on his watch from the dresser. His wedding band stared back at him as he clasped the stainless steel piece to his wrist. He twisted it on his finger. *Despite everything, Angie had not taken her wedding ring off.* He wondered how long that would last with the BS he had going on.

Breana: **I didn't trap u Derek. Need I remind u how many times we had sex while in da Bahamas?**

Derek: **No need I've been suffering because of it ever since.**

Breana: **Harsh. So F how I feel ending up prego with your baby? This situation isn't ideal 4 me either.**

He knew he shouldn't be taking his anger out on her and that maybe he should consider her feelings in all this, but his family was torn apart because of her. Unfortunately everything Breana meant destruction to him.

Breana: **My parents aren't exactly going to be thrilled hearing about their youngest divorced daughter pregnant by a married man.**

He wanted to find some sympathy for her, but he couldn't, so he texted back:

Derek: **What do you want from me Breana?**

Breana: **I want you to be there with me when I tell my parents.**

He thought that was strange.

Derek: **What are you, 12?**

Breana: **36. But my parents are very influential in my life, so it would be better me telling them I'm pregnant with you there.**

Okay, for some reason he thought they were the same age or maybe she was a bit younger than he was at thirty-three. But meeting her parents? Her being pregnant with his child from a mistake was bad enough, he didn't want to have to deal with her parents too.

"Daddy we're ready!" Dena said excitedly from his bedroom door.

Derek turned to face her. "Ok baby. Give me a minute then we'll leave."

"Okay Daddy." Dena walked away.

Breana: **Please Derek. After that, all I ask is for you to be an active part in our child's life.**

He wasn't feeling this, but replied:

Derek: **Ok**

Breana: **Thank you!!!!!! I will let you know when**

Derek: **Ok**

He placed his cellphone in his jeans pocket then went to leave his bedroom. His cellphone chimed. He pulled it out. It was Breana again.

Breana: So what are you doing today?

Derek: We're not on that level so don't ask!

He'll be there for his child, but he wasn't about to become chummy with her. Texting her back and forth for so long was already too much for him. Thankfully she got the hint and didn't reply back.

****

"You look beautiful as always."

"Thank you!" Angie blushed. She had on a red sweater dress that hugged her curves and stopped above her knees, black tights and black knee high leather boots. She had on a stylish beanie covering her classic bob hairstyle and protecting her head from the cold December temperature. She sat down in the seat he pulled out for her at the dinner table. "So do you Mr. Urban Chic."

He grinned, showing off perfect teeth. "Coming from you, that means a lot sweetheart." He returned to his seat.

"Like you don't hear that all the time."

"I do," he admitted smugly. "But who says it matters most."

She smiled, showing no teeth. *Is he flirting with me?* She brushed it off. "Brian I hope you didn't invite me to dinner to talk about Derek. I'm sure you know that he got Breana pregnant."

"I do."

Angie shook her head. "Well soon he'll be able to marry her so they can have a *happy* family."

"You think he's still sleeping with her?" He signaled the waiter with his hands, to give them a minute.

"Honestly I don't care," she lied. But she would never admit it. The thought of Derek marrying Breana or any other woman made her nauseous. "Anyway, I don't want to talk about them."

The waiter came and took their drinks and dinner orders.

"So how are things with you, how's business?" She asked after taking a bite of one of the breadsticks the waiter left on their table.

"Business is great! Why wouldn't it be, I'm the owner."

"Modest are we," she joked.

"I'm just confident in what I do."

"Hmmmm."

"Only issue is juggling my time between the DMV and New York. I like to be hands on with my clothing stores, got to make sure these managers handling my businesses right."

"That explains why business is going well. You keep them in line when you let them know you're watching."

"Yup. So how do you handle dealing with all those rugrats all day?"

"I have some tough days, but for the most part I love teaching. And this year I got some really great students, haven't had many issues."

"That's what's up," he drawled. He took a sip of his potent drink. "When do you think you'll be ready to start dating again?"

His question threw her for a loop. She took a sip of the fruity alcohol beverage she'd ordered. She didn't remember the name of it. But it tasted good. "Ahhmm. I haven't thought about it. But I know I will eventually."

He acknowledged her answer with a head nod. "Tell me, are you going to do one of those divorce parties people have been doing lately?"

She was beginning to question if Brian was really Derek's friend. What true friend does that? Ask your best friend's wife when she would be ready to date again and if she would throw a divorce party before she even filed for divorce?

"No! I won't exactly be excited about ending my marriage. I'm only doing so because I don't think I would be able to survive if I stay."

Their food arrived and for the rest of the evening the conversation flowed smoothly, helping Angie to forget all about her woes.

Twenty-Five

Angie picked up her purse, then messenger bag from her desk and started for the classroom door. She was going to get Dena and Devon from aftercare then head home. The door swung opened just before she reached it. Aron walked in closing it behind himself.

"Hey, did Arnold forget something in his desk?" She asked.

"No. I wanted to come back before you left to...I know you told me things were *complicated* with you right now, but wanted to chance asking you to accompany me to my work Christmas party this Saturday."

Cat caught her tongue. She was stuck, she didn't know how to respond. Just a few days ago Brian was asking her when she thought she would be ready to date again, and now this. Things were complicated weeks ago because she was still trying to figure out if she wanted to work things out with Derek, but now, she definitely wanted a divorce, so that made things, uncomplicated.

"Things just became *uncomplicated*." A flirtatious smile crept upon her face.

Aron grinned, causing her heart to skip a beat. "So that's a yes?"

"Yes!"

"That makes me a happy man." He pulled a card out of his pocket. "My cellphone number is on there. Send me a text later so I can have yours and we'll make arrangements."

Angie took his business card and slipped it into her purse. "Okay."

****

"So you're actually going out with him, huh," Pauline said, sitting Indian style on Angie's bed watching her pull dresses out of her walk-in closet to try on.

"Yup!" Angie held up an emerald colored, chiffon, floor length dressed with a thigh high slit on the left. She'd bought it last year and hadn't worn it yet.

"Well you know how I feel about it, so I'm going to keep quiet about that."

"It's just a date Pauline."

"Dates lead to other things."

"I'm grown!"

"You're married!"

"Soon divorced!" Angie countered.

Pauline shook her head. She wasn't going to be a party pooper. Besides, she was happy to see Angie not moping around the house anymore. She'd been through a lot these past months, so a night out would be good for her, she thought. She had volunteered to babysit tonight and she and Benjamin had a fun night planned for Dena and Devon. It made them look forward to all the fun things they wanted to do with their kids. She couldn't wait to be a Mommy one day herself.

"I like the green one. Aron won't be able to take his eyes off of you," Pauline complimented.

Angie turned to look at her. "Oh, so now you're trying to help me get my kitty scratched?" she smirked.

"I thought it was just a date?" Pauline asked, taking the bait.

Angie laughed. "You sure are team Derek." She shook her head. "I don't plan on sleeping with him. You know Derek's the only man I've been with, so I'm not trying to take it there…yet."

"I'm team you, and you know that. I just don't want you to make a mistake and get caught up in some mess. You're emotionally vulnerable right now Angie. So take your time."

"Thank you! And I will." She undid her robe, then stepped into the emerald dress to try it on. "Zip me up." She turned so Pauline could help her. "What do you think?" She asked now standing in front of a full length mirror.

Pauline looked her over, as if she was contemplating her decision. "Yes! Aron's eyes are going poke out of his head when he see you. You look HOT!" Pauline high-fived Angie.

Angie turned around, checking herself out from the back. "You think my butt looks too big?"

"You know how many squats I do in a day to get a butt like yours. Some white chicks like me have to work a little harder to get what you have."

Angie playfully grabbed Pauline's toned behind. "And you got buns of steel girl." She slapped her on the butt causing Pauline to laugh.

"Girl get!" Pauline pushed her away. "Being around you I can't be walking around with a wall butt. Anyway... you look great! Wear that tonight."

Angie looked herself over some more in the mirror. The dress fit her perfectly and she had the perfect accessories to complete the look.

****

Angie smooth her hands nervously down her dress. She'd just stepped into the lobby of the hotel where the architectural firm Aron worked for was hosting their Christmas party. She had declined his offer to pick her up. She agreed to the date, but she wasn't ready for the whole 'should I, shouldn't I let him in, good night kiss, etc., etc.' when it would be time for him to walk her to her front door. She looked down at her left hand, it felt naked without her wedding band on. She slipped it off and placed it in her jewelry box right before she walked out of her bedroom earlier. She figured if she was going to do this whole dating thing, she couldn't still have another man's ring on her finger. *Taking it off doesn't mean you're not married*, her conscious told her, but she brushed the thought away as soon as she saw Aron walking toward her.

He was...brother was fine as all get out! She lustfully checked him out in his tux. He looked so good she was almost questioning her self-esteem and if she was good enough to be his date. *Derek would look scrumptious in that tux.* She shook her head when that thought popped into it. Derek was the last person she wanted to think about.

"If I knew how sexy you would look in that dress, I would've manned up and asked you out a long time ago." He greeted her with a hug. Angie almost melted in his strong arms, and darn his cologne for revving up her sexual need. *Gawd, how am I going to survive this night remaining a lady?*

"And you look like you just stepped away from a photoshoot for designer suits."

"Only the best for you Ms. Monroe." He winked at her after releasing her from his embrace. "Are you ready?"

She smiled. "Yes."

"Good. I've been bragging about you since I got here, telling all my colleagues I have the best looking date of all."

She giggled. "You didn't."

"I did. And you wearing that dress will prove my point, no doubt!"

****

Derek could think of a million and one things he'd rather be doing right now, than sitting in the uncomfortable seat in an overly priced restaurant in the hotel he was in waiting on Breana's parents to arrive.

"They should be here any minute now," Breana told him seeing how impatient he was becoming.

He said nothing while he checked his business emails on his phone. He busied himself by replying back to his clients and reviewing his schedule on the calendar for next week.

"I know you don't want to be here, but can you promise to be cordial when my parents arrive?" She asked, referring to the fact that he'd completely ignored her the whole fifteen minutes they had been waiting for her unpunctual parents to arrive. The only reason he was there was because Breana wasn't the only one to blame for their ordeal. But after this his only obligation to her was the child she was carrying.

Derek nodded acknowledging her, but kept his eyes on his phone screen.

Moments later. "Mommy, Daddy," Breana stood up to greet her parents. Derek did the same, wanting to get this meeting over and done with ASAP. He placed his phone in his coat pocket.

"Mommy, Daddy, this is Derek, Derek my parents: Dr. Bruce Sutton and Mrs. Susan Sutton." Derek shook both her parent's hand. Moments later they were all settled at their dinner table. Drinks and food orders were placed. However Derek declined placing a dinner order. He didn't want to stay there longer than he had to.

"You are positively glowing sweetheart. Does Derek here have something to do with that?" Mrs. Sutton asked.

Breana smiled nervously. "Actually yes Mommy. That's why I wanted you and Daddy to fly here before your trip out of the country." She shifted her gaze between her parents. They waited anxiously for her to continue. "I'm...I'm pregnant," she blurted out.

Mrs. Sutton's eyes grew big like saucers. Dr. Sutton turned angry eyes toward Derek. "Does that mean you're marrying my daughter?" He asked Derek.

HELL NO! "I'm already married," Derek answered.

Mrs. Sutton looked like she was about to pass out. Dr. Sutton slammed his hand on the table causing the glasses, plates and silverware to bounce, which subsequently caused a few items to fall onto the carpeted floor. Thankfully there glasses were only filled with water awaiting the waiter to arrive with their drinks.

Recovering from the shock, Breana used the napkins on the table to dry up the spilled water. An eerie silence fell over the table. A waiter came and asked if they wanted another table. Dr. Sutton silently declined by shaking his head. However new glasses and utensils were placed.

"How stupid could you be Breana?" Her father boomed. He didn't care if he was creating a scene. Now a retired neurosurgeon, he'd worked too hard to provide a good life for his three children, teaching them to have good morals, and values only for his youngest child to end up pregnant by a married man. *Where did I go wrong with this child?*

"Bruce!" His wife admonished him.

"No sweetheart. I'm not sugaring coating it. First she was married to that con artist that, thank God she finally divorced, before he got her caught up in his mess that sent him to jail for fifteen years a few months ago. But now she gets pregnant by a married man. You're thirty-six years old, when the hell are you going to grow up and stop making dumb decisions?"

Breana's eyes were filled to the brim with tears. She was completely mortified.

Derek for once, felt badly for her. No wonder she wanted him to be there when she spoke to her parents. "Dr. Sutton, Breana isn't the only one at fault here."

"You're damn right she isn't! What kind of man are you to step out of your marriage? Have you no morals, no shame? And now you're going to bring an innocent baby into your mess!"

Derek knew he was all kinds of messed up for what he'd done. But he wasn't going to be chastised by this man. "Watch your tone with me Sir!" He gritted through his teeth. "You may not like me, but you for damn sure going to respect me enough to check your tone before you speak to me. Until you become Jesus Christ Himself, don't sit there throwing judgment my way. I know I screwed up so I don't need you or anybody else pointing it out."

Breana was now in full blown tears. "I'm sorry Daddy!"

Dr. Sutton shook his head.

"I'm not marrying your daughter Sir, but I will take care of my responsibilities when it comes to my child she's carrying."

"And what about your wife? Do you have children?" Dr. Sutton asked him.

"I'm here tonight regarding Breana and our unborn child. My wife and kids are not open for discussion."

They were all silent as the waiter filled their table with their dinner orders, then he left.

"The situation isn't ideal, but at least you're taking on the responsibility. I will definitely hold you to that," Dr. Sutton told Derek.

"Yes Sir."

After making sure Breana was good, Derek left the dinner table. He fulfilled his obligation for tonight, so he was done. He didn't know how he felt about having Dr. Sutton as his child's grandfather, but it was too late to be concerned about it.

Derek's steps halted as he made his way out of the restaurant, into the lobby of the hotel. He could point her out anywhere, his entire body was always awakened when she was around. Angie. She looked positively radiant. Since they've been back from Florida, she'd been keeping her distance from him. Whenever he came to pick up or drop the kids back to her, she was cordial, but kept all conversation about the kids only and on a need to know basis. And even that was mostly just a yes or no response from her. Anything detailed about the kids she would text or send him an email, just to keep from having to engage in conversation with him for more than five minutes. He'd made his bed of thorns and was painfully lying in it. For the sake of peace and to not hurt her further, he didn't pressure her about giving him another chance. *How could I expect her to accept and help raise a child I'm having with another woman anyway?* He knew he couldn't ask her to do that.

But the sight of Aron on her arm had him ready to kill dude right there on the spot, and what escalated his spiking rage was when dude reached over and kissed her on the cheek.

Derek was standing in front of them within seconds. It took every ounce of God given strength he possessed not to clutch his hand around Aron's neck and choke the life out of him. "You're on a date with this dude Angie?" He was breathing so hard he wouldn't be surprised if smoke started puffing out of his nose and mouth.

The fear of God came upon Angie when she saw the rage in Derek's eyes. She'd never seen him so angry.

"She is and what's it to you?" Aron spoke with voice of steel.

"She's my wife mutha—" Derek thundered.

"Derek, please!" Angie begged. She knew if pushed Derek would go ballistic on Aron's behind. He had the bite to back up his bark and then some.

"Soon to be ex-wife—" Before Aron could finish Derek clocked him, snapping his head back. Derek got a second punch in on his face before Aron found his balance and was able to defend himself, getting in some hits of his own.

"STOP IT PLEASE!" Angie screamed frantically watching the men brawl.

They both pushed away from each other, heaving from the exhaustion. Both of their faces were battered up and articles of clothing torn. But each held their own.

"What the hell is your problem Derek?" Angie asked. She saw in the corner of her eyes security guards heading their way and a crowd had formed spectating. *So embarrassing.*

Derek wiped his bloody mouth with his hand. "You're still my wife so the *only* man that supposed to kiss up on you is me! So if you don't want me to kill this nigga end that shit now!"

Angie's mouth dropped. Was it wrong for her to be turned on right now? She knew he had some hood in him, but it didn't come out often. "This coming from a man that's having a baby with another woman." She turned to walk away from him.

Derek stopped her by pulling her back toward him. "Try me if you want to Angie, but I'm serious." And as crazy as it might sound, he meant that. He still had connections from his old stomping grounds in New York and could have Aron disappear in a blink.

"What is going on?" The security officers demanded when they approached.

"Just a misunderstanding that we got sorted out," Derek told them while looking at Angie. She cut her eyes away from him, then looked Aron over asking him if he was alright.

"Alright, but y'all still have to leave!" They were being escorted out of the premises.

"Next time I ain't gone stop til you're laid out!" Aron threatened Derek.

Derek smirked. He was giving Angie forty-five minutes to get home without that flake or all hell was gonna break loose.

****

Derek: **If you dont pick up ur phone n tell me ur home without that dude I'm coming over.**

Angie picked her phone up off of the bathroom counter looked at it, then placed it back down. Derek had been blowing her up since she stepped in the door fifteen minutes ago. She still couldn't believe the scene at the hotel. *How embarrassing*. And in front of Aron's colleagues. Thankfully he was able to defend himself well, so both men came out equal. *But still*. Now Derek was calling her back to back and just resorted to sending a text message.

She had gotten out of her dress and was now in the bathroom removing her makeup. Minutes later the doorbell rang. *No he didn't!* She walked out of the bathroom and grabbed her robe off of the bedroom door and slipped it on, covering herself only dressed in a bra and thong underwear.

"You have completely lost your marbles tonight!" She spat through the security screen glass door. She had no intentions of letting him in.

"Are you alone?" He asked ignoring her rant. He looked her over in her bathrobe and bare face. He thought she was even more beautiful without the makeup.

"And if I'm not?" She knew she was playing with fire, but he'd pissed her off and he needed to get a taste of his own medicine.

"Baby, you don't want to play this game with me." She was his wife, point, blank, period, whether they were separated or not. And he would not tolerate her being with someone else. Yeah he screwed up with Breana months back, but he'd been nothing but faithful before and after that incident and he expected her to be the same. He'd made a mistake, who hasn't in their relationships, but he had no intentions of hurting Angie like that ever again.

"If I want to date I'm going to date and you won't stop me. We're separated Derek and soon will be divorced so as far as I'm concerned I'm no longer married to you." She held up her bare ring finger to solidify her point.

He took a key out of his jacket pocket and unlocked the door, to Angie's disbelief. He'd had keys made months back during the times she'd allowed him to be at the house with the kids when she wasn't there. But he'd never used it, wanting to respect her privacy. But he got copies so he could have easy access to check on his family if need be.

"How…how long have you had those?" She asked backing away from him.

Derek closed then locked both doors behind him. "Angie I know you're trying to hurt me by what you just said, and I get it. Cheating on you was foul and I'm sorry. I will regret it for the rest of my life." He stepped predatorily towards her. "But you are my wife and I'm your husband. You will *always* be my wife in my eyes, whether you wear your wedding ring or not." He backed her against a wall in the kitchen. His fingers trailed down her face then he tilted her head up towards his. Her lips trembled, not in fear, but in anticipation. He bent and captured her mouth with his in a loving, then chastising kiss. He bit down on her lip, then soothed the pain by sucking on it. He reached down and undid the tie to her robe. She didn't put up a fight so he was going to take it as far as she allowed. His hands caressed her smooth mocha skin, rubbing her thighs, then palming her butt. He trailed his fingers up her body and slide the robe off of her shoulders letting it fall to the fall. His eyes hungrily roamed over her body.

"You wore this under your dress for your date?" He was pissed that she chose such sexy undergarments for her date with that prick. But pleased to be the one to see her in them.

She said nothing. Her breathing was ragged. Her body was on fire, she hadn't been touched, kissed, in weeks since the last time she broke down and gave in to his sexual lures. Altogether, they'd had sex three times total since he told her of his affair almost four months ago.

Derek unclasped her bra then filled his hands with her bountiful breasts. He bent and captured a nipple in his mouth, then moved on to the other. Her body creamed from the sensation. She didn't want him to stop, but she couldn't find her voice to speak. Derek knelt down before, ripped her thong off of her body then buried his face in her treasure. Angie lost it. In less than a minute she was raining down on him.

"So you want to go on dates with other men, huh?" He pulled her over to the counter and bent her over it, she obediently obliged. Before she knew it, he was buried deep inside of her. She hollered his name repeatedly as he punished her unmercifully with pleasure. Almost an hour later she was begging him to stop because she didn't know if her body could handle another orgasm.

They had somehow made it into the family room. Satisfied that he'd punished her enough, Derek lifted her limp body off of the couch and into his arms. He took her upstairs and into the master bathroom. He placed her feet on the ground, but kept her now sleeping form close to his bare chest. He reached and turned on the shower, when it was hot enough, he walked inside with her and cleaned them both up. Minutes later he had Angie dried and tucked in bed. Sitting on the edge of the bed, he gazed down at his sleeping wife.

"I love you Angie," he whispered.

She stirred a little, but was obviously still sound asleep. "I love you Derek." He heard her mumble. His heart swelled with joy. He hadn't heard her say that in months and was beginning to think she didn't love him anymore. And even though she said it unconsciously in her sleep, he was happy to know that her love for him was still there.

Derek stood up to leave. He hadn't planned to come and have sex with her tonight, he just wanted to make sure Aron wasn't in his house with her. He was surprised she didn't stop his advances. But after that comment she made about dating, he lost it. He had to remind her that he was the only man in her life. Now how he was going to deal with it if and when she filed for divorce

– he didn't know yet. But like he told Angie, she will always be his wife in his eyes – legally married or not.

He found his articles of clothing downstairs and put them on. He set the alarm and locked up on his way out.

Twenty-Six

Pauline pulled the blinds open letting light into the bedroom. "Girl, get up! We've been to church and everything, its twelve-thirty and you're still in bed." She sat on Angie's bed and nudged her.

"Hmmmm," Angie turned onto her side. "What?" She was disoriented.

Pauline laughed. "Okay, I really want details on your date with Aron. You look like you're in a different world."

Angie moved her legs and that's when the pain hit her causing her to groan in pain and in pleasure from the memories of last night. Being mindful of her aching body, she carefully got up and out of bed. She really needed to pee. Every step she took toward the bathroom made her want to cry. Derek had worked her out punishing her so well.

"Okay, what in the world did you get into last night? You're walking like an old woman needing a walker." Pauline watched her friend curiously.

Angie handle her business in the bathroom. She popped some aspirin into her mouth and drank water from the tap to swallow it down.

"Okay, talk!" Pauline had her arms crossed over her chest while sitting with her back against the headboard.

"Where are the kids?" Angie made it back into bed and pulled the covers over her.

"They're downstairs eating lunch and watching a movie."

Angie closed her eyes, recalling the events of last night. "I can't believe I slept with him," she whispered. She didn't want to go there with Derek again. She'd given into him a few times during their separation but she really didn't want to have sex with him *again*. It complicated things more. After he told her Breana was pregnant, she knew more than before that she wanted a divorce. She couldn't stand by his side and watch him have a baby with the woman he cheated on her with. She had to wean off of him. She knew it was going to be hard, but she had to get used to doing things on her own. She had to get used to making decisions on her own, taking care of the household and more on her own. He had been her husband for nine years and they'd dated a few years before marriage, so despite everything, letting him go wouldn't be easy. And last night just set her back.

"You did not sleep with Aron last night!" Pauline said in shock. *OMG did Angie cheat on Derek too?* Her mouth formed an o waiting for Angie's response.

Angie opened her eyes slowly and turned her head to look at her friend. "No I didn't sleep with Aron. I had sex with Derek."

Pauline was beside herself with the news. "Uhm, how did that happen?"

Angie told her what happened at the hotel last night and up to the point where Derek showed up on her doorstep. She left out the juicy details of what happened after, but Pauline got the gest.

"Whoa," Pauline said after Angie was finished. "So, are you still going to go out on dates?"

Angie closed her eyes waiting for the pain medicine to take effect. "I've got to move on with my life Pauline. If he's so worried about me dating and being with another man, he should have never cheated."

"I know and I agree with you one hundred percent." Pauline wanted Derek and Angie to get back together and thought that would've happened, until the news of Breana's pregnancy. And as much as she was still rooting for Derek and Angie – she knew it would take a lot for any woman to accept her man having a child with the woman he cheated on her with. So she couldn't fault Angie for wanting a divorce.

"I need to contact Aron and see how he's doing," Angie said sitting up to reach for her cellphone off the nightstand. Looking at it she noticed missed calls and text messages from Aron. And a text from Derek asking how she was feeling this morning. *God that man*. She didn't know if he was sincere or making sure she got his point about not dating. She wasn't in the mood for dealing with him right then, so she decided to respond to Aron's text messages letting him know that she was okay, because he'd asked. She also texted him to find out how he was. He responded instantly saying he was good and if she wanted to go see a movie with him that upcoming Friday. She smiled, thankful that he wasn't pissed about last night. She responded telling him she would love to.

"Seems he put a smile on your face," Pauline said when Angie placed her cellphone back on the nightstand.

"Yeah. We're going out to the movies this coming Friday."

"Hmmm, you better be careful before Derek gives you another spanking," Pauline laughed.

"Derek is out there about to be daddy to his third child. He has no right to dictate what I can or cannot do." *Though I wouldn't mind another spanking*, she smirked. But quickly shook the thought out of her head. *Weaning off of him remember? Weaning off!*

Twenty-Seven

"So many nights I dreamt of you, holding my pillow tight, I know that I don't need to be alone, when I open up my eyes, to face reality, every moment without you, it seems like eternity, I'm begging you, begging you come back to me...Can we go back to the days our love was strong, can you tell me how a perfect love goes wrong, can somebody tell how to get things back, the way they use to be, Oh God give me a reason, I'm down on bended knee, I'll never walk again until you come back to me, I'm down on bended knee..." The lyrics to "On Bended Knee" by Boyz II Men were speaking to Derek's soul. He wasn't much for love songs, but it seemed every sad and breakup song that came on the radio spoke about his broken heart for not being with his wife and kids. He didn't know how he'd survived for so long.

Derek was going hard on the treadmill at the gym listening to music from his iPhone through his earbuds. He'd been there for two hours working out on different types of machines. Working out, work and spending time with his kids — kept him sane. It had been a few days since seeing Angie and Aron on a date, and she had distanced herself even further from him — if that was even possible. Seeing her with another man was like putting a bullet into his chest. Just the thought of it angered him.

He flicked his wrist to see the time. He had an hour and half to go to his condo, shower, change and be on time to pick up Dena and Devon from school. It was Thursday, and his weekend to have them, so he was excited about that. They'd been telling him about all the gifts they wanted for Christmas which was only two weeks away. He'd pretty much gotten all of their gifts already. So this weekend, like he'd been doing since Dena could talk, he was taking the kids so they can pick out the gifts they wanted to give Angie for Christmas.

"Daddy we've been staying at Aunt Pauline and Uncle Benjamin's house," Devon said out of nowhere as they sat eating an afternoon snack at Chick-Fil-A. "So Aunt Pauline made a huge fort with pillows and sheets in the family room for me and Dena to sleep to make it fun."

"What!? How long have you guys been sleeping there?" Derek automatically thought it was because Angie had a man, Aron to be exact, coming over to his house.

"Since Monday." Dena told him before sucking lemonade through her straw. "Mommy said the furnace isn't working and she has to get it fixed, so we've been sleeping there until."

Derek blew a mental sigh of relief. But was upset and hurt with the fact that Angie didn't call him to let him know. He would've had someone over there to fix it ASAP or he would've checked it out himself. He didn't want his family in a cold house in the dead of winter.

Derek made a few calls and arranged for someone to be at the house within an hour to fix the problem with the furnace. He called the babysitter Tina and arranged for her to watch the kids while he met the technician to fix the furnace.

****

"Hi Derek," Pauline greeted after opening the front door for him.

"Hey Pauline. I need to talk to Angie." He knew she was there because her car was in the driveway.

Moments later Angie met him in the foyer, he didn't have any intentions of staying long so he waited there.

"Why didn't you tell me about the furnace?" He asked as calmly as possible. He knew she was still pissed with him for obvious reasons, but her and his children's wellbeing was of utmost importance to him and he didn't like not being aware of what was going on.

"Because I was going to have it fixed," she answered, standing her ground while folding her arms under her breast.

"You should have called me Angie."

"We're separated. I don't have to or need to call you whenever something breaks in the house. I can handle it. That's not your responsibility anymore."

Now she pissed him off. He didn't want to start an argument with her, especially since all of their recent angst has been his fault, but he wasn't going to tolerate her not keeping him in the loop about issues in a house he was paying the mortgage for. "I messed up Angie, yeah I get that, I'm paying for it every miserable day without you and my kids, but I'm still your husband and Dena and Devon are my children so that makes all of you *my* responsibility. So I want to know when something isn't working – especially when it forces you all to have to stay somewhere else. I may not live there anymore, but I'm still the man of the house and I'm going to make sure my family is okay," he told her with no sense of humor.

"I wasn't trying to keep it from you, if that's what you're thinking. But we're getting a divorce, I don't need you coming over to fix things that I can handle on my own."

"Angie," he said with steel in his voice.

"I'm no longer your responsibility. Now if it's anything regarding Dena and Devon's safety of course I will let you know, other than that, I will take care of what needs to be done around the house." She wasn't going to have him thinking he can run her house. Yeah she got that he wanted to make sure that they were good, but at the same time she couldn't continue to rely on him. It was bad enough he tried to sex her into submission about not dating a few days ago, which almost worked, but no way was she going to allow him to think he was going to know all the ins and outs about the household he forfeited.

"Dammit Angie, what the F—" He stopped himself. He didn't like cursing at her. "I need to know what's going on with my family."

She didn't want to hurt his feelings, even after all the BS he'd put her through, but they had to face reality. "Like I said, anything pertaining to Dena and Devon you will know about. But us staying here until I fix the furnace isn't a big deal. Someone will be out tomorrow."

Derek blew a frustrated breath. "It's already fixed. It was fixed just a few minutes ago. So you can go back home whenever you're ready."

She looked at him with surprise. He always did make sure his family was secured, it was one of the things she loved about him, and would miss. "Thank you! How much was it to get fixed?"

"Please don't insult me Angie." He turned and walked toward the door.

"Derek whether you want to face it or not you need to stop seeing me as your responsibility." Each word she said piercing her heart.

He stopped and turned around to look at the love of his life. He never in all the years he'd known her thought they would be at this place in their lives. "You need to stop thinking that's ever going to happen." With that he was gone.

Twenty-Eight

"Derek, you sure have made me a very happy man! I should have come looking for you before I went into business years ago, I would've been a millionaire by now," Mr. Nelson, owner of an electrician company, said giving Derek a handshake before leaving his office. They'd just went over the increase in sales for his company since he'd hired Derek to help garner more business.

"You followed my advice about getting the customer service training for your staff which I provided and you've partnered up with that electrical supplies company in New Jersey, so now business is just falling into your lap. You'll be a millionaire in no time."

"Thanks to you man."

"Don't forget my check when you make your first million though," Derek joked, clapping the man on the shoulder as they walked toward his office door.

"Get me there in a year and I'll gladly write that check for you," Mr. Nelson told him.

"Deal. Take care man."

Derek walked back to his desk, he was happy about his client's success which meant business for him was doing well too.

"Mr. Monroe," Latoya called on the intercom.

"Yes."

"Ah, Ms. Sutton is here to see you." Latoya rolled her eyes behind Breana's back. She didn't get into her boss' business but she just knew this chick had something to do with Derek and Angie's breakup. She hadn't seen Angie in months and didn't want to overstep bounds by reaching out to her personally. But she'd been trying her best to dig up some dirt on little Ms. Debutante standing here like she was Queen Sheba, that she could use against her. Derek had been a walking depression for months. She saw that he tried his best not to look it – and if she hadn't been working for him for so long she would be fooled – but she wasn't. And she knew it was because of Breana.

"You can go in," Latoya told Breana giving her a fake smile. *I'm gonna find out what you're up to, trick.* Latoya didn't like anyone messing with her family and Derek and Angie were her family. Derek gave her a chance with this job when everyone else had given up on her. Because of his generosity she was able to afford her own place, car and pay all her bills without stressing. She owed a lot to him and finding out what that snake was up to would only be a small way of giving back.

Derek rolled his eyes the moment Breana walked into his office. She'd been finding the liberty to call or show up at his place of business whenever she felt like ever since she told him she was pregnant.

"How can I help you Breana?" He asked after she took a seat in one of his visitor chairs.

She seductively crossed her legs showing off some thigh covered in brown tights. Derek shook his head, aware of her show and tell. He wasn't interested. "I thought we could go out to lunch."

"We both know that's not going to happen. So what else is there that you want?" He was already tired of her presence – pregnant with his child or not.

"Seriously Derek, you're still going to treat me like a nobody? I'm the mother of your unborn child," she said, placing her hand on her small belly. "And as two people that will be having a baby together in a few months, we should spend time getting to know one another," she argued.

"All you need to know is that I'm going to be a father to my child. And as long as you don't try to prevent me from doing so, we won't have a problem."

"Of course I won't stop you from being there for our child. But come on Derek, there's so much about you that I don't know. I want to get to know the father of my child."

Another reason why I shouldn't have succumbed to your charm and slept with you in the Bahamas. We know nothing about each other. So he knew she had a point – they were virtually strangers, strangers that were expecting a baby together. *Damn!* Every time he thought about the mess he'd gotten himself into, he cringed. "What is there you want to know Breana?" He leaned back in his seat.

She smiled. "Let's chat over lunch, I'm starved." She rubbed her belly for emphasis. "This baby is a greedy little thing." She added to sway him in her favor.

He knew what she was doing, but figured it wouldn't hurt to have lunch with her. She was right, they are having a baby together and should get to know one another more. He didn't even know if she would be a good mother or not. Something he didn't have to worry about with Angie – she was the perfect mother to his children. "Okay, I'll have my assistant reserve us a table for a restaurant here at the harbor so we won't have to wait long."

"Hmmm you mean your *rude* assistant." She stood up.

Derek gave her a scathing look. "Latoya is very professional, so if she was rude she was picking up on your attitude," he stated.

"You're taking up for her?" She asked placing her hand on her hip.

Is she really trying to catch an attitude with me right now about my assistant? He arched his brow picking up the phone. "Miss Simms, please reserve a table for two at Rosa Mexicano," he told Latoya. "...Yes, thanks!" He stood up.

"For you to be running a Business Consultation firm, you sure have snotty help," Breana said, walking behind him to the door.

He ignored her. If she thought he was going to argue with her about Latoya she was greatly mistaken. Besides Angie, Latoya had been a big help to the success of his business, which was why she was his only full time employee. He hired subcontractors on a needed basis, but for the most part he and Latoya ran his firm expeditiously. Besides, Breana wasn't of great concern to him even if he wanted to check Latoya on her presumed rudeness toward her.

Breana sucked her teeth under her breath after realizing he wasn't taking her bait. She just brought up Latoya in an attempt to invoke some empathy out of him for her concern, but it didn't work.

"Your table is reserved." Latoya told him when he walked toward her desk.

"Thanks!" He pressed the button for the elevator.

Breana rolled her eyes at Latoya as she walked by her desk. Latoya bit down on her tongue to prevent herself from cussing her out.

After Derek and Breana got on the elevator and the doors shut, Latoya picked up the phone. "Hey girl, I need a favor," she said to her cousin who worked at a private investigation firm in DC. "You know that real estate developer Breana Sutton...You know, the woman that has her picture on those billboards around PG County?...Yeah her. Can you find out whatever you can about her?... Just do me this favor...Yeah...Oh and I think she's pregnant, get me details about her doctor's office, everything you can...Okay, thanks! I got you chica."

Twenty-Nine

Derek didn't know what it was, but lately he'd been feeling Brian was on some slick stuff. He knew he and Angie were separated but Brian had been inquiring, a bit too much for his liking, about his interactions with his wife. Then Derek thought maybe he was just feeling some type of way about Angie seeking a divorce and it was causing him to trip on his boy, but something about Brian just felt foul to him and he couldn't put his finger on it.

"So hey, when was the last time you talked to Angie? I know you said she has been giving you the cold shoulder since that bust with her and homeboy," Brian asked. He remembered asking Angie about when she was going to start dating, but he sure as hell didn't intend for her to go out with some other dude.

Derek was sitting on one of the huge beanbags in his living room playing a video game. He had Brian on speaker phone while he played. "It's been a minute man. All I can do is give her space. I don't want a divorce, but I can't make her stay married to me either." It never got easy admitting that. He shook his head.

"I hear ya man. Shoot I still can't believe you got old girl pregnant."

"Me either."

"So what you gonna do, try to start something with Breana since she's having your baby?"

"Hell naw!" Derek yelled. If she wasn't pregnant with his seed, he sure wouldn't miss never seeing her face again.

Brian laughed. "I hear man. But hey, Angie's filing for divorce, and having Breana as a baby mama won't be bad, she sure is easy on the eyes. So getting with her probably won't be a bad thing." *Cause I need your focus off of Angie. It's my chance now.*

"No woman will ever replace Angie. Breana having my baby doesn't change that," he stated adamantly.

"Waxing her tail every so often would have its benefits. You could only be in a drought for so long," Brian stated. Although Derek cheated on Angie while in the Bahamas, Brian knew his boy wasn't the cheater type and he probably hadn't been with anyone else but Angie since their separation. And he wasn't feeling that one bit.

"Why you concerned about my sex life? I'm good, bruh," Derek said a bit defensively. He wasn't in the mood for the conversation, especially if all Brian wanted to talk about was the doom of his marriage. "Look, I'll hit you up later."

"A'ight cool."

Derek ended the call and refocused his full attention to the wide TV screen ahead of him.

****

"You know they know what we're doing down here right?" Pauline said cutting a piece of wrapping paper. She and Angie were hiding out in the basement trying to quickly wrap Dena and Devon's Christmas gifts. They had them occupied upstairs watching *A Charlie Brown Christmas*.

"They don't, they're watching the movie that would keep them busy for another forty minutes." Angie pulled some tape and finished wrapping the Lego set she got for Devon.

"So I have a Christmas gift for you. I wanted to wait until next week, but I just can't keep it a secret anymore," Pauline said. She placed a huge red bow on the big gift she just finished wrapping.

Angie stilled her hands and looked at Pauline sitting across from her on the carpeted basement floor. "Is it something I have to unwrap?"

Pauline shook her head.

"Oh my GOD, you're pregnant! You're pregnant aren't you?" Angie asked with a huge smile on her face. Her hazel eyes twinkled with delight.

Pauline smiled placing a bow onto her flat shirt covered belly. "Yes! Benjamin and I are finally having a baby. Merry Christmas!"

Angie pushed the gift away from her and leaped over to hug her friend. "Girl I'm so happy for you guys!" She squeezed her friend. "How far along are you?" She pulled back from her embrace.

"Almost three months."

"You heifer!" Angie exclaimed jokingly. "You've kept this from me for three months?"

"I wanted to tell you as soon as I found out, but Benjamin and I just wanted to wait and be in the safe zone before we told our family and friends. And if it makes you feel any better, you're the first I'm telling besides Benjamin. We plan on telling everyone for Christmas."

"Okay, that does make me feel better. And I can understand why you guys wanted to wait." Angie hugged her again. "This is awesome! I'm gonna be an Auntie!"

Minutes later they were back upstairs with Dena and Devon.

"Shoot, it seems everything wants to act crazy now that I'm the one that has to take care of it." Angie stood by the sink in the kitchen flipping the switch on and off for the garbage disposal.

"I can ask Benjamin to come and check it out for you," Pauline offered. She was sitting at the island stuffing her face with some turkey soup Angie had made earlier. Now that Angie thought about, Pauline had been eating a lot lately.

"Thanks!" The doorbell rang. Angie went to go see who it was. "Hey," she said to Brian. She stepped aside to let him in and to close the door quickly to not allow too much of the cold air from outside in. "To what do I owe this visit?" She asked walking back toward the kitchen. She and Brian had become very friendly lately since her separation from Derek. He was a good sounding board when she wanted a male perspective on her feelings regarding the fall of her marriage.

"You know I like to do my occasional drop ins," he told her while watching her hips and behind move as she walked ahead of him.

"Yeah," she said over her shoulder.

"It smells good in here," Brian mentioned after walking into the kitchen. "What's up Pauline?"

"I'm good, how about you?" Pauline was at the sink rinsing out her bowl.

"I'm good. No complaints."

"I made turkey soup earlier, do you want some?" Angie offered him.

"Yeah, I'm down for some home cooking." He sat on one of the high back stools at the kitchen island.

"Okay Angie, I'm heading home for a much needed nap," Pauline announced after drying her hands with a kitchen towel. "I'll tell Benjamin about your garbage disposal." She turned to Brian. "I'll catch up with you later Brian." She walked out of the kitchen and went to tell Devon and Dena that she was leaving.

"What's wrong with your garbage disposal?" Brian asked Angie.

"I don't know, but it's not working."

"I can check it out." He got off the stool and went to the kitchen sink. He flipped the switch off and on, and got nothing. He then opened the cupboard under the sink to check things out. "Do you have some tools I can use?"

"Yeah. Be right back." Seconds later she was standing near him with Derek's tool box in her hand. "Here, anything you need should be in there. Thanks for looking at the it for me," she told him, placing the tool box beside where he sat on the floor looking under the sink.

Angie went and sat with the kids for a few minutes in the family room. They were now watching Madagascar Christmas movie while eating popcorn. She walked back into the kitchen moments later after making sure the kids were good.

"I got it working. You had a couple spoons stuck in there stopping it from turning on." He showed her the destroyed metal.

"Thank you! That must have happened when Dena volunteered to wash the dishes to earn some Christmas shopping money."

Brian washed his hands at the sink. "No biggie. If there's anything else you need fixing around here just let me know." He turned and gave her one of his panty dropping smiles.

Angie blushed despite herself. "Well it's only fair that I feed you now." She went to the cupboard to pull out a huge bowl. Then she walked over to the stove to spoon out some turkey soup for him.

Seeing the opportunity, Brian stepped close behind Angie as she stood at the stove. He ran his hand down her arms. Startled, and very uncomfortable with his closeness and forwardness, she tried to step out of his reach which caused some of the soup to spill onto her pants. She bent slightly to wipe the hot liquid off, which allowed Brian to gently hold her waist bringing her butt in direct contact with his manhood.

"Brian, what the hell!?" She exclaimed, turning to look at him.

Driven by lust, he said nothing while cupping the back of her head and bringing her lips to his. His kissed started off gentle then his hunger for her overtook him causing him to dive deeper. He'd wanted to for so long and could no longer help himself...and oh was it worth the wait. *Forbidden fruit is always the sweetest.*

"Mommy!" Devon exclaimed in horror. "Why is Uncle Brian kissing you?"

Angie pushed Brian away forcefully. She couldn't believe he just kissed her. She wiped her lips with the back of her hand. She wanted to slap the living daylights out of him, but she didn't want to create more of a scene in front of her six year old son.

"Get your ass out of my house!" She gritted through her teeth for only his ears to hear. "Baby it was nothing, Uncle Brian was just giving me a hug because he helped fix the garbage disposal." She turned to tell her son.

"Oh." Devon stood there in the entryway to the kitchen watching them closely, then moved to grab a juice box out of the cupboard. He turned and went back into the family room with it. She normally didn't allow them to eat and drink in there, but since it was the holiday season she was giving them a pass.

"Come on Angie, it was a harmless kiss," Brian said with a smirk.

"You're a snake! Derek probably learned how to cheat because of your grimy behind." She couldn't believe she fell for his nice guy act, calling to check in on her to see how she was dealing with her separation from Derek. Popping up to sit and chat, taking her out for dinner. She was so heartbroken from learning of Derek's affair that having his best friend on her side made her feel a bit vindicated. But now she knew his true reason for *support*.

"You don't mean that." He went and sat at the island as if nothing just happened. "I'm sorry for overstepping. But honestly I've wanted to kiss you for a long time Angie, you are a beautiful, desirable woman." He schmoozed.

"Are you serious right now?" He disgusted her. "I'm your best friend's wife!"

"Soon to be ex-wife." He corrected.

"Wow!" Her mouth formed an o. "Wife, ex-wife, it should all mean for you to stay away from me." She shook her head. "Do you men only think with your dicks?"

He laughed, pissing her off further. "It was just a kiss Angie, far less than what I really would like to do with you if you give me a chance. Unlike Derek, I wouldn't be dumb enough to let you slip out of my fingers if given a chance."

"Get out of my house and don't ever come back or call me again!" She snapped.

"Come on Angie it's not as serious –"

"Get out!" She slammed her hand onto the counter.

Brian got the clue and got up and left. *She'll come around*, he told himself cockily. He licked his lips, he was already addicted to her taste.

Thirty

Angie smiled while reading the text message she just received from Aron. She was laying across her bed with the TV on watching a Christmas movie. He and Arnold were in Texas for Christmas, and he'd just texted her to wish her a happy Christmas Eve.

Angie: **Happy Christmas Eve to you too.**

Aron: **Wish you were under the Christmas tree as my gift.**

She didn't know how to respond to that. Things were moving at snail pace with them, but she liked him. Though she had yet to even kiss him on the lips. She'd only allowed him to kiss her on spots like on her neck, cheek and forehead, she just wasn't ready to move things along in that arena for now. Her fingers danced over her phone as she contemplated how to respond.

Angie: **Hmmmm, maybe U have to wait until U get back to get UR, gift.**

After sending the text she wished she could take it back. Did she want to take things there with him? *Please take it as a joke, please take it as a joke.* Her heart beat rapidly as she waited for his response.

Aron: **Forget spending Christmas with the folks, I'm coming back to MD to get my gift**

Shoot! Think fast Angie.

Angie: **LOL don't disappoint UR fam. I was only referring to a small gift not the BIG gift, yet.**

Aron: **I wld leave them to come n get that too**

Angie laughed out loud.

Angie: **Pucker ur lips Im sending you virtual kisses** 😚

Aron: **Oh damn that's the first n best virtual kiss I've ever got. U make me want to come n get the BIG gift now.**

Angie blushed. She felt like a teenager texting him. Since it was all fun and games she replied...

Angie: **And will UR gift 2 me be just as big?**

She bit down on her bottom lip as she waited for his response. She'd never been this flirtatious with a man other than Derek, so it was exciting.

Aron: **You've got to unwrap it to find out. N I hope u can handle it**

Her whole body tingled as she read his response. She knew she was probably playing with fire, but he was in Texas and she was still there in Maryland, so it was harmless in her eyes. Plus the kids spent the night at Derek's and won't be back for a couple hours, so why couldn't she have some fun?

Angie: **I think I can handle it, but can you handle what I'm gifting?**

She was being bold and loving it. Derek was the only man that ever received her gift.

Aron: **Baby I can show u better than telling. You about to make me hop on a plane.**

Angie: **And what would u do once you got here?**

Aron: **I don't know what's gotten into U but I'm loving it.**

She was loving it too.

Angie: **Send me a pic**

Did she just text that? Yup and she was surprised by her own self.

Aron: **Angie don't make me pull out the beast if UR not here to greet him personally.**

Damn! She bit down on her lip.

"Angie," Derek said walking into the master bedroom.

PLOP!!!

Her cellphone fell onto her face from being startled. She removed it and looked at Derek standing by the door. She felt like she was just caught doing something naughty.

He wondered what she was so engrossed with on her cellphone that she didn't even hear him coming in the house and up the stairs.

"What are you doing here?" She asked while sitting up. She put the phone down on the bed and stood up.

Derek's eyes raked over her body. She was dressed in leopard print pajama pants and a long-sleeved shirt that showed the imprint of her braless breast. He groaned internally.

"Why didn't you ring the doorbell? I don't like you just using that key you made a copy of without my permission," she vented.

"Why didn't you hear when we came in?"

"What do you want Derek and where are the kids?" She walked past him toward the door.

"They're downstairs, they wanted to bring you breakfast from IHOP," he told her.

Her cellphone chimed on the bed just as she walked out. Curious as to what she was busy doing, he walked toward the bed then picked up her cellphone. He'd never went through her phone before, but something had her mind so preoccupied she didn't hear him and the kids come into the house, what if they were a burglar?

Aron: **I'll be back on Tuesday, then you'll have the liberty to unwrap UR gift as slow or as fast as you want to.**

Derek wanted to haul her cellphone across the room and smash it against the wall. Not giving a care, he unlocked her phone by putting in her code. *She didn't change it.* He scrolled through her texts with Aron. He wanted to hurt somebody badly and that person was Aron. But what the hell was Angie doing being so forward with this dude? *Asking for a pic?* He was sick of this guy, but would getting rid of him stop Angie from dating others? Derek sat down on the bed. He had to get his emotions under control before he went back downstairs and jacked things all the hell up. He felt like he was about to explode with rage.

Minutes later.

"Are you guys ready to go?" Derek asked Devon and Dena once he made it back downstairs in the kitchen where they were with Angie, she was eating her peppermint pancakes.

"Mommy are you coming with us?" Dena asked. "Daddy's taking us to the Christmas workshop in the mall."

Angie wanted to spend the day with her kids, but she knew they all had to start adjusting to doing things separately. "Not this time sweetie. You guys go and have fun with your Daddy."

Derek was hoping she would say yes. *Maybe texting Aron is more important.* That still had him pissed and he wanted to question her about it, but thought it wise not to in front of their kids. He didn't want to be held accountable for what may fly out of his mouth.

"We'll be back at three. Maybe then you'll notice when we arrive." He turned and started for the front door. Angie watched his retreating back questionably. Dena and Devon were right on his heels after kissing and hugging her goodbye.

Back upstairs in her bedroom, Angie picked her cellphone up off the bed. She went to reply to Aron's last text message, that's when she noticed he'd texted her again after she'd left the room. "He read my text messages," she said out loud while sitting down on the bed. She didn't know how to feel about Derek going through her phone. Yeah they were separated and she told him she was dating, but for him to actually read her flirty texts to Aron had her feeling like she betrayed him in some way.

Thirty-One

"Here you go Mommy, this is your Christmas Eve gift from me and Dena." Devon handed Angie a gift box. They had made a tradition of opening one gift from each person on Christmas Eve, and to not ruin the experience for the kids, Angie was okay with Derek staying for the gift exchange.

"Thanks baby!" Angie opened the gift as her kids and Derek looked on. She pulled out a t-shirt that read: Best Teacher Ever! "I love it!" she said, holding the purple shirt up.

"That's from the money I made doing chores," Dena said happily.

The kids had already opened their one gift each from Derek and Angie, and Angie just opened her gifts from the kids. Derek had already opened his gifts the kids got him. But this year Angie didn't get him a gift and she hoped he didn't get her anything either. It was awkward enough having him there knowing that they probably won't be doing this together next year. And she was still feeling some type of way about him reading her texts to Aron.

"Mommy, Daddy, did you get a gift for each other?" Dena asked bouncing on the floor with excitement. She loved the American Doll Derek got her for Christmas, and Angie got her clothes and accessories for the doll since Derek had texted her to let her know months back that he was getting the doll.

"Uhmm, not this year sweetie," Angie told her. She shifted her gaze to Derek, he was looking at her intently. She could tell he was still pissed from what he read in her text. But it was his fault for snooping.

Derek pulled his cellphone out of his jeans pocket when he felt the buzzing. He had it on mute. It was a text message from Breana.

Breana: **I have a surprise for you and please don't tell me no. Meet me here in thirty minutes.**

He wasn't in the mood for her and he was tired of telling her to only contact him if it had something to do with her pregnancy or the baby. But of course she didn't listen. Seconds later she texted him an address in Accokeek, Maryland.

Angie watched him as he looked at something in his phone. She wondered if he just got a text from Breana or some other woman. She swallowed the jealousy that soured her taste buds. Here she was concerned about his feelings from reading her text messages to Aron and he probably had a woman waiting on him.

"I guess it's time for you to leave." Angie stood up from the couch, she didn't bother hiding the bitterness in her voice. Having him there, though nice for the kids' sake, was torture to her. Her feelings for him had been so conflicting lately. Yes he cheated, yes he'd gotten Breana pregnant – but he was still the love of her life. She was trying to move on, she knew she had to do it, but his presence, his thoughtfulness for their wellbeing, his love for their kids, was making it so hard to just let him go. But she knew she wouldn't be able to handle him having a baby with another woman. She hated him for cheating on her and his child with Breana would be the constant reminder.

Derek looked at her. He wanted to stay a little longer to spend time with his kids, with her, it's not like he had anything at home to go to. But he wasn't going to stay if she was ready to put him out. Besides he was going to be there bright and early tomorrow morning to watch the kids open all of their Christmas presents.

"Yeah I guess I'll head out." He texted Breana back letting her know he'll be there but he wasn't going to stay long so she needed to make whatever it was, quick. He stood up and followed Angie in the kitchen where she had walked off to. "Merry Christmas Eve." He pulled a small box out of his pocket and placed it on the kitchen island. He turned and then left the house, after telling the kids he would be back in the morning.

Angie stared at the neatly wrapped gift Derek left on the island. *And I didn't even bother to get him anything.* She picked it up, inspecting it from the outside, then she tore it open. It was a diamond and birthstones, white gold tennis bracelet. And it was absolutely gorgeous, obviously custom made, and obviously expensive. The pattern was four rows of diamonds, then changed to four rows of birthstones: amethyst, ruby, aquamarine, and emerald. Each birthstone representing hers, Derek's, Dena and Devon's birth months. She was in awe. She ran her fingers along it. Then clasped it onto her wrist. It even fit perfectly. She loved it!

****

Derek sat in his car in the driveway of the house address Breana had given him. It was a nice house in a housing development. It was similar to the home he'd bought for his family. *Maybe this is one of her projects.* He hopped out of his car before he got the chance to change his mind.

"I was wondering when you were going to get out of the car," Breana said opening the door for him. She had on a wrap sweater dress that showed a tiny baby bump. The sight of it made her pregnancy a little bit more real to him.

"Yeah I almost didn't. Why am I here?" He asked after she closed the door behind him. She had a nice home, outside and in. Seemed she was doing better than he thought in the real estate biz.

"Come, let me show you." She went to hold his hand, but he looked at her letting her know with his eyes that she better not. So she walked ahead of him and he followed.

She walked over to her ten foot Christmas tree that was beautifully decorated with purples and silvers. She turned to face him then seductively undid her dress. She dropped it to the floor and there she stood, in red heels and an emerald green lace panty and bra set. Her body was banging, even with her small baby bump. It took Derek a second or two to look away, but he did. It had been weeks since he'd had the luck and misfortune of punishing Angie with sex, and to say he was starved for sex would be an understatement. But the only woman he wanted to stroke his manhood was his wife. Any desire he'd had for Breana on those three days in the Bahamas, where they created the baby she was carrying, had vanished.

He started for the door.

"What? Why are you leaving?" She was disappointed that her blunt attempt to get him in her bed didn't work. She too had been sex starved and had hoped to be fed tonight by her baby's daddy.

"If that is your surprise you can keep it. I'm not interested Breana." He turned the knob to the door.

"Derek!" She called out walking toward him. "Why are you so hard toward me? We obviously had some chemistry in order for us to have created this baby?" She placed her hand on her belly. "I...I just want us to...since things didn't work out with your wife...I mean I assume they're not...that we can try to work on us having a romantic relationship."

He wondered what she knew that he hadn't told her. "Why do you assume that things aren't working out in my marriage?"

"I don't. I just figured –"

"Don't concern yourself about my marriage!" He stated with finality. "And no I'm not interested in anything but being cordial to you for the sake of our unborn child."

"Dammit Derek! Stop treating me like some worthless bitch that just so happens to be pregnant with your child. I have feelings too." She cried, causing him to stop his exit.

He didn't mean to be so hard toward her, but shoot, that's just what it was. Sleeping with her was a huge mistake which was costing him his marriage, and now they were bringing a baby in the mix, so yeah, he didn't have any warm and cozy feelings when it came to Breana. And the fact that she kept pushing him for more when he had repeatedly told her he wasn't interested only built his repugnance towards her.

"Look, I'm sorry for my callous attitude toward you, but it doesn't help when you keep pushing for something that I've told you is not going to happen. I love my wife Breana, with everything that is within me, and I'm sorry, but you only remind me of all the hurt I've cost her. So no, I'm not interested in going out to lunch or dinner, and definitely not a romantic relationship with you. But I'm sure we'll find the best way to co-parent our child." He finished turning the knob, walked out the door, to his car then left. That was all he had to offer her and if she couldn't accept that – oh well.

Breana locked the door behind him completely deflated.

Wife: **Thank you for the gift, I LOVE it (smiley face)**

Derek smiled after hearing Angie's text message through his Bluetooth while he drove down 210 Highway. He knew she would, but receiving her text made him feel great. He wasn't sure how she was going to respond to it though.

"Message to wife: I'm happy you LOVE it, baby (smiley face)" Derek recited a text message back to her.

Wife: **Derek, sorry for rushing you out tonight. The kids really enjoyed the Christmas Eve tradition.**

"Message to wife: Does that mean I can come back to spend the night?"

He was trying his luck, he knew, but it was worth a try.

Wife: **Sure. The guestroom is available. You know the kids hardly sleep on Christmas Eve, up before dawn which means you would have to be here by then otherwise.**

Derek had a huge smile on his face. Yeah she was offering their guestroom – but she was cool with him spending the night, so he was going to take what he could get.

"Message to wife: Be there in 20."

Thirty-Two

"Man, sometimes I think I need to root for another team," Derek said, pulling the beer bottle from his lips after taking a swig. His attention was on the football game playing on the large flat screen TV on the wall behind the bar. It was late January and the snow had melted giving people the opportunity to escape cabin fever.

"The Deadskins ain't about this football life," Benjamin laughed.

"Yeah man, time you join the winning team, Cowboys!" Brian chimed in laughing. He was surprised when Derek called asking him to meet him at the bar for drinks and to watch the game. It had been a while since they'd hung out together. But the fact that he called meant Angie hadn't told him about the kiss. He figured she wouldn't, but wasn't sure. He knew he would lose his friend over it – but oh well.

"Hell naw! I'm Redskins for life, although if I was a betting man they would have cost me all my damn money," Derek said, they all laughed.

"You from New York and go for the Skins?" Benjamin asked.

"Yeah, my mom's people from Maryland," Derek answered.

"But Redskins in DC, why not the Ravens, you're chances of winning would be better," Benjamin said.

"Man just shut up! I'm a Redskins fan, don't matter how I became one, I just am." One of the reasons he stuck with the team was because his mother was a diehard Redskins fan. And since she died years ago from cancer, cheering for the team, in some ways, felt as if he was doing so with his mother.

"You'll come to your senses after another losing season," Brian said. His attention was quickly drawn to the tall, chocolate honey that just walked into the bar. "Ahhmm, shorty is fine as hell."

"That's like the fifth chick you called out since we've been here." Benjamin took a swig of his beer.

"Yeah, ain't God good?" He asked still admiring the woman that walked over to a table where another, less attractive woman, Brian thought, sat at.

"Dude, when you going to settle down with just one?" Benjamin continued.

"Actually, I've been working on that," Brian admitted. He brought his attention back to his boys. Angie was playing hard to get, but he planned to wear her down. He loved a challenge, and her being the prize was more than worth it to him.

Derek and Benjamin looked at him in disbelief.

"She must be a Queen for you to want to give up the player card," Derek said. He'd never heard Brian talk about wanting to settle down with one woman.

"She is man." Brian smiled thinking about Angie and her soft lips. "She making me work a lil hard to get her though, but I will," he vowed.

"You haven't won her over with your charm?" Benjamin mocked.

"Yeah, but she's dealing with a situation with her ex, so once that's resolved I'm going in full force," Brian told them. Wanting his best friend's wife made him feel a little guilty – *but his loss is my gain.* The right woman would make a man do all kinds of crap he never thought he would, just to have her.

"Best of luck with that! You deserve a great woman in your corner," Derek told him. They all clicked beer bottles in a cheer.

****

"You know what I find interesting?" Pauline asked after swallowing a piece of chicken off the chicken wing she was munching on.

"What's that?" Angie had her eyes on Dena and Devon playing video games at the arcade.

"You haven't mentioned anything to me about talking to your lawyer about drawing up divorce papers. Does that mean you have a change of heart?" Pauline asked hopefully. She licked her fingers free of barbecue sauce then wiped them with a wet-nap.

"I just haven't gotten around to it yet," Angie answered nonchalantly. "And it's been snowing like crazy."

"Hmmmm. Has your busyness had anything to do with Aron?" Pauline arched her brow.

Angie turned to look at her with a smile she couldn't hide. "Maybe."

"Yeah!" Pauline laughed. "Well you know despite what's going on with you and Derek, I'm team Angie and Derek all the way. But Aron is a cool dude.

"He is. But we're only friends right now. I'm not ready for a relationship."

Pauline burped loudly, then excused herself.

Angie laughed. "Dang, that baby has you eating everything in sight and burping like a grown man.

Pauline rubbed her small baby bump. "This baby has my body changing like crazy and I'm only a few months in."

"Trust, there's more changes coming as you progress. Hopefully nothing that's uncomfortable or too annoying."

"I only hope so. But I'm blessed just to be pregnant after trying for so long, so I'm not going to complain either way."

"Good afternoon beautiful," Aron said to Angie from behind them. He stood there handsomely, looking down at her sitting in the booth.

"Hey," Angie stood up to greet him with a friendly hug. She'd invited him to stop by briefly. Like she told Pauline, he was only a friend, although it had been really hard to deny the strong attraction she had for him, and not to act on the sexting she'd done with him over the Christmas break. Also, she didn't want to introduce a *new* man to her kids, so having Pauline there as a buffer was a benefit. "Thanks for coming."

"Of course," he said with a smile. He turned his attention to Pauline. "How are you Pauline?"

"I'm good. How about you? Glad to escape out of the house after that crazy snowstorm?"

"I'm good. Yeah I was. Arnold was going crazy being indoors for two days. He was excited to go over to my mom's." Aron sat down in the booth next to Angie.

Angie peeped to make sure the kids were still occupied with the games in the arcade. "Yeah my kids were acting like it was extreme torture to be snowed in."

"Looks like you ladies love your chicken wings." Aron observed the tray filled with chicken bones.

"Believe it or not, that's all Pauline's," Angie said, laughing.

"Oh yeah?" He looked over at Pauline with surprise. "Well there's nothing wrong with a woman that likes to chow down."

"Yup, especially if she's eating for two," Pauline told him.

"Congratulations! That explains your glow," he complimented.

Pauline blushed. "Thank you!"

Angie looked at her friend rolling her eyes in amusement. *Yeah right, team Angie and Derek?* But she couldn't deny that Aron had that charm that made it easy to like him.

"So how have you been?" Aron asked closely to Angie's ear which sent a shiver down her spine.

Pauline read Aron's desires and care for Angie all over his face. *Angie may be in the friend zone but not Aron.* She got up to excuse herself so she could play with Devon and Dena, giving Angie and Aron some privacy and to keep the kids occupied and away from the table.

"I've been good, thanks for asking," Angie told him.

"That's a nice bracelet." Aron said admiring the tennis bracelet on her wrist.

"Thank you!" She smiled looking down at Derek's Christmas gift to her. She'd been wearing it ever since and it was now her favorite piece of jewelry. She wasn't about to tell Aron that it was a gift from Derek though, even if they were just *friends*.

"So when am I going to have the pleasure of taking you out on a date again?" They'd only been on two dates: his work Christmas Party and the movies. They'd been talking a lot over the phone and would chat briefly at school when he brought or picked his son Arnold up, but nothing besides that.

"Aron I..."

"Have things gotten complicated again?"

She shook her head 'no'. "It's just...I'm not ready for anything serious right now."

He thought about what she said for a couple seconds. "We don't have to make things serious now. We're still getting to know one another, so we can take it one day at a time," he said sincerely.

She smiled, heightening his urge to kiss her for the first time. So he did just that, throwing caution to the wind. Her lips were soft and welcoming and it took everything in him not to indulge longer. The kiss was short and sweet, but perfect for their budding relationship.

"That was perfect!" She told him. But remembering her kids were there, she turned in their direction to see if they saw them. They were still preoccupied with the game, both showing Pauline how to play. She blew a mental sigh of relief.

"Yes it was." He brushed his thumb along her cheek looking at her admirably.

"So I know I invited you to stop by for a few, but like I told you on the phone, I don't want to introduce a man to my kids now. Thankfully they didn't see you kiss me."

"Yeah I understand. Just wanted to see you." He stood up and she followed.

Angie smiled. "I wanted to see you too!" They hugged goodbye and he left after she agreed to go to a comedy show with him next weekend.

Thirty-Three

Angie tapped her feet nervously as she sat at her desk. She was busy grading papers afterschool, but stopped to make a phone call. "Good afternoon, may I speak to Ms. Flowers please?"

The call was picked up after being transferred. "Hi Mrs. Monroe, how are you?" Ms. Flowers asked.

Angie cleared the frog in her throat. "I'm okay," she responded woefully.

Ms. Flowers noticed the sadness in her client's voice. "How can I help you?"

"I'm ready to file divorce papers," Angie said with a shaky voice. She couldn't believe she was actually making this call but it was one she felt she needed to make.

"I see. And you're sure of this? Things didn't work out with counseling?"

"No things only got worse." Angie closed her eyes, the thought of Derek having a baby with another woman was still very painful. "Derek's having a baby with the woman he cheated on me with. So no, counseling didn't and won't work."

"I'm sorry to hear that. I can have everything written up and ready within a few weeks. Hopefully it will be uncontested by your spouse and you won't have to go to trial."

"Okay. Hopefully he won't have any issues with the terms, but you and his lawyer can negotiate things for us," Angie said.

"Yes. So I will keep you abreast with everything, you'll hear from me soon."

"Thank you!" Angie ended the call and placed her cellphone onto her desk. She hoped Derek would make the divorce as painless as possible. She wanted everything to be fair for the both of them and wasn't out to be vindictive. She just wanted it over and done with so they both can just move on with their lives – separately.

****

A couple weeks later.

Derek ended the call after speaking with his lawyer. Angie was filing for divorce and his lawyer was contacted about the terms for Derek to review. He knew it was coming, though hoping that it wouldn't — but now knowing that she was actually going through with it — hit him violently in his chest. He looked like a man that was just told he had an incurable illness and only had a few days left to live.

He didn't know how to feel or react. One of his greatest fears was coming to fruition and he felt helpless in preventing it from happening. He suppressed the urge to cry. He wanted to punch something, anything, to get the pain and aggression out.

"Daddy look, I'm almost beating your high score," Devon said sitting on one of the beanbag chairs in Derek's living room. He pointed his little finger to the TV screen mounted on the wall. They were playing a racecar game together, but Derek's mind was now elsewhere after talking to his lawyer, so his son had overtaken him on the race track. It was just the two of them hanging out since Derek had dropped Dena off at one of her friend's house for a couple hours.

Derek pushed aside the sadness that was quickly consuming, to respond to his son. "Yeah, looks like you are catching up." He ran his hand over Devon's neatly trimmed hair. If not for his children, he didn't know if he would survive the pending divorce. Derek picked up his controller and tried his hardest to get back into the game. But his headspace was just filled with turmoil.

Out of nowhere Devon says, "I saw Uncle Brian kissing Mommy in the kitchen."

Derek's head snapped back, he blinked, unsure of whether he heard his son right. "What did you say?"

Devon, with his eyes still glued to the TV screen said, "I remember seeing Uncle Brian kissing Mommy in the kitchen one day..."

Derek's blood pressure rose to violent levels. He was ready to rage war on the whole damn state. He gripped the game controller so tightly in his hand he almost crushed it.

"...I thought only daddies were supposed to kiss mommies. But Mommy said that Uncle Brian kissed her and hugged her because he fixed the garbage disposal," Devon continued oblivious to the effect his words were having on his father.

It took Jesus and His Angels to keep Derek rooted on the beanbag chair. All kinds of crap was going through his head, messing with this headspace. But he couldn't take it any longer, he jumped up from the beanbag chair and started for his bedroom.

"Daddy, we're not finished," Devon called out.

"Be right back," Derek said to Devon. He dialed Angie's cellphone while walking toward his bedroom. He didn't want to lose his cool in front of his son. "When did Brian fix the garbage disposal?" He asked her as soon as she picked up. His voice was laced with rage.

"What?" She was thrown off by his question and tone.

Derek cursed under his breath, he was hanging on by a thread. "When did Brian fix the garbage disposal," he gritted through his teeth.

"Okay, you need to fix your tone with me. But he fixed it the week before Christmas. Why?"

"Are you sleeping with him?" He couldn't believe he was asking that question, but he needed to know.

"What!? NO!" She answered adamantly. "We may be getting a divorce Derek but I'm not scandalous enough to do something like that."

"Why did he kiss you?"

Angie sighed deeply. "I take it Devon told you he saw that."

"Angie I'm about to lose my effing mind. Why did he kiss you?"

"Heck if I know. He said he wanted to for some time, but there is nothing going on between us. I didn't lead him on. We've been talking a lot since you told me about the affair, but I didn't know he was only being friendly to make a move on me. And I didn't tell you because he's your friend..."

Derek couldn't believe what he was hearing. Brian, his friend since college, was behind his back trying to take his wife. "He's obviously not my friend. And he could've been my father and I would've wanted to know this shit!" He spat.

"I handled it, okay. It's not like we're together anymore Derek," she had to add.

"You're still my wife Angie! It's my job to handle it," he reiterated, he didn't give a damn about her wanting a divorce.

"Goodbye Derek, I don't have time for this!"

"You should have told me," he said in a nicer tone.

"Okay now you know. I dealt with it. You hurt me when you cheated on me, but I would never do something like that to hurt you. I only saw Brian as a friend. That's too close to home."

"And what about you dating that gay dude? You don't think that bothers me?" He had a death warrant out for him and now Brian.

Angie smirked. "Aron's not gay. And it's none of your business but he and I are just friends."

"Friend that you ask to send a picture of their dick?" He was heated.

"You had no business snooping in my phone, so what I do is none of your concern unless it's about our kids."

Derek huffed a breath. He ran his hand over his smooth bald head. "I love you Angie. Despite what I've done that's never changed. Being away from you and the kids is driving me crazy and now knowing you dating other guys..." The thought of it was too much.

Angie sighed, he was touching a soft spot in her heart. *You have to wean off of him.* "Derek...I can't stay married to you. You, Breana and the baby, it's just too much. This is for the best, I would only grow to resent you more if I stay."

"Baby, please. Just tell me what I have to do?" He wasn't one to beg, but if it would help keep his wife, he would get on his knees and do whatever he had to. His heart was shattered and only she could put the pieces together. She was the glue. Hearing from his lawyer today that Angie was definitely filing divorce and then learning of Brian deceiving him had him emotionally overwhelmed.

Angie swallowed the lump in her throat, she loved her husband, she really did, but she just couldn't stay married to him under the conditions. The trust was shattered and now a baby would be added because of his affair. "Derek I can't...I've got to go." She lied, if she stayed on the phone any longer she would give in to his plea and she felt it wouldn't be good for them in the long run. She hung up to not give him a chance to refuse.

Derek pulled the phone from his ear. Vengeance like no other began to fill his veins, bringing back a side of him that he had tucked away years ago.

****

A truck door slammed shut then moments later footsteps where heard against the stone sidewalk making their way toward the front steps of a house.

"It's about time you showed up." It was eleven, thirty-nine at night.

"The F—Derek?" Brian halted, caught off guard. "What the hell you doing sneaking up on me man?" He almost pissed his pants. He looked around in the dark, now trying to be more aware of his surroundings. He'd been meaning to change the light on the porch but never got around to it. His neighborhood was secured so he didn't worry about burglars. "Where'd you park?"

"Doesn't matter. I wanted to talk, got a lot on my mind," Derek said casually walking onto the front step to Brian's house.

"Damn you should have called and let me know you were coming over." Brian went and unlocked the front door.

"I did, you never answered."

Brian laughed, thinking about the chick he just left. "Yeah, I was caught up in something."

Derek nodded his head that was covered with a dark hoodie. He stepped behind Brian into his house.

"So what's up?" Brian threw his keys on a table by the door, shook off his coat then threw it on the couch. He then made his way toward the kitchen. He pulled two beers out of the fridge, opened them then offered one to Derek.

Derek took the beer, threw his head back and took a long swig.

"So what's going on?" Brian asked again. He now went into the living room, turning the TV on before plopping down on the couch. He put his feet up on the coffee table. His was beat after a marathon sex session with his latest conquest.

Derek sat in a chair next to the couch, he pulled the hoodie off of his bald head. "Something I found out that's bothering me man." He took another swig of the beer, sitting back comfortably in the chair.

Brian turned his neck to look at his friend. Something about Derek was off to him, and why was he being evasive about what he came there to talk to him about? "What is it man, something to do with Angie or Breana?" He yawned.

"So tell me about this chick that got your nose wide open?" Derek asked, ignoring his question.

Brian looked at him sideways. It was too late for small talk and he had some business to take care of at seven the next morning. But thoughts of Angie was always welcomed. "She's perfect man, what can I say? Just waiting for her to sort things out with her ex."

"Hmmm," Derek nodded his head. "What's her name, anyone I may know?" He looked Brian dead in the eyes.

Brian sat up on the couch. His mind raced thinking of what it was that Derek may know. "Naw, man I don't think you know her," he said. He nervously lifted the beer bottle to his mouth to take a swig.

"What's her name?" Derek demanded with a smirk. "I just may know her."

"Man look, I'm tired after dealing with this chick I was just with and I got to get up early." Brian stood to dismiss him.

"Why you don't want me to know who she is, think I may try to *steal* her from you?" Derek taunted. Fire flickered in his eyes.

"I'm not worried about anything like that, you just don't know her. Her name is Ang...Amy, Amy Moore if you must know."

Derek stood up leisurely. "Amy, huh?" He arched his brow. He stood arm length away from Brian. "So answer me this, why were you kissing my wife?"

Brian shook his head. Now that it was out there, he wasn't going to deny it. Shoot, he knew this moment would come soon enough. "Look man, it's not as serious as you may think?"

"Really?" Derek questioned as calmly as possible. Before Brian could blink Derek rammed his fist connecting it to Brian's mouth. Blood gushed everywhere. "Nigga if you knew what I was thinking you wouldn't be standing here trying to play me," Derek barked.

Brian was almost knocked to the floor from the punch, and Derek was only taking it easy on him. He charged toward Derek, and then it was on. Each man blocking, receiving and connecting punches; and cussing each other out in the process. It was like two daredevils let loose in the living room. But Derek had the rage of man losing his entire world and the betrayal of a friend to allow him to easily overpower Brian. He had his hand clutched in a death grip around Brian's neck as he kneeled over him on the floor.

"You must have forgotten there is another side to me from the suit and tie I wear every day for business," Derek told him. With his free hand, he pulled out the Glock that was secured behind his back and pressed the metal against Brian's temple. His finger itched to pull the trigger.

"Come on man," Brian pleaded. He knew of that *other* side of Derek.

Derek had given up that lifestyle a year after starting college. He had lived a life of crime that awarded him with a lot of street cred and thousands of dollars that allowed him to pay his way through college without help from his parents. But Derek had given up that life to live one on the straight and narrow, however moments like this brought the other side of him out. Being Derek's friend from their first year in college, Brian knew that his friend was capable of murder. How he thought he was going to get away with trying to be with Angie behind Derek's back, he had no clue. Frankly he wasn't really thinking about the consequences, until now.

Brian acted and sometimes dressed like a thug, but he really wasn't about that life. He was a lover not a fighter. He'd grown up privileged and everything he'd learned about the hood was through Derek, TV and rap music.

Tears spilled down Brian's face as he struggled to get out of Derek's grip. "Don't..." He began to cough. "Don't kill me man," Brian begged, he felt he had too much to live for to go out this way. The look he saw in Derek's eyes was like the devil's.

"If you haven't given your life to Christ yet, I'mma give you two seconds before you meet your maker," Derek said with no trance of remorse in his tone. "How you think you can kiss my wife and I turn a blind eye to it, huh?" He didn't play when it came to his wife and kids – and Brian of all people should've known that.

"I'm...sooorry...man," Brian struggled to talk, he was slowly slipping away with the grip Derek hand around his neck. "I...I messed up, I'm sorry."

Derek released the hold he had around his neck, letting his head fall back onto the floor with a thud. "I will kill your ass before I allow a man I once broke bread with be with my wife! The fact that I used to consider you a friend is the *only* reason I'm letting you live, *this time*." He stood up, tucking the gun securely behind his back.

Brian heaved deeply trying to restore the oxygen in his lungs. He'd never been so close to death in his life. Trying to go after Angie wasn't worth it after all.

"Try me again and I will murk you before you could even think about calling the authorities." Derek pulled his hoodie over his head and started for the door, leaving Brian struggling for his life.

****

The next morning Derek's cellphone rang angrily on the nightstand near his bed. He turned over onto his side and grabbed it. "Hello," he answered groggily.

"What did you do Derek?" Angie asked with terror in her voice.

"Do about what?" He asked opening his eyes so they could adjust to the sunlight seeping through the blinds in his bedroom.

"Oh my GOD!" She exclaimed on the other end of the phone. "On the news...All of Brian's clothing stores in Maryland, Virginia and DC were set on fire last night even the ones in New York."

Derek yawned loudly. He was unfazed by her outburst. "How are you this morning?" He laid on his back.

"Are you serious right now? Did you hear me Derek, *all* of Brian's stores caught on fire last night."

"I heard you, but you didn't answer my question?" He was cool as a cucumber.

"Ugh! Derek please, please tell me you had nothing to do with the fire. I mean it's impossible for you to be at all of those places at the same time, but..." It didn't seem like a coincidence.

"I had nothing to do with it," he told her. Well not literally setting the fires himself, but she didn't have to know that. He handled the issue with Brian, he was still playing nice with her *friend* Aron. He knew he couldn't go on a rampage with all the guys she may potentially date – but Brian definitely had to be dealt with for crossing the line. His level of disrespect was not to be tolerated. He still wished he had killed him last night. Oh well, he'd have fun doing it later if it came to that. But the side of him that was trying to live a life of faith, told him it was best he'd let Brian live. He shouldn't be playing God when it came to someone's life.

Angie breathed a sigh of relief. She wasn't totally convinced – but she was going to take his word for it. "Have you called Brian to see how he's handling the news?" Brian crossed the line by kissing her, but she still had sympathy for him.

"I have no need to call him and neither do you!" He said with finality.

She hated how he felt the need to tell her what she could and couldn't do. "Are the kids still asleep?" She asked changing the subject.

"Yeah. You know they sleep late on Saturday mornings." It was only six-fifteen.

"Okay. I just wanted you to know about Brian's stores."

"You still haven't answered my question baby," he said huskily sending a chill down her spine.

She smiled. "I'm fine. I'm going back to sleep."

"I'm surprised you're up this early anyway."

She didn't want to tell him that she was up early talking to Aron before he boarded the plane for his early flight to Texas to attend his cousin's wedding. He'd invited her to attend, but she declined because she wanted to keep them in the friend zone. They had kissed a few more times since the first time, but nothing beyond that. "I was just up, but now I'm going to get some more sleep."

"Okay, go back to sleep. I love you!" He had to remind her of that every chance he got.

"Bye," was all she said before hanging up.

Thirty-Four

Latoya pulled up Derek's schedule on the computer screen to type in a speaking engagement he would need to be at in two weeks. Her cellphone rang pulling her attention away from the desktop computer. She dug into her purse for it then pulled it out.

"Hey, what's up?" She asked her cousin Sherry.

"So all I found out about the Breana chick is that she's divorced and her ex-husband was sentenced a few months back to fifteen years for fraud. Her dad is one big shot neurosurgeon, now retired though. Her real estate business isn't doing too great, but thank God for her moms and pops that she could mooch off of. No criminal records, just a couple speeding tickets. And she is pregnant."

Latoya was upset that there was nothing incriminating. She at least hoped Breana was lying about her pregnancy. "So she's really pregnant?"

"Yup according to the nurse I paid off," Sherry told her.

Latoya got more details from her cousin Sherry about Breana then told her that she would pay her later that day for the info she provided. *So she's really having Derek's baby.* Latoya shook her head after ending the call with her cousin. That put a damper on things. She was hoping to find something to oust Breana, now all it seemed was she was going to have to work on her fake smile whenever she showed up on her weekly visits to Derek's office. UGH!

****

Pauline burst into Angie's classroom. It was an early dismissal day so it was one-sixteen in the afternoon. Angie was busy entering her student's grades into the school's computer program. She looked up when she saw Pauline walking through the door.

"You entered your students' grades already?" Angie asked turning her attention back to her task. Report cards would be given out in two days.

"I just got off the phone with Benjamin, he said that Brian was in the hospital," Pauline told her. She pulled one of the student's chairs near Angie's desk and sat down.

"What? When?" Angie shifted shocked eyes toward her friend.

"Yeah, he was there for two days but just got released today. He had gotten beat up pretty badly. Benjamin said he called Derek to ask him if he knew about t it, but Derek told him he wasn't effing with Brian anymore."

Angie hated to think that Derek may have had something to do with not only burning down Brian's clothing stores in three states and the district, but he may have been the cause of Brian being in the hospital for two days. It just didn't seem like a coincidence. *What the hell?*

"Do you know if Derek and Brian had some type of falling out?" Pauline continued.

Angie looked like a deer caught in headlights. She hadn't told her about Brian kissing her that day in the kitchen. "Ummm, yeah Derek told me things weren't cool with him and Brian anymore." Which was technically the truth, no need for her to go into the details. This whole situation was starting to freak her out. She knew Derek had a dark side to him, he'd told her a little bit about his past – but maybe there was more to him that he didn't reveal. Surprisingly she was intrigued and frightened all at the same time. Would she be a freak right now by being turned on by him protecting her honor? But her common sense kicked in. If Derek was involved in what happened to Brian – would he get caught? Would Brian report him and have him arrested? Fear gripped her.

"Are you okay?" Pauline saw the distress on her friend's face.

"G...give me a minute, I want to call Derek. I'll come to your classroom later when I'm done."

Angie snatched her cellphone out of her desk draw as soon as Pauline left and closed the classroom door behind her. She called Derek and he answered on the second ring. "Hi, did you know Brian was in the hospital?"

There was silence on his end. "Honestly I'm a bit pissed that the only two calls I've received from you in the past couple days were about him," Derek said, not hiding his ire. Angie didn't call him often and when she did it was only concerning the kids, so for her last two recent calls to him to be about Brian's punk behind didn't sit right with him.

"I just found out he was in the hospital for two days, did you put him there?" She pressed.

Derek sighed loudly. He didn't need Angie concerned or asking questions about him *handling* Brian, it was already a dead issue for him. He trusted that his people hadn't left any trances of the incident that would lead back to him. He was too smart for that. "Why are you so concerned about Brian?" He wanted to know.

"Look, yeah he crossed the line when he kissed me, but he was still your friend. I've known him just as long as I've known you so it would only be natural for me to be a little bit concerned. What happened to him just doesn't seem coincidental, Derek."

"I hope you don't think or are about to say that I had anything to do with it." He needed that thought out of her head, quick! This was why he'd tucked that side of himself away – the liability, now with his wife and children, was too great. He knew he was straight though, he wasn't concerned about Brian spilling the beans, but didn't need Angie questioning him either.

"Derek..." She was so scared that something might happen to him, her gut told her he had something to do with it, but she understood that her mentioning it could cause problems. She may be seeking a divorce, but he would always be her first love and the father of her children. She didn't want to be taking the kids to prison to visit him. "Just tell me you're going to be okay."

Derek smiled. Just knowing that she was scared and concerned for his safety spoke volumes. She didn't say the words 'I love you' but he took it as that. "I'm straight," he confirmed confidently.

Angie relaxed back into her seat. That's all she needed to know. She would forget about the fact that he committed a crime, whether he admitted it or not. "Good! Okay I've got to finish up entering these grades –"

"You know it would be nice if you can just call me to talk without it just being about the kids." He didn't want to let her go. He missed having conversations with her, talking about any and everything. She was his best friend – not Brian. She was the one that always had his back. "I miss you Angie." He was a man not afraid to express his feelings.

Her heart rate speed up. Every time he got sentimental it was like a wave of desire would overtake her. This was why she limited all communication between them about the kids. He could so easily cause her to forget all the pain he'd caused her – the betrayal, Breana, their baby. "Derek–"

"Baby, before all of this, we used to be friends."

"Things are so different now and you know it," she bit out. *And it's all your fault.*

"But can you admit that you still love me? You still have feelings for me?" He didn't beg just simply asked, in order to keep some of his manhood intact. But he yearned to hear her *consciously* admit that she still loved him.

Of course I still love you, she screamed in her head. But anger and hate were not too far behind. "I don't want to talk about this, but regardless, I still want a divorce. Talking about this won't change that."

"Then why don't you want to admit that you still love me?" He pushed.

She closed her eyes to suppress the tears. "Derek, you were my first everything, there will always be a piece of you with me," she finally admitted.

"Enough for you to stay my wife?" He was grasping for straws, but he was fighting. He was already a shell of a man being separated from her – divorce – he didn't know what would come of him then.

There was a pregnant pause. Angie wished that it was enough...*is it enough?* "No," she said with it leaving a bitter taste in her mouth.

Derek didn't know how much more torture his heart could take – but he'd asked and she answered his question. As much as he'd thought of kidnapping and tying her down and forcing her to remain his wife – that wouldn't work. He didn't want to force her to stay, he wanted her to want to remain his wife on her own. He didn't have to coerce her to marry him nine years ago, so he wasn't going to do so to make her not file for divorce.

"Mr. Monroe, your two o'clock appointment is here," Angie heard Latoya's voice on the other end of the phone. She hadn't seen that girl in months, she made a mental note to check in on her soon.

"Give me a few more minutes," Derek told Latoya. "Duty calls," he said to Angie. He still didn't want to let her go, but he had a business to run.

"Yeah, I've got to get back to what I was doing too." She was relieved the conversation was ending, it was getting too intense for her. She didn't want to be an emotional basket case the rest of the day. "Bye Derek."

"I love you Angie."

"Okay." She ended the call. Sighing, she placed the phone on her desk. She loved hearing him say he loved her and lately she'd been biting her tongue not to tell him it back.

Thirty-Five

"I got your popcorn, Raisinets and Coke," Aron told Angie as he walked toward her with his hands filled with refreshments. They were on another movie date. They were safe, friendly dates that she preferred with him. The dressing up and wining and dining – she wasn't ready for all that yet. *And you're still married*, her conscious would tell her. And no matter how hard she fought it, Derek still owned her heart.

"Thank you!" She blessed him with a radiant smile. She looked down at the ticket stubs, he had given her to hold, to see which theatre room their movie was in. "I think our show is that way," she pointed her finger. But when she turned, the sight in front of her surrendered her immobile.

Angie hadn't seen her since that night she found out she was the woman Derek slept with while in the Bahamas. Breana had just walked out of a theatre with the same Hispanic woman who was with her that night at the charity event. But what drained the life out of Angie was the sight of Breana's small, but obviously pregnant, belly bump. The evidence of Derek's affair was plain to see. She felt sick to her stomach. The pain of that fateful night came rushing back to the forefront of her mind in spades.

"Angie, Angie, are you okay sweetheart?" Aron asked with concern. He had been calling her name repeatedly but she hadn't responded. She was lost in a daze.

"I think I'm going to be sick!" Angie exclaimed. She made a beeline to the lady's room, pushing people out of her way and holding her mouth with her other free hand. As soon as she stood over the toilet, she deposited the contents of her stomach. The bile bitter in her mouth and hot tears flowed down her cheeks. A headache flooded between her temples like a tsunami. She slid down to the dirty ground of the bathroom stall. Actually seeing Breana pregnant was more than she could take. *How could he?* She screamed in her mind. She was supposed to be the only woman to give Derek children, no other was supposed to come after her – at least not while she was alive and still his wife. Angie cried uncontrollably.

Aron paced back and forth outside the ladies bathroom. Angie had been in there for fifteen minutes. He was worried out of his mind. He asked a few women going into the bathroom to check on her, but they all said she had her stall locked and was just sitting on the floor crying. He couldn't take it any longer, so when the bathroom was cleared, he walked in. He could hear Angie sniffling and went to stall she was in.

"Angie, I'm worried about you, please open up," he pleaded. He knocked gently on the stall door. He could see her boots peeping out from underneath.

She continued to sniffle.

"Angie, sweetheart please. You don't want them to throw me out the theatre for sneaking into the women's bathroom, do you?" He hoped a little humor would work. She was breaking his heart with her crying. *What the hell happened?*

Seconds later, her boots feet disappeared, he could hear her standing up, and then the stall door opened. She looked like a basket case. Puffy red eyes and tear stained cheeks. Aron pulled her into a hug immediately.

"What happened?" He rubbed her back. He prayed his strong embrace would soothe some if not all of her pain. He walked her toward the sinks so he could wipe her face with a wet paper towel.

Angie didn't respond, but she allowed him to wipe her face. Then she went and rinsed out her mouth and wash her hands. She avoided looking at herself in the mirror, she knew she looked like a nightmare. Women were a bit startled when they walked into the restroom and saw Aron, but once they realized he was assisting Angie who looked obviously distressed, they went about their business paying the couple no mind.

Finally out of the bathroom, Aron asked her again, "Angie, what happened, what's wrong?" His eyes were filled with so much concern.

"I'm sorry, but I just want to go home." She had driven herself to the theatre, she still wasn't ready for him to know where she lived, and he understood and respected that. Though she knew he wanted to pick her up and drop her off whenever they went out.

"Okay. But can you please tell me what happened, what made you breakdown like that? Who upset you?" Because he wanted to beat them down, badly.

"I...I saw the woman my husband cheated on me with, and she's pregnant." She had never told Aron about the issues in her marriage. Quite frankly he never asked, so she never disclosed or was forthcoming with the information. All he knew was that she was separated and getting a divorce.

That took Aron by surprise. He wondered why Angie and Derek were separated, but chose not to know – as long as she was divorcing him that was all his concern. "I'm sorry." He hugged her. He was genuinely sad for her. Angie allowed his strong arms and intoxicating male scent to soothe her. "I'm going to follow you home, just to make sure you arrive safely." He wasn't going to take no for an answer.

"Okay," she replied in his chest.

****

A few days later, Regina Flowers slid documents over to Angie then placed a pen down in front of her client. She'd filed many divorces for clients over the years, but looking at Angie today, was by far one of the first cases that affected her deeply.

Angie stared down at the documents that were placed in front of her. With just her signature she would be consenting to the end of her nine year marriage. The pain of it all was almost crippling. Ironically, in exactly two months from today's date, would be the ten year anniversary of her and Derek's marriage. She should have been finalizing the last minute details for their vow renewal somewhere on a tropical island. She had always wanted to renew their vows on the beach. Instead today she was going to sign away her marriage.

Angie couldn't help the tears that spilled from her eyes as she picked up the ink pen. Her lawyer had already explained everything to her. Derek should be receiving his papers today as well. After they both signed, all was left was for the documents to be filed in the courts then they would receive their divorce decree. With shaky hands, Angie sealed her fate. She pushed the documents back over to her lawyer, then stood up. She left the office not saying anything. Regina understood, she watched her client walk out of her office with her head down and shoulders slumped.

****

The last thing Derek expected after opening his door for the delivery man, was to open divorce documents. He collapsed on the beanbag chair with the papers in hand. The day he was hoping would never come had finally arrived. He stared at the papers which called out the cancellation of his nine years of marriage. He didn't realize he was crying until a tear dropped onto the paper.

Angie wanted their marriage to end and it was all his fault. He wanted to rip the papers up in shreds, then burn them to ashes. How could he sign away his marriage? He made one stupid, irreversible mistake that was costing him his family. Hadn't he suffered enough? Hadn't months of living separately from his wife and children been enough? Derek got up and got a pen out of the kitchen drawer. He didn't want to, God knew he didn't want his marriage to end. But no judge was going to make Angie stay married to him if she wanted out. He would only prolong the inevitable if they went to court. So he wouldn't do that. All of their assets and custody arrangements were fair, so he had no reason to contest.

Derek stared down at the papers now on the kitchen counter. He needed a drink, he couldn't do this sober. He needed something to numb the pain. He grabbed a bottle of scotch he had left in the cupboard, opened it and took it to the head. The burning down his throat was welcoming. He picked up the pen then signed his signature. He pushed the papers to the side, grabbed some more alcoholic beverages and went to his bedroom to drink his sorrows away.

****

Angie wasn't much for alcohol, she didn't like the effect it had on her body, but today of all days she felt she needed it. She wasn't drunk, but she was pretty darn close and being in the house alone, listening to breakup songs nonstop, while Dena and Devon were with Pauline and Benjamin, wasn't helping. The alcohol wasn't numbing her pain from signing divorce papers today fast enough.

"Hey, can I come over?" She said into her cellphone.

Her question caught Aron by surprise. She'd never been over to his place, not that he hadn't wanted her to, she was just strict with keeping their relationship friendly, and so she'd always decline his offer. "Yeah, that would be cool." Arnold was with his grandmother so Aron was free. "I'll text you my address." It would be a lie if asked and he said he wasn't excited about her visit to his house.

"Thanks, I'm heading over now." They said goodbye to one another. Seconds later Aron's text came through with his home address. He lived in Waldorf as well and was only fifteen minutes away. Angie grabbed her purse and keys and started for the front door.

Aron finished straightening up his house for Angie's arrival. He didn't live sloppy, but Arnold had some of his toys lying around that Aron put away in his son's toy box. This would be her first visit over so he wanted his place looking right. He went into the kitchen and grabbed a bottle of Febreze the cleaning company that came to clean once a week, left there. He sprayed it lightly over the fabric couch to freshen things up a bit. *Women like these flowery scents*. The doorbell rang after he returned from the kitchen to replace the Febreze. He checked his breath – still minty.

"Hey," he answered the door casually. Before he could get a chance to check Angie out in her purple jogging suit, she threw herself at him. She pulled his head down toward her, then buried her tongue into his mouth. She didn't have to convince him. He kicked the door closed with his foot, then took the first opportunity he'd had, to feel her shapely behind with his palms. He squeezed, enjoying the feel of her delicate body pressed against his.

Angie's kiss was eager and desperate. She was tantalizingly sucking the life out of him and he was aroused by every second of it. His desire rose, piercing her in her stomach through his basketball shorts. His thick, long stiffness startled her, she jumped back staring down at it. Derek's was the only one she'd encountered before. Neither one of them said anything as they caught their breaths. Angie was beginning to second guess her reasons for coming over, and Aron was praying that she would resume what she'd started.

"I need something to drink," Angie spoke. She pulled her eyes away from his tented shorts and up to his handsome face.

"Ummm, water, soda, juice?" Aron asked.

"Something stronger." She finally looked around his house from the foyer. He had an open floor plan that she liked. "You have a nice home," she told him.

"Thank you!" He adjusted himself best he could in his pants, then started for his mini bar near the dining room. Angie followed him. "You have a particular drink in mind?" He opened the cabinet so she could see his selection.

Angie was naïve when it came to alcohol so she just decided on some Patron with salt and lime. She had seen it somewhere on one of the TV shows she'd watched and figured it was worth a try.

Several shots later, Angie was drunk and giggling at the simplest things that Aron would say out of his mouth. They were now cuddled up on his couch with a movie playing on the wide flat screen ahead of them. Although drunk, Aron liked the fact that she was relaxed and carefree. He was a little tipsy himself, but figured, what the heck, they were chilling and having a good time. Days like today didn't come often.

Angie sat up, then positioned herself to straddle Aron's lap. She aggressively pushed his shoulders back, then gave him one of the most mind-blowing kisses he'd ever experienced. She started dry humping him while pushing her breast into his chest. The feeling was heightening every one of their senses.

"Make love to me," Angie whispered into his ear sending the message to both of his heads. She sat up and seductively unzipped the jacket to her track suit. She took it off revealing her white tank top. Then she pulled her tank over her head showing off her lace bra.

Aron watched her in total lust. His mouth literally watered at the sight of her mocha mounds. He kissed her stomach, her lavender scent filled his nostrils.

"Make love to me," Angie repeated. She cupped his head with her hands, lifting it up so he could look into her eyes. The desire and need he saw there left him with no other choice.

"There's something in this liquor girl, I'm looking at your figure whoa

I just want to see you strip right now, baby let me help you work it out, oh

Girl you look so good, I just want to get right to it, oh

I could beat it up like-like a real nigga should, baby when we do it, whoa..."

-Chris Brown

Thirty-Six

Angie's head was pounding and her throat was like the Sahara desert. She rolled over on the bed onto her back. She slowly tried opening her eyes, but even that was painful. So she kept them closed.

"Good morning beautiful," Aron said looking down at Angie. He gently stroked her cheeks.

Angie's mind reeled with uncertainty. Why was she on a bed with Aron next to her? She recalled coming over to his house, the shots, her asking him to make love to her. She pitched up into a sitting position on the bed, forgetting her throbbing head. Her eyes opened and she looked at Aron sitting on the edge of his bed. She looked around his master bedroom, then back at him.

"I thought you were never going to wake up," he told her. "I made you breakfast, but it would have to be warmed up now."

Angie was starting to panic. She couldn't believe she had sex with Aron. *Oh my God, NO!* She was too ashamed to even look at him any further.

"How are you feeling, we had a rough night last night." He looked her over with concern.

"I need to pee, and I need some pain pills." She kicked the covers off of her and made her way to the door she assumed was the master bathroom. She couldn't look at him, she felt like a slut. How could she have gotten drunk and sleep with another man? Derek was her only.

Minutes later Angie made her way to the kitchen. Aron had breakfast on the kitchen table for her: eggs, pancakes and bacon. And a bottle of pain pills. She was famished and wanted to eat despite her slight hangover. "Thanks," she mumbled taking a seat at the table. Shame was overwhelming her with Aron so near. She had so many questions about the night before.

Aron placed a steaming cup of dark coffee in front of Angie, then sat down next to her. "About last night..."

Angie put her head in her hands. She wasn't ready for the details.

"...Nothing happened."

Angie looked up at him with disbelief. That explained why she still had on her jogging pants and tank top.

"I want you Angie, really, really bad." He shook his head. "But you're not ready yet and I would never take advantage of you. You put up a fight though when I told you no last night." He laughed remembering the events of the night before. He told her how she started cussing him out because he wouldn't have sex with her and how she tried to fight him when he tried to get her to lay down to sleep the alcohol off.

Angie was stunned. She couldn't even remember ever getting drunk before, and from what he just told her, she never wanted to again. But she was relieved that nothing happened between them last night, well other than kissing and heavy groping. And even that had her feeling terrible. If she was honest with herself, the only reason she really pursued going out with Aron was to hurt Derek as much or close to how he'd hurt her with sleeping with Breana. However along the way she did like Aron – but only as a friend.

"Thank you for not going through with it." She finally looked into his eyes. "I signed my divorce papers yesterday and I was just...I was a mess. I just wanted to do something to take the pain away," she said honestly.

Aron reached over and affectionately stroked her cheek. "I figured something was off with you. But no worries, your self-respect and dignity are still intact."

"Thanks!" She picked up the fork and ate some pancake.

"I know we're still in the friend zone, but you and me both know there's a strong attraction between us. So, I'm going to pull back. I want you Angie, more than just a friend. But right now you need time to heal." That fact was made loudly clear to him last night. He'd wanted Angie from the first day he saw her at Arnold's school orientation, but he wanted her whole. And maybe he was wrong for wanting a married woman from the get go, but he just did. She needed time to adjust to being divorced and getting over her ex.

Angie nodded her head. She knew he was right. She wouldn't be good for any other man if Derek still dominated everything within her. "Thank you for being so understanding Aron. I really appreciate your friendship." She smiled.

"Backatcha. Besides, you're still Arnold's teacher for a few more months until school ends in June. So we'll still see each other."

"Of course!"

"Now eat up. And I heard your phone ringing a few times, so I'm sure there's people wondering where you are."

"Yeah, I texted Pauline and told her I'm good. Dena and Devon slept over at her house last night." She picked the fork back up and continued eating breakfast. She and Aron chatted while she did, then afterwards she left to head home.

Thirty-Seven

Derek had been running only on fumes for a week ever since signing the divorce papers. All he could do is wake up each morning and thank God for life. But truly he felt like he had died and was a walking zombie. He needed to get himself together, he knew it. But knowing that he would soon officially be a divorced man was hard for him to accept.

He hadn't seen Angie in over a week. When he did pick up the kids, instead of going inside like he used to, he just waited in the car. Seeing her would only intensify his pain of losing her as his wife. He heard once that divorce was like death – and he could truly relate. He was in a state of mourning. A dark cloud had taken up permanent residence in his life.

"She's here," Latoya said after she stepped into Derek's office.

Derek had his back to her. He was staring out the floor to ceiling window at the view of the Potomac River. He'd been doing that for hours. He hadn't been productive all today and it was already two-thirty. He turned around in his chair to face Latoya standing at the door. That was the first time he'd heard disdain in her voice about a client — she always kept it professional no matter how obnoxious some of them may be. That must mean the visitor was Breana. He'd picked up on Latoya's dislike for her over the past few months.

"Send her in," he spoke. He wasn't in the mood for Breana like any other day, but she was pregnant with his child.

Latoya nodded her head then backed out of the office. Seconds later Breana entered. She had a bright smile on her face. Derek looked her over, he had to admit — pregnancy suited her very well. Her belly was much more noticeable now and she still had good fashion sense. She wore a black jumpsuit with a tan cardigan over top.

"Here!" She practically sang placing an ultrasound picture on his desk. "Since I'm seven months pregnant I found out the sex of our baby today."

Derek looked down at the ultrasound then up at her. The feeling of joy, still had yet to make its appearance whenever *their* baby came up. "Why didn't you let me know, I would've came with you."

Breana sat in one of the visitor's seats. "Really, whenever I call you ignore me. I don't ever know when would be a good time to talk to you about our baby," she shot back.

Because she was right, he left it as that. He looked at the 3D image of their baby and tried to determine the sex for himself. "So, what is it?"

Breana's megawatt smile returned. "A boy!" She exclaimed excitingly. "We're having a boy."

Still, no joy, no excitement. But for her sake Derek forced a smile onto his face. He hoped it looked convincing. "Wow, a boy. I'll have two sons." His heart ached.

"Yes! So I've been thinking about names. Brandon, Diesel, Brun, Benjamin, Dru or Derek Jr.? I didn't know if your son was a Jr. or not."

Derek Jr. That didn't work for him at all. And he didn't want to be picking out a name for a child he felt no attachment to. "I prefer not to make him a Jr., but other than that, how about you choose a name."

"Yes but I wanted your input," she frowned. She was really hoping he would be more excited about having another son.

He sighed deeply. "I like Benjamin and Dru."

"Yay, Dru is my favorite too! So Dru Benjamin Monroe, how does that sound?" She was so happy, he didn't want to rain on her parade.

He pulled out another fake smile. "Perfect!"

"Great! Okay since I wanted to wait to find out what we're having before I purchased a crib and decorate Dru's room, I want you to come with me."

Derek was shaking his head before she even finished her sentence. "I won't be much help with that." A complete contrast to when he and Angie were expecting Dena and Devon. Derek was so overjoyed with being a dad, Angie had to practically beg him to allow her to purchase new things for the baby of her own. He went crazy buying baby clothes, furniture, toys, and wanted their rooms to be nothing but perfect for their arrivals.

"Really Derek? What do I have to do to get you to at least be a little bit excited about this baby? You said all that mess about being supportive but every time I bring up the baby or anything regarding the baby you just brush me off." She was visibly hurt by his constant rejection. Her eyes filled with tears. She really didn't expect having her first child to turn out this way. Even her doctor was impressed with her great health and progression in the pregnancy considering she was thirty-six years old. So for her only concerns to be about Derek not being fully involved was irritating. This was supposed to be a great experience for her all around.

Derek stood up and walked over to where she sat. He lightly placed a comforting hand on her back. He didn't want her to cry. "I'm sorry." He blew a breath. "I'll go baby shopping with you. You're right, I did say I would be supportive and I'm sorry." He was truly sincere. He knew he needed to stop treating her so badly. "Tell me when ahead of time and I'll clear my schedule."

Breana's face lit up. "Thank you Derek! I know our situation isn't ideal, but I want us to be great parents to Dru." She already loved the fact that they had a name for their son. "Can you make it this Saturday?"

Derek didn't have Dena and Devon this weekend, so he guessed that would work. "Yes, that should work." He hoped he would find some enthusiasm by then.

"Yay!" She jumped up out the seat and hugged him spontaneously. Derek stepped back. His touching her on her back was one thing, her hugging him – he wasn't for that.

Breana looked hurt by another one of his rejections, but she quickly recovered when he placed his large hand on her protruding belly. *Maybe touching it may help me feel some type of connection.* He felt a flutter over his palm. He smiled looking down into Breana's eyes. She was smiling too.

"I think Dru is happy that you've agreed to go shopping with me too," she said placing her hand over his. Derek allowed it for a second, before drawing his hand back.

"Yeah, I guess he is." He stepped away from her. "Let me know the time for Saturday so I'll be ready," he said, dismissing her. He started for the office door. "I need to handle some business now."

Happy with the progress she'd made with Derek today with him actually agreeing to go baby shopping with her, Breana picked her purse up off of the chair and met him at his office door. "Okay, I call you later and let you know."

After Breana entered the elevator and the doors closed, Derek turned to Latoya. "Come see me in my office for a moment."

Latoya took a seat in a chair in front of his desk. She smoothed her hand over her pencil skirt anticipating what it was he wanted to talk about.

"I know you may be wondering why Ms. Sutton has been showing up so often. I really appreciate you keeping my privacy by not trying to intrude by asking a lot of questions. But despite the fact that we keep things formal in the office, you know that I see you not only as my assistant, but a little sister too…"

Latoya smiled. She knew that and was very grateful for it.

"…So I want to make you aware of the fact that…I cheated on Angie with Breana, which is the cause of our separation. It happened while we were on the business trip in the Bahamas…"

Latoya nodded her head fully aware of the circumstances, his office walls were thin, even though she never intentionally eavesdropped. But she kept a stoic expression on her face because of what he was revealing.

"…Breana is seven months pregnant with my baby," Derek breathed out. He knew Latoya may have put the pieces together already over the course of the past months, but he wanted to finally come out and tell her personally.

Latoya stared at her boss. She didn't know how to respond. But she finally said, "Congratulations?" She arched her brow.

"I know you don't like Breana. You and Angie got along well, so I don't expect you to do cheers for Breana, but try to be a little pleasant toward her. She isn't the only guilty one in all this."

"I was hoping you and Angie would work things out."

Derek painfully shook his head. "Angie filed for divorce."

That was news to Latoya. The shock of it smacked her in the face. "What!?" Derek and Angie had that type of relationship she had wanted to obtain – so this was a real blow.

Derek didn't say anything. It was still too raw, too painful. And seeing the pain in Latoya's eyes prickled his heart more.

"I'm...I'm so sorry Derek. I know how much you love Angie, even though you messed up with Breana, I know you love her."

"I do! But, I really can't blame her for getting a divorce. I was stupid enough to cheat and get another woman pregnant – so now I have to deal with the consequences."

Derek and Latoya chatted for a while before they both left the office for that day.

Thirty-Eight

The next day, Angie had called in a substitute and had Pauline take Dena and Devon to school on her way in. Angie made an appointment to see her doctor to remedy whatever she was coming down with. She didn't want to risk getting her kids and students sick with her germs.

She had just arrived back home at eleven-eighteen that morning from fulfilling her prescription, at the pharmacy, which her doctor had prescribed. All she wanted to do was crawl into bed and sleep forever. She hadn't felt this terrible in years. After parking her car in the driveway, she walked to the mailbox to retrieve the mail. She mindlessly shuffled through the mail while walking back toward the house, it was mostly bills and coupon booklets. But one envelope in particular caught her attention. After walking into the house and locking the door behind her, she ripped the letter open:

Angie,

I hope it's not too late, but if you want your husband back, go get him! Breana isn't pregnant with Derek's baby.

Signed: Only want the best for you two.

Angie stared at the letter in her trembling hand. Her mind was racing trying to figure out who wrote it and if what they wrote was true. She flipped the letter and envelope over checking all sides in hope of finding out the author of the letter. But there was no clue. She read the letter again. Her heart galloped in the cavity of her chest. *Breana isn't having his baby?* She knew deep down that if Derek hadn't told her that Breana was having his child, that perhaps they would've been able to mend their marriage. It would have taken a lot of work and more counseling with Dr. Williams, but she felt she would have been able to trust Derek again. But Breana's pregnancy threw a wedge in there. *Now...now all this time Breana could be lying about the baby?*

Angie turned around and retraced her steps to her car.

****

"How are you able to call me during the mid-day?" Breana said into the phone. She was sitting behind her desk, in her office in Fort Washington, Maryland.

"I was able to get a cellphone snuck in here, no thanks to you," her ex-husband breathed through the phone.

"You know I'm not going to jeopardize myself by doing any such thing," she spat. "What do you want? I'm busy."

"Damn Bre, that's how you're treating me now? I mean nothing to you know since I got locked up?" You could clearly hear the hurt in his voice.

Breana sighed loudly. "You know I care about you. But you are in jail."

"Yeah, and you promised me that you would come see me at least once a month. It's been months since I've seen you Bre. I thought you're supposed to be holding it down for me baby."

Breana rolled her eyes. "We're not married anymore. And you have a fifteen year sentence. No woman in her right mind would hold things down for a man that long."

"You promised me Breana! Besides, you've got to come see me eventually, bring my baby to come see daddy."

"I'm not pregnant with your child!" She almost shouted into the phone. But she quickly remembered that she was in her office and other ears were around.

"That's not what you told me before I got locked up. I saw the pregnancy tests Bre, I know you're pregnant with my baby."

The door to Breana's office swung open.

"I've got to go, bye!" Breana slammed the phone down then stood up to greet her guest.

Angie calmly closed the door shut behind her then walked with an air of ease towards Breana's desk.

"How can I help you?"

SMACK! Angie backhand slapped Breana so hard she thought her neck would snap. Breana had to hold onto the edge of her desk to stop herself from crashing to the floor. She slid gently to the ground eventually while holding her stinging face.

"You lying bitch!" Angie spat looking down at Breana looking pitiful on the carpeted floor. "I divorced my husband because of you. You're lucky you're pregnant with *another* man's baby or else I would be beating you all around this damn office."

Angie turned and marched out of the office. Breana's secretary, she presumed, who wasn't sitting at her desk when she had arrived, ran into Breana's office to see what was wrong after hearing the commotion. Angie faintly heard Breana telling her that she was okay and not to call security.

****

Minutes later, Angie burst into Derek's office. "Derek," she breathed. She stood in the doorway with tears streaming down her face. Derek was behind his desk and Latoya was sitting in one of the visitor chairs. They were going over some reports for one of his clients. But now both their eyes looked at Angie with shock. It had been a long time since she had stepped foot in there.

A smile tugged at the corners of Latoya's mouth. She rose to her feet and quickly made herself disappear. She closed the door behind her.

Derek stood to his feet, stepped from behind his desk then walked toward Angie. She was still standing by the door crying, but making no sound. Derek didn't know what to feel: fear, hope, gladness, or sadness. Why was she there?

Angie lunged at him, throwing her arms around his neck and taking his lips hostage. Derek felt weak in the knees. He couldn't believe this was happening, but he held her tight and succumbed to her kiss. They felt so right, so perfect, so at home.

"I'm so sorry Derek, I'm so sorry," Angie cried between kisses.

Derek pulled his face back, but kept her snuggled in his arms. "What's wrong, why are you crying? Why are you sorry?" He was confused. Was she sorry about the divorce?

"I shouldn't have divorced you." She looked up into his eyes. Her hazel set showed nothing but sadness. "But after knowing about you getting Breana pregnant, I just knew I couldn't stay your wife."

Derek used his thumbs to smooth the tears away from her eyes and off her cheeks. "But now you think you could now?"

She nodded her head.

"Are you sure? Breana is due to have the baby soon." He needed to know if she was serious about what she was saying.

"Breana's not having your baby, I am. And now we're divorced." She sobbed burying her head in his chest.

Derek stood completely still. His mind and ears were playing tricks on him he was sure. Did he hear Angie correctly? "Baby...baby what did you just say?" He stepped back, pulling her away from his chest. He tilted her head up so she could look at him. "What did you just say?"

"I'm pregnant. I just found out today. I've been feeling sick for a while, but it's so different from when I was pregnant with Dena and Devon that I didn't go to the doctor sooner. Plus I've been having light periods. But Dr. Wright said everything is normal and I'm four months."

A joy like no other bubbled up inside of Derek. He gently pulled Angie back into his chest and buried his tongue into her mouth. Every ounce of love he had for her was poured into the kiss. He loved her beyond description. "We're having another baby?" His mahogany face lit up making him even more handsome.

She nodded her head.

"Thank you baby!" He exclaimed. Then he remembered. "But you said something else. Breana's isn't having my baby?"

Angie pulled the letter out of her pocket then handed it to him. Derek read it. His face transformed from joy to anger in a flash. The letter crumbled in his palm. "Do you know who sent you this?" He was on the verge of rage. *That bitch played me?*

"No. But Breana didn't deny it when I confronted her."

"You confronted her? When?"

"Before I came over here."

Derek was willing himself to calm down. He didn't know he could hate a person as much as he did Breana at that moment. She had been playing with his life for months. He had been a pawn in her game, a game that helped pushed him further away from his wife and children.

"Derek," Angie said pulling him out of his thoughts of retribution. "I want you back. I want to be your wife again."

Derek shook his mind free of Breana. The only thing that mattered at that moment, was him and Angie. "You will always be my wife," he confessed. He stepped to her and ran his hands down her arms.

"But the divorce?" She questioned.

"I never got around to mailing the papers." He looked down at her bewildered face. Every time he passed the papers on his kitchen counter, he kept telling himself he would get around to mailing them eventually. "You're still legally my wife."

Angie reached up on her toes and kissed him on the mouth. "Thank you! I love you so much!"

Thirty-Nine

Breana confessed to being a month further along in her pregnancy than she had told Derek. She was pregnant by her ex-husband. She had planned to seduce Derek on the business trip to the Bahamas. She had purposely sought his services to pretend as if she was interested in his assistance with landing some business deals on the island. But it was all to get him away from his wife, in a foreign country to set her plan in motion. And slipping something into his drink every day during the trip helped with the three days of seduction. But she wasn't dumb enough to tell him that part. She did it because she knew if her father found out she was pregnant with her ex-husband's baby that his financial support would cut off. So she needed someone else to act as proxy. And Derek was it.

"The only reason I'm going to let this slide is because I have my wife and children back, but you best believe, if you ever come near me or my family again, you will have serious problems to deal with." Derek promised Breana when he confronted her himself after his reconciliation with his wife.

That night he and Angie wasted no time telling the kids that they were officially back together.

****

"I can't believe you were able to pull this off so quickly." Pauline turned to view herself in the full length mirror. Her pregnant belly was more prominent now at eight months pregnant. "And I can't believe you convinced me to still be your maid of honor with this huge belly of mine." She smoothed her hands over her round front. Even with the extra weight she gained, she looked beautiful in her sunny yellow chiffon dress. Her brunette hair was pulled up in an elegant high bun.

"Well mine isn't too far behind yours." Angie checked herself out too, now fully dressed in her own white chiffon dress with crystals along the waist and up to the one shoulder strap. Her bob hairstyle was gone, her hair was styled in a side ponytail bun, with ringlets along her edges.

"You look beautiful!" Pauline exclaimed. Her eyes started to fill with tears.

"Thank you! So do...oh no you don't, stop that crying!" Angie exclaimed. "If you cry I'm gonna cry especially with these pregnancy hormones and our makeup artist already left."

Pauline fanned her face while trying to suck the tears back into her eyelids. "I'm sorry, it's just I'm so happy for you and Derek."

Today was the day of their ten year anniversary and Angie and Derek were renewing their vows at a resort in Miami. Since Pauline was a month away from her due date, her doctor advised her not to travel out of the country, and Angie couldn't imagine not having her best friend there to celebrate her day. So a quick flight to Miami it was.

Angie pulled Pauline into a hug. "I know, I'm happy too! We were so close to being divorced. But I'm so thankful that we're here today. We made it through all of that mess from last year. God truly has that man as my one and only husband."

There was a rapid knock on the suite door. Angie and Pauline pulled out of their embrace. "Yes," Angie called out. She went to open the door.

"Show time, everyone's in place," the bubbly resort coordinator said.

"We're ready." Pauline walked up behind Angie carrying their bouquets.

Derek looked at his bride with nothing but love. It still stung his heart every time he thought about how close he came to losing her. But today, under the splendor of the heavens above, the clear, scenic ocean behind them, and family and friends before them, they were renewing their love and commitment to one another. His heart was filled with absolute love and gratitude. There was no other woman in the world for him – Angie was it. So today meant even more to him than when he'd married her ten years ago.

He kissed her passionately after the minister told him to kiss his bride. That was all he wanted to do when he saw her walking toward him, looking like an angel, with her bare feet sinking into the sand. Their guests cheered them on when their kiss took longer than the few seconds rule. The loudest to be heard were their kids. Dena and Devon were overjoyed to see their parents together and happy again. Everything was now perfect in their world.

Thank you for reading! Please do me a favor and leave a review, it's very helpful to authors and other readers looking for good reads. I will really appreciate the 1 or 2 minutes of your time to do so ☺

Please connect with me on social media:

Instagram: @IntrovertedKhara

Facebook Page: Khara C.

Website: http://kharacampbell.blogspot.com/

Check out my other titles:

Not My Will

Purple Tears

Bahama Love

Island Girl

Can't Love What I Don't Trust Part 1 & 2

Made in United States
North Haven, CT
15 September 2022

24179972R00236